WE USED TO BE FRIENDS

WE USED TO BE FRIENDS

A novel by

AMY SPALDING

AMULET BOOKS • NEW YORK

PUBLISHER'S NOTE: This is a work of fiction. Names, characters, places, and incidents are either the product of the author's imagination or used fictitiously, and any resemblance to actual persons, living or dead, business establishments, events, or locales is entirely coincidental.

Cataloging-in-Publication Data has been applied for and may be obtained from the Library of Congress.

ISBN 978-1-4197-3866-1

Book design by Hana Anouk Nakamura and John Passineau

Published in 2020 by Amulet Books, an imprint of ABRAMS.

Printed and bound in USA
10 9 8 7 6 5 4 3 2 1

ABRAMS The Art of Books
195 Broadway, New York, NY 10007
abramsbooks.com

To my friends

Jessica Hutchins

and Christie Baugher

CHAPTER ONE

August after Senior Year

JAMES

By the time you realize you're thirsty, it's too late. You're already dehydrated. Therefore, it stands to reason that if you feel the end coming, you're already there.

I've had four heartbreaks. The first was Tony Aldana, who kissed me at our sixth grade dance and then laughed about it the next day in the cafeteria. Back in grade school, I'd gotten teased—not exactly *constantly* but *enough*—for being a girl with a boy's name, and this dragged into middle school for a while. I might have been worthy of kissing during a semi-dark sixth grade dance, but I was still seen as too much of a weirdo for Tony to be OK with it in the bright sunlight of lunch.

The story behind my name is so boring that now it's funny to me that it, briefly, marked me as *weird*: Mom and Dad expected a boy, and the boy was to be named James McCall the Third. When I showed up a girl, Dad apparently *cried* about his family legacy until Mom—in an epidural haze—agreed.

Bryce Bradley was my first real boyfriend, if eighth grade boyfriends count. We went on long walks around our neighborhood after school every night while discussing the day's events. Dad thought he "seemed like a fine young man." (Mom merely said, "way to go, James" in a knowing tone I'd never heard from her before.) Then suddenly Bryce didn't have time for the walks, and our texting looked lopsided in my direction. He didn't tell me; I had to walk into homeroom and hear Lilah Boyer telling Jessamyn Williams that Bryce had taken her on a real date the night before, and she was pretty sure it was *the real thing*. In retrospect, she was probably quoting something she'd heard in a TV show, but at the time, between that and her sleek pixie haircut, Lilah was improbably chic and mature. No wonder Bryce was over me.

Then there was Javier, who showed up the summer before sophomore year. He was staying with his aunt and uncle—our next-door neighbors—and we somehow managed to hit every boy-and-girl-next-door cliché that existed. There were flashlights and signs and climbing up trees to second story windows. We kissed in my bed, under my covers, which felt dangerous and sexy and important, even though our clothes stayed on. I dreamed of scenarios that kept him in LA, but none of them mattered, because two weeks into August he had to go home, back to Texas. I can't explain why I knew it was over. Phones and social media exist. But when he hugged me good-bye, I knew that it was for forever. I hardly ever cry, but I cried every day of that third week of August.

I told myself I'd never let anyone get that close again, because the risk was too big. I fell for Logan anyway, which didn't even matter. I hadn't been looking in the right direction to know where the real danger was coming from.

After all, the boys added up—Tony, Bryce, Javier, and I guess Logan, too—didn't come close to this. There are breakup tunes and lovesick ballads and celebrating-that-he-was-gone anthems. It was easy to believe that romance was the only heartache out there.

• • •

Dad keeps all the yard equipment in neat rows in the garage, so I know where the shovel is. Now that I'm helping to build homes on a regular basis, I even know how to use it properly.

I remember being fourteen, which felt grown-up at the time, starting high school. I'd dedicated a page in my journal to a list of ideal time capsule contents, while Kat made her choices more impulsively. We laughed later about a future historian finding the box and trying to make sense of this point in history by one very well-organized teen and one who took a much more scattershot approach.

This printout of Justin Bieber's Instagram must mean something extremely significant, Kat would say in the voice of a stuffy old man, and before long we'd be in tears from laughter.

Luke is probably still mad at Kat for burying the newest-at-the-time Game of Thrones book, but our younger selves were convinced that it would be historically relevant.

But we knew what would actually be the most important later, and we were right. I sweated over my letter to Kat because writing does not come easily to me and laying out my feelings is even tougher. So of course, after unearthing our high school time capsule, it's the first thing I look for. When I pick up the envelope with my name written on it in metallic pink marker, I see how much thicker it is than the envelope I sealed myself, four years ago.

Dearest James (ha ha ha),

OMG can you believe we are 18? I mean, we are 18 now, when you are reading this letter and I am reading whatever you wrote to me, which is probably like *Dear Kat, You are a good friend, Sincerely, James* because I know you hate stuff like this. This is why you are the greatest friend ever. You go along with all my ideas even when they annoy you because they matter to me.

I'm trying to picture what we will be like when we graduate. You'll probably get some special award for being good at sports (or whatever) and I just hope Mom and Dad don't freak out when I get accepted at a school super far away. (PLEASE LET ME GET ACCEPTED AT A SCHOOL SUPER FAR AWAY.) We'd better both have really good grades AND super cute boyfriends, because both are really important.

I know it is cheesy, but I seriously think you are amazing, James. Also, it's sort of a secret you're so amazing. Ms. Bedrosian always refers to you as my quiet friend, which is pretty weird, but I'm also like, ha ha, if you only knew, Ms. Bedrosian. You're like an exclusive thing only the coolest people know about, and the coolest person in this case is me. But you are so funny and good at sports and smart about boys AND school. I know this is all still true now, which is the future for me but the NOW for the you reading this letter. Whoa! Just thinking about it is kind of crazy.

I am so glad that in kindergarten we got paired up for that dorky graduation ceremony and that our moms decided we should hang out. What if I got paired with some random girl and she was my best friend now? Actually I think that is impossible. If I'd gotten paired with anyone else, you and I would have become friends at some point anyway. But everyone loves how cute we were when we were only six wearing those little caps and gowns, and I actually love it, too. I love knowing we'll have new pictures by the time you read this of us walking together at high school freakin' graduation!! (I sorta hate those old pictures because that was before I figured out PRODUCT and so my hair looks like a frizzball but it's adorable we're holding hands like the besties we were destined to be.)

Speaking of that, sorta, thank you for tripping Andrew Mitchell when he called me an electrocution victim after I got that bad haircut. Thank you for shutting down that rumor I went to third freaking base with Caleb Weintraub after his birthday party. Thank you for pretending that Luke doesn't think you're cute because it's super embarrassing. Thank you for being so nice all the time to my parents like THAT is not super embarrassing. (Ugh they're such dorks sometimes but it doesn't bother me like maybe it should? Am I destined to be super uncool? OMG since you're in the future you already know the answer to this. CRAZY!)

Anyway, I guess I am just thanking you for being my friend. It sounds like not a big deal but you are not a little thing to me! And I am really REALLY excited to watch your face as you read this because you'll be embarrassed and I'll already have finished your short little note already and I'll be waiting. Ha!

Love, your best friend forever,

Kat

• • •

I'm not sure what I expected to get out of doing this, but this couldn't have been a good idea. It's like pushing a bruise, though; now that I'm in it, I feel the urge to stay here. The dumb mementos and the four-years-yellowed copy of the *Burbank Leader* and the letters.

Though—the letters, plural? I'm holding the one Kat wrote, more like clutching it, and it becomes wrinkled and ruined in my hand. I search for the other envelope, a glimpse of my handwriting in sensible blue ink and no sparkles at all. I wish I could remember the letter more, because that would be a glimpse, too. It's impossible to remember the last time Kat felt like the kind of friend who would write me this letter, and if I'm being honest, I can't remember being the friend who would get this letter anyway.

The things I said the last time I saw her weren't untrue, but I didn't say them well. Maybe I didn't say things for so long because that was easier than figuring out how to say them right.

I dig and dig through the box, and when that proves fruitless, I turn it upside down over my bedroom floor to separate the mess into piles. By now I wish it had stayed beneath the earth. Justin Bieber and Westeros and Kat's Dr Pepper–flavored Lip Smacker and a tiny scrap of paper where Joel Vega had written *cool* and approximately fifteen other mementos that meant something then.

But there's nothing for them to mean now, because it doesn't matter how many times you write *BFF*. Forever can go away before you even know it.

And I don't know why the letter is gone, but my stomach clenches at the ridiculous symbolism of it. Whatever I'd written to Kat, four years ago—back before Kat's mom died, or my mom left—isn't here. Just like Kat.

I wonder where she is right now. It's likely she's been where she's been since we met: down the street at her home. Her summer won't have been practically ruined by this, though. Kat is probably feeling just fine. And a few blocks have never felt so far away.

• • •

Logan stops by while we're loading Dad's car and I'm texting Hannah, already making plans for tonight. I hadn't asked Logan to be here, but I'd be lying to say I wasn't happy to see him.

"I got you a gift," he says, loping up in that casual way of his. Hands in pockets, hair effortlessly shoved to one side. We—Kat and I—used to joke that his glasses would be askew if he could do that and still manage to see.

"You didn't have to," I tell him.

"Well . . ." He grins. "You haven't seen it yet."

I wait while he takes his hand out of his pocket, and then he places something heavy in my palm and closes my fingers around it. It feels substantial.

"Oh," I say as I open my hand. "A roll of quarters. How . . . thoughtful."

"You'll thank me the first time you do laundry," he says.

I wrap my arms around him. He feels substantial, too.

"Sorry I didn't ask before stopping by," he says.

"I know it's hard for you not to follow rules," I say, which makes him smile. "So I guess I think it's cute."

"James." Dad walks up with a stack of my boxes. "Hey, Logan! It's good to see you, man."

They do their usual semi-secret handshake ritual. After all this time, I have no idea when they would have had the opportunity to come up with it.

"It's your move-in day, too," Dad says. "Shouldn't you be on the road?"

"Sophomores actually move in next week," Logan says. "And my trip's a lot shorter. But I'd make time for James anyway. Especially when she so nicely asked me not to."

I elbow him but give up trying to hold back a smile. I've been picturing this day ever since I knew what college was, and in my head the send-off had always been much bigger. After this year, I'm honestly glad anyone showed up at all.

"I don't want to ruin the fun," Dad says, "but—"

"We need to go," I say to Logan, but as nicely as I can. And he knows anyway.

We stand there in silence for a second or so before Dad takes a hint, says good-bye to Logan, and gets into the SUV.

"This is not over," Logan says, and then at my expression: "I hope not, at least."

"We'll see." I blink back tears, because Logan has never seen me cry, and I'm not about to start today. "But thank you. For the quarters."

He leans in to hold my face in his strong steady hands. I know that he's asking permission, so I slide off his thick black-framed glasses, and then we're kissing. We're kissing like we never stopped, like this year never happened, like I didn't say any of what can't be taken back now. The kiss is time travel and infinite possibilities.

Except when we step back from each other, I have to remember everything else I've lost and how kissing Logan won't bring any of it back.

It's certainly not bringing Kat back.

"Hey." Logan touches my face, and I realize against all my best efforts, I'm crying. Logan is seeing me cry. "Your future's *bright*, McCall."

I look away from him and grin. "I'll text you later."

"It's a date—sorry, it's whatever you want it to be."

"You'll have to settle for *whatever*," I say. "For now, at least."

"I can handle *whatever*."

"I hope you're still in it, though," I say. "However it works out."

"Well, here's the thing," he says with a grin. "Stuff goes away, and then, luckily, stuff comes back. Stuff's cyclical nature and all."

"I hope you're right." I can tell he thinks this is about us, but I hope that it's about Kat, too. It still hurts, every day, in a way I didn't know that it could. I remember the morning after my first Habitat for Humanity build how muscles I didn't even know I had were aching. Losing Kat is a build, and my heartache is the unknown muscles. But

I can already feel that, just like with construction, your body learns how to turn pain and effort into newfound strength.

"Call her," he says, because of course no matter how seemingly cocky Logan can appear, he understands other people—maybe especially me.

"She doesn't want to hear from me," I say.

"Text her, then. Instagram the grossest thing you can order through a drive-through and tag her because you know she'd love that shit."

A laugh bursts out of me, even though I didn't think that was possible on this topic anymore. "We'll see."

"I know she misses you," Logan says, not with his normal bravado but with a confidential almost-whisper. I don't want it to, but my heart seems to seize forward to grasp at this possibility.

"I wish." Even a month ago, I probably never would have just admitted that. Much less to Logan. It's so real and eggshell-fragile, and now here it is, just sitting out there, between us.

"Don't forget that I'm frequently right," he says.

"Normally I'd call you out on that, but my therapist talks a lot about cycles, too," I say. His ego doesn't need the rush of knowing he also practically read my mind. "So I'll let it stand."

"Therapy, huh?"

"I should have started it long ago," I say. "But Dr. Edelstein keeps saying that it's not too late."

"It's never too late, McCall."

I agree and hope that that's not only about him or therapy.

He gives me a gentle hug, and then he's gone. I turn back and stare at the house. It won't be so long before I'm back, but I know it won't be the same. By Thanksgiving, I'll be a visitor.

"Kid." Dad sticks his head out the window. "Are you ready?"

I appreciate that he doesn't add a *finally* to that question.

"Yes," I say without even having to think about it. "I am."

I get in the car and say it without dwelling on it for too long first. "I know we're in a hurry, but can we stop by Mom's on our way?"

Luckily, he doesn't make the face that he's overly proud, and so I don't feel overly embarrassed. "Of course, James."

Even though she isn't expecting me, Mom answers the door right away.

"Aren't you on your way upstate?" she asks.

I gesture at Dad's car. "Almost. I wanted to say good-bye in person."

Mom does make the overly proud face, but I guess that's fair.

"I also wanted to . . . well, do you remember you asked me to challenge myself to something this year?"

Mom appears to take a huge breath. "Honey . . . I was going through a lot."

It hits me how . . . *herself* she looks. For some reason, I think I wanted Mom's new life to be a mess of selfishness and destruction, but Mom's just Mom.

"No, it's OK, you—"

"James, if anything I said made you feel—"

"You were right," I say. "I wanted to take photos to show you everything I did, but . . . taking photos of volunteer work seems . . ." I try to find a word that doesn't sound yanked from Kat's vocabulary, but it's the only one that sounds fitting. ". . . braggy."

Mom laughs. "Oh, god, doesn't it? Like my cousin Sandra."

I laugh, and we say it together: "Hashtag *amvolunteering*!"

"But," I continue, "I just want you to know that I did things. And I'm going to keep trying to help when I'm up at college, even if everyone warns me my schedule will make it impossible."

"I have faith in you, James." Mom hugs me so tightly I don't breathe for a moment. "I'm really sorry for making your year harder than it should have been."

I stay right in her arms, like when I was little. "I am too."

She makes me promise to text once I've arrived, and we hug again before I get back into Dad's car. He's nonchalant even though he must have seen the hugging, and for the millionth time, I'm grateful for him.

I take out my phone and hold it for a few moments as Dad navigates out of Mom's neighborhood to the 170. With Logan's words echoing in my ears, I type.

> I know we're going off to have new adventures, learn new things, and meet new people, but I'd like to keep our Christmas Eve tradition, if you'd want to pencil me in. See you at Porto's?

As soon as I tap *send,* I power my phone down. This drive shouldn't be about waiting for her. This is for me and my next steps, and I guess a little for Dad and me, too.

Then he tries to turn the radio on to NPR, and I have to override him with my running playlist. I associate the songs with movement, of putting one foot in front of the other and not looking behind me.

I smile. That's what I'm doing today.

CHAPTER TWO

September of Senior Year

KAT

I can't believe how he tells me.

"We're at *school,*" I say.

"Yeah?" Matty says, then shrugs. Matty is *shrugging* mere moments after dropping a horrible life-changing bomb. Matty is making the face he always makes, somewhere between bemusement and cockiness, and for maybe the first time ever, it does nothing to me.

It does nothing *good,* at least.

"How many times?" I ask, even though I don't know what I want him to say. Since the answer won't be zero, does it matter? If he slept with Elise Penderson once, twice, forty-two times, what's the freaking difference?

"Kat . . ." He reaches out to push my curls back from my face, a move he's mastered by this point. When I've listed all the things I love about being Matty's girlfriend, his care with my Medusa hair always gets a mention. Some guys know to bring you chocolate or take you to special places you'd never find on your own or kiss you with an almost incomprehensible intensity. But Matty takes care.

He did, at least.

"Why?" I ask. It's now that whatever magical resolve that was holding me together disappears completely, and my voice breaks on that one word. And now Matty is seeing me cry.

It's not like he hasn't seen me cry before. Matty showed up only moments after my mom died almost two years ago. We weren't even serious then, but there he was with James, my perfect pair of support beams. After that, though, I didn't want to be the girl who cried. To Matty, I wanted to be the cool girl he deserved. To Matty, I *was* the cool girl he deserved. Or I thought he deserved, at least.

"You know I believe in honesty," he says, like he's proud. "I messed up, and I'm telling you."

"Good for you, Matty," I say. "Super great. I'm so happy while you were doing it with someone so"—Elise Penderson, blonde, fun, probably never has to send dresses back to ModCloth because she can't fill out the top—"*not me* that it was only under such strictly honest terms."

"Babe," he says, and I've always teased him for that,

babe, like we're some cozy married couple in our forties. That's how it always sounded to me. "I love you."

"You don't," I say, full tears now. For me, full tears involve snot. I go straight from girl to beast. "If you did, you wouldn't have . . ."

"It wasn't like that," he says.

"Then what was it like?" I slam his locker door shut. Whoever wasn't already looking at us is looking now. "Why?"

"I . . . I dunno." He scratches his head and shrugs again. "You were out of town. I was bored."

"You were *bored*?" The locker door didn't completely latch, so I yank the door open and slam it again before slapping its cold metal side. "Good-bye, Matty."

"Kat," he says, the way only he can say my name, the way his lips curl around the syllable. The first time I heard my three letters in his voice, it practically brought me to my knees in an all-but-literal swoon. "This doesn't have to be a thing."

"Yeah," I say. "It does."

I walk off like I'm the brave one.

James runs up alongside me. She's built for track-and-field and so my faux confident strut is no match for her. "Sofia told me you tore the door off of Matty's locker."

I laugh so hard I snort, and snot from my tears flies in all directions from my nose. James, true BFF that she is, doesn't flinch.

"Honestly it was easier for me to believe that you"—she makes air quotes—"'hulked out' than that you and Matty . . ."

"Oh, god." My laugh feels yanked out of my body, and for a second I think I'll never feel anything but sadness and anger again. I'm not capable of strutting at all, much less in such a confident manner.

"Let's get out of here," James says.

I take a step toward my first period class.

"No, Kat, *out of here*," she says.

"Like skipping?"

"More than *like* it," she says. "Come on."

She links her arm through mine and steers me down the hallway. Since the first bell hasn't rung, people are milling about everywhere, including in front of the school. James and I blend in until we're magically not on school grounds anymore.

I think about our lunch table, right in the center of the courtyard. Last year, James and her boyfriend, Logan Sidana, sat in the two most prominent spots, but since Logan graduated this past spring, Matty and me sat in the center, with James right at my side. I'm not someone who set out to be popular, and in a school as big as Magnolia Park, literal popularity might not actually be possible anyway. It feels like some leftover idea from old movies about teens and like it has less to do with my actual life.

But the thing is, you can't even go outside to eat lunch

without seeing us and our crowded table of athletes and top students and couples who get crowned prom king and queen. So where does that leave me today? And for the rest of the year?

Today, I feel safer when Magnolia Park High School is behind us. It's like out here, Matty's still mine, and I'm no table's centerpiece.

"Do you want to talk about it?" James asks gently.

"Matty fucked Elise Penderson."

James flinches when I say the f-word, because I do not say the f-word.

"When I was in Indiana. Or maybe when I was in Ohio. Maybe both."

"Yeah," she says. "That's what I heard."

"When?" I ask. My heart thuds like it also spots all the worst possibilities. "Right before you found me today? Did people know before I knew? Did *you* know? Did you know and, like, not tell me?"

"*No*, geez," she says. "I'm not sure of the exact time-line. I think Elise might have told people. I had literally just heard, so I was coming to find you. And then I ran into Sofia and she told me about the fight."

"Why are you yelling at me right now?" I ask.

"Kat, I'm not," she says, and I realize she's right. Her voice is raised just the slightest bit, but that's so rare from James it might as well be a scream.

Or maybe I can't judge anything right now.

"I'm sorry." I lean my head against her shoulder as we walk down Keystone Street. My heartbeat seems OK now, despite my heartbreak. "Everything just feels out of control. I know it sounds stupid, but sometimes I kind of hoped Matty and I might be together forever."

"It doesn't sound stupid," she says. And why would it to James? Her parents fell in love in high school and they're still the happiest couple you could imagine.

"I mean, I at least assumed we'd be prom king and queen." I'd already pictured the crown glittering in my curls and how handsome Matty would look as he led me to the dance floor.

"It's a fair assumption."

"I can't believe this is our first Friday as seniors," I say. "We were supposed to go out tonight."

"We were?" James asks.

"No, me and Matty," I say. "His parents are going out tonight so . . ."

"So it's more that you were supposed to stay in tonight?" James asks with a smirk. Her mouth quickly straightens out. "I'm sorry. I somehow forgot for a moment."

"Me too," I whisper. I try to imagine it, Matty and me in his bedroom, but instead of my face, it's Elise's.

"What do you want to do?" she asks.

"A burger." I realize it as I say it. "The biggest cheeseburger you can dream up."

"I thought you were vegan now," James says.

"Well, *yeah*, but me and Matty . . ."

James grins. "Dump a vegan, eat a burger?"

I'm not sure it counts as dumping someone when they betray you first, but I guess I did technically break up with him. I dumped Matty Evans, the bicycle-riding, hybrid-driving, violence-protesting vegan.

And it might only be eight o'clock in the morning, but suddenly the only thing I can think of is the taste of red meat.

• • •

I'm home, alone, when Dad walks into the house that evening. Since we got back from Indiana without Luke, this is our new normal. Our *new* new normal, because you can't have your mom gone for only two years and be completely used to her absence already.

I can't, at least.

"Your school called me," Dad says as he puts his bag down on the counter. Mom used to pack a lunch for him every day, and at night he'd carefully take out all the empty reusable containers and load them into the dishwasher. Now I don't know what Dad eats during the day. His bag only carries his laptop to work and then home again.

"What about?" I ask.

"Nice try," Dad says, and I remember that I skipped

school today. This morning feels so long ago, and the decisions made like someone else's. "I covered for you. Figured you had a good reason."

I nod. "Matty and I . . ."

"Sorry," Dad says, though his posture's different now. It reminds me of when I wrote *tampons* on the weekly grocery list for the first time after Mom was gone. Dad's so great at so many things except when he remembers I'm a girl with girl feelings and girl needs and a whole girl life.

I don't understand why that has to be a scary revelation.

"I'm sorry I skipped." I try to sound innocent even though Dad probably hasn't forgotten that I used to skip school sometimes even when I wasn't going through a major life crisis. Before Mom was gone, I didn't worry so much about rules. I barely even thought about them at all.

"It's fine." His back is already to me as he roots around in the freezer. "How about this lasagna thing? It's got those soy bits in it you like so much."

"I'm eating meat again," I say.

"Oh, yeah?" He turns around and grins. "That's my girl."

"Don't be so happy," I say, but I haven't seen him smile like this in a while. I realize I'm smiling right back at him. "I'll still eat the lasagna."

"No way," he says. "Not until times are more desperate,

at least. Can I take you out to dinner? Or is it too embarrassing to be caught with your old dad on a Friday night when your friends are all doing parties?"

"'Doing parties'?" I giggle. "*Dad.* You can't possibly think that's how normal people talk."

"I never claimed to be normal," he says. "Come on."

"I have to change," I say, because once James and I finished eating burgers at Carl's Jr., we came back here and I traded my new flowered romper for a tank top and old baggy yoga pants. The romper had been the favorite thing I'd bought during back-to-school shopping, but now it's tainted by Matty and the rest of today's events.

"Well, go change," Dad says. "We're getting steaks."

The romper is on the floor of my bedroom, and I realize that I don't want it to only be the thing I was wearing when I was part of a humiliating public breakup. So I put it back on, fluff my curls, fix my eyeliner, and dust powder over my face in the hopes that I no longer look like I was crying most of the day.

I've lost the ability to judge if I do or not.

We see him as soon as we walk outside. Dad silently gets into the car, and suddenly for the first time in years I'm glad we don't have one of those relationships where I tell him everything. If Dad knew about Elise he might back his Subaru Forester right over Matty. And I might hate Matty now, but I don't want him dead or my dad in jail.

Matty shoves his hands in his pockets. "Hey." Honestly,

if anyone looks like they've fallen apart, it's not me and my romper.

"What?"

"Kat, I *love you,*" he says like he's giving me a gift.

"Stop saying that when it can't be true."

"We've been together for two years," he says. "I thought you were committed to this. To *us.*"

I stare at him, the messy brown hair I normally can't keep my hands out of, his slightly crooked nose, the tiny scar over his lip he got wrestling with his brother when he was only five, the way his dimples settle in like they're sneaking behind the corners of his smile. If you've memorized someone's details, how can it be possible that maybe you don't actually know him at all?

"You're willing to just give up on this?"

"OMG." I shake my head. "You cheated on me, Matty. Because you were *bored.* You don't get to make me the mean one now."

He grabs me around my waist. "Elise means nothing to me."

"You know what?" I pull out of his grasp. "That doesn't make me feel better. Honestly it makes me feel worse. You ruined this for *nothing,* and I'm not taking the blame."

He doesn't move as I walk toward Dad's car, but I pretend that he's gone. Dad seems to have extra worry lines on his forehead, so I'm genuinely relieved he just backs out of the driveway. I sneak my phone out of my purse to text James, but I lose track of that original goal because I haven't looked at my phone in ages, and my screen is lit up with texts from basically everyone in my contacts list. *Are you ok?* and *He's an idiot!* and *WHERE ARE YOU???* and *I feel like I can't believe in true love anymore.*

"She'd know what to say," Dad says. "If she were here."

I blink back tears and don't say anything. It would be so much easier if he wasn't right.

My phone lights up again. *Text from James: How are you doing, Kat?*

I reach for the chain around my neck and pull on the gold monogrammed letters. Mom's initials in engraved swirls, her eighteenth birthday present from her parents. And I miss her so much it's like an injury, and while Sofia's text was overdramatic, I might not believe in true love anymore, either.

But I have a lit-up phone and a dad driving me for breakup steaks. It's not enough, but I'll try to pretend that it is.

• • •

James shows up early the next morning, dressed in her sleek running outfit. She knows my schedule better than practically anyone, but I still feel like a total slacker because I'm in my pajamas with sleep crusty in my eyes.

"Come on," she says. "Get dressed. Let's go get breakfast."

I make a grumpy sleepy noise, but James just shakes her head.

"Matty doesn't deserve your wallowing."

"I'm not wallowing!" I say. "It's, like, six A.M., you freak."

"This is the only way we can get Porto's without waiting in line for an hour," she says, which is unfortunately the truth. I let her inside and quickly change back into my wallowing clothes, which are fine with James because she doesn't know they're my wallowing clothes. Athletes are much more comfortable with stretchy clothes in public, so I'm able to get away with a lot. If we were out with a larger group, someone would definitely call me out on these yoga pants.

The line is fairly short, as expected, and James insists on ordering dozens of pastries in two boxes. I know that one box is for her family and one is for mine, and I know that Dad will smile when he sees the familiar yellow, gray, and white box. Porto's is a Cuban bakery with rows and rows of sweet and savory pastries and desserts beyond what your mind could even dream up. They're magically cheap, too; James pays only twenty dollars, total, for both boxes.

"What do you want to do today?" she asks, once we're seated on the patio with little cups of coffee. I'm still learning to appreciate its bitterness; we both know once we're done here I'll walk up the street to the proper coffee shop for something milkier and sweeter.

"I thought you were hanging out with Logan today," I say. Logan Sidana, James's boyfriend, is a new freshman at UCLA. He and James have the most mature relationship of anyone I know. By next year she'll be at UCLA as well, and I already have ideas about anecdotes I'll tell in my speech at their wedding when we're twenty-five or whenever.

I've actually been thinking a lot about Logan in the last twenty-three hours. James and I were getting ready to go to junior prom last year, and Logan showed up early. He didn't want to get left out of the conversation, because Logan's not one of those guys who doesn't like hanging out with girls. He has two sisters and he'll compliment your hair or notice if you get new shoes. So he stood outside James's closed bedroom door, chatting with us while we finished getting ready. James, of course, was ready much earlier than I was, so she joined Logan in the hallway.

Matty's running late! I'd called when I got his text. James called back a *No problem! We have time!* but I clearly heard Logan mutter something about *that douchebag*. I still remember how chilled I felt by his words, because I *liked* Logan. Everyone at Magnolia Park liked Logan, because he was handsome and polite and ended up giving a valedictorian speech that brought the majority of the audience to tears. And back then I loved Matty—a mere twenty-four hours ago I loved Matty, after all—but I had this deep *respect* for Logan. So instead of thinking about someone like Logan thinking that my boyfriend, the love of my sixteen years of life, was a douchebag, I decided that was where Logan and I would never agree.

And it's hard to explain, but something was never the same from then on.

"We're hanging out later," James says, and takes a sip of her coffee. "But we don't have to, if you need me. Or you could come with me."

"I'm not coming with you," I say. "You haven't seen him in weeks. You guys need to make out and stuff. Like, full contact stuff."

"We're going to a party," she says, like a full-blown grown-up. "You could go. You could have one of those ill-advised rebound hookups I've heard about."

"I am super not in the mood for an ill-advised rebound hookup," I say. "Probably no one will ever touch me again, and I'll turn to stone."

James grins. "I'll check with Logan, but I don't think that's physically possible."

"Why would Logan know about that?" I shriek.

"Because he's pre-med," she says. "Not because he's never been touched. Don't worry. Logan is fine."

"Turning to stone isn't a medical thing," I tell her in between nibbling on a guava and cream cheese pastry. "It's a curse. Doctors can't help with curses."

"You're not cursed, Kat," James says, in such a warm calm tone that I burst into tears. She doesn't look embarrassed that this is happening while we're out in public; she just takes my hand and holds it. And it always feels safer to cry when James is holding my hand.

• • •

James offers up several more invites, but I manage to escape the UCLA party. It would have been fun to tag along with Matty in tow; he's so in his element at parties. Crowds always end up forming around him, even if he barely knows anyone when the evening starts. And I liked being the girl at his side, the one laughing first at his jokes and anticipating his moves. I've been one of a pair with James since we were little, but I liked being one of a pair with Matty, too.

Anyway, maybe someday I could imagine being at a party not as a pair of any sort and having a good time, but tonight's not it. I do hope at some point it sounds good to kiss someone else, but right now I might as well have a little cage around myself, or one of those cones our neighbor's dog wore so he wouldn't chew on stitches after leg surgery.

Dad is working at the kitchen table on his laptop when I get back from hanging out with James, and he grins as I set the pastry box on the table.

"Do I tell you enough that you're my favorite daughter?" he asks.

"Ha ha," I say. "So, is your boss making you work again this weekend?"

We both know that it's very rare that Dad's forced to work on weekends, or even late evenings. Since Mom's been gone, we're both happy to pretend that he's not just trying to fill his time.

"Uh, sure, Kat," he says, and I notice the words on the window he's minimized. *Online Dating*.

"Dad!"

He turns to look at me. "What?" And then his eyes see where mine are looking. "Oh. It's . . . it's nothing. I didn't even sign up yet. You're right, it's dumb."

"No," I say, correcting my tone. "It's not dumb. I didn't say that. I just didn't know you—"

"I won't do it if you don't want me to," he says.

"It shouldn't be up to me," I say, because my deep down honest answer would be that I don't want him to. But I'm not about to make Dad's life even worse with brutal honesty. I hate myself for even *thinking* brutal honesty, and I feel my heart speed up.

The symptoms of cardiac arrhythmia are so vague—a freaking "fluttery heart"? Lots of things can give you a fluttery heart, like kissing someone or seeing otters at the aquarium. It's hard to be constantly vigilant. Dad let me get a second and then a third opinion after Mom died, but if Mom didn't know something was wrong until it was way too late, how can I trust them?

"You should totally do it," I say with all the enthusiasm I have. "Go meet someone!"

"What should I say are my hobbies?" Dad asks, instead of ducking out of the topic, like I expect him to. "I've never had to worry about having hobbies."

"Cooking," I say. "Cooking sounds good on a dating site, right?"

"I don't think heating up your weird lasagnas counts as cooking," he says.

"But you used to, sometimes. The salmon with veggies, and spaghetti. Your spaghetti was always better than Mom's."

Dad sighs, and I feel that I've done the wrong thing by bringing her up.

"You could also—"

"Maybe I'll wait to do this until I don't have to lie about having hobbies," he says.

I feel something in me settle, even if that isn't at all fair.

• • •

The next time I emerge from my room, thinking about maybe watching TV, I find Dad in the living room doing exactly that. It's my first Saturday night as a senior, and I'm having literally the same evening as my forty-six-year-old father. Maybe worse? He was at least thinking about dating. He's not cursed.

"I'm going to walk to Von's," I tell Dad. "We're out of . . ."

I can't think of what we're actually out of, but luckily

he just gives me cash and waves me off. It feels good to be out of the house again, and I hope that it's not a bad omen of my future that it also feels good to be alone.

Up ahead of me, I hear a dog barking—but not any sort of threatening barking. It's the sound of tiny yapping, and when I turn the corner onto Pass Avenue, a little black-and-white dog makes a beeline for me.

"Catch him!" someone shouts, and I don't question it. I've never been athletic like James, but I can be fast in short bursts. And within moments, the dog is in my arms, continuing to yap in protest.

"Oh my god, *thank you.*" The dog chaser catches up with me, and I realize it's someone from school. Magnolia Park is big, so there are a lot of people like this girl who I recognize on sight but couldn't name if I was being held at gunpoint.

Not even under much less stressful circumstances.

I hold on tightly to the loud squirming dog, who's clearly already plotting another escape. "Is this your dog?"

"He's my aunt's dog." She reaches out to clip a leash to the dog's collar. "She's letting me watch him this weekend and . . ."

"It's going super great?"

She laughs and pushes her hair back from her face. Her hair's tall in front, short like a boy's everywhere else, swooped up and over, and it stays put where she shoves it. "Oh yeah, super great for sure."

I tentatively set the dog on the ground and breathe a sigh of relief when the leash keeps him from escaping. "He seems angry."

"My aunt works from home, so he's not used to being without her. It's pretty codependent," she says. "It's lucky you were here, though. Especially because you have super strength, ripping doors off of lockers and all."

Oh, no.

"Oh, god, I'm sorry," she says, and everything must be apparent on my face. "I just thought that it was funny—I'm an asshole."

"You're not an asshole," I say, which I can feel, even if I don't really know her. It's easy to forget sometimes that while others might get lost in the crowded halls of Magnolia Park High, Matty and I were visible. We were one of *those* couples, and it doesn't hurt that Logan and James had been, too, up until graduation last school year.

"I accidentally am." The girl holds firm to the leash as the little dog strains against it. "All of the time."

"Me too." I think of Dad and how his face looked thinking about Mom's spaghetti. "It's hard not to be. Maybe for some people it's not? For me it is."

She watches me for a moment or two. "So where are you heading? *None of your business, Quinn,* is an acceptable answer, obviously."

"I'm just going to Von's to buy . . ." I shrug. "Whatever. Nonvegetarian lasagna."

“Please don’t buy premade lasagna,” the girl—Quinn—says. “My mom’s half-Italian. Microwave lasagna is an affront to our people.”

This is how I end up in Von’s with a dog hiding in my bag and Quinn loading a plastic grocery basket with lasagna ingredients. She shops with the confidence of an adult, decisively selecting meats and cheeses and pasta and asking me questions about my family’s spice cabinet.

We walk back to Quinn’s aunt’s house to drop off the dog, and then I lead Quinn back to my house. Dad looks understandably surprised to see so much activity in the kitchen, but Quinn has such a command of everything that it somehow normalizes the situation. I don’t really help, but I don’t think that it matters.

“I guess I should go,” Quinn says once she’s slid the lasagna into the oven. She turns and flashes me a smile. “Check on Buckley.”

“Who’s Buckley?” I ask, and she laughs.

“The beast from hell who ate your ChapStick,” she says, because that ended up being the only consequence of hiding the dog in my purse.

“Good luck,” I tell her. “And . . . thank you for helping me.”

“Tell me how it turns out,” she says with a nod to the oven.

I take out my phone to get her number. There are *five* new texts from Matty, and while a strong and brave person would delete them immediately, I know I'll read them as soon as I have a moment alone.

"I like your friend," Dad says once Quinn's gone. "Why hasn't she been around more?"

It suddenly seems silly to admit I'd never even spoken a word to Quinn before tonight, so I just smile and shrug.

• • •

OH MY GOD.

Is everything OK?

THIS LASAGNA!!!

Oh, god. Now I really need to know. Is everything OK?

❤❤❤

I'll try to remain humble, but. It's a good recipe.

Thank you so much for rescuing me and my dad from the frozen kind. You're a saint.

I'm not sure if saints ever wanted to murder an innocent dog, but, thank you.

INNOCENT?!!! He tried to escape! He ate a ChapStick!!

Well, you've got him there. Escape and ChapStick-eating are capital offenses. California will have to bring back the death penalty.

I text Quinn until I fall asleep, and it's not until I wake up the next morning with an imprint of my phone on my arm that I remember there were five texts from Matty I haven't read yet.

I still love you.

Kat, 😻 I miss you.

We could go to Summers' party tonight.

Fine, ignore me. I'm going by myself. See you there?

drnuk miss yo

I screencap them, all in a row, and text them to James, and for the first time I wish I would have talked to Quinn about Matty, because I can feel how funny she'd think these were. But knowing a new person is a special kind of magic, because they don't have to see everything. Quinn doesn't know my mom is dead or the intricacies of Matty and me. And even though I can imagine her laughter, especially at "drnuk miss yo," it's nice knowing that, for Quinn, I'm a new person, too.

CHAPTER THREE

June of Senior Year

James

"This is pointless," I mutter while pulling a hair elastic off my wrist so I can sweep my long hair off my neck. We're practically high school graduates, and instead of sitting inside having to do relatively little in the air-conditioning, we're outside in the suffocating Burbank heat rehearsing graduation.

"Why are you in such a crappy mood?" Mariana asks. She and Sofia are walking behind us. It's a funny combination because all four of us have barely been together since very early in the school year, before Kat relocated the two of us to the other lunch table. Technically at this point they're just walking behind *me*, though, because (unsurprisingly) Kat's nowhere to be found.

"We just have to walk down the aisle and take seats," I say. "I don't know why we have to rehearse that."

"Some people are really stupid and need the run-through," Mariana says, in the most sugarcoated voice imaginable. I've missed her brand of salty and sweet. "This seems like a weird thing to get hung up on, James."

I'd text Logan to find out how useless he thought graduation rehearsal was, but it could send the wrong message. It's incredible how many things can be interpreted as *I miss you and want you back and also deeply want to have sex with you* when the recipient is desperately seeking that meaning.

"James, I feel like we haven't hung out in so long," Sofia says.

I shrug, instead of saying that it's because that's an accurate fact. Last year, a day didn't go by that Mariana didn't say something so snarky that we'd laugh until we cried, and Sofia had some overly heartfelt thing to share with us (that inevitably led to another snarky comment from Mariana). Our lunch table seemed like the center of Magnolia Park, and not the way that sort of thing went in stereotypical movies about high school. Sure, people like Matty & Co. could border on being assholes, but on the whole, we just weren't like that. I can so clearly picture sitting right between Logan and Kat while laughing so hard at something that I couldn't even eat my lunch. Senior year should have been more of the same; it was all I'd wanted. Everything felt straightforward and decided back then.

"Are you walking alone?" Mariana asks me.

"No one's walking alone," Sofia says. "If you're a friendless loser, school admin will pair you up with another friendless loser."

"Aw!" Kat bounces over, finally. "Maybe that's how people fall in love."

"The rom-com no one is waiting for," Mariana says, and I grin.

"To answer your question," I say, "I'm walking with Kat. At least, I signed up to walk with Kat."

"OK, yes, true, but here's the thing." A giggle escapes her lips, and I wonder just how immoral it is to wish unhappiness on someone. Logan would probably have an answer for that, too.

I miss Logan too much for words. Is it possible that my fingers literally itch to text him? Maybe the truth is that a simple question about rehearsal or immorality *would* be a secret message about missing and wanting and loving. I hardly want to admit that, though. Not to Logan. Barely even to myself.

"So now that Raina and Gretchen are together, they really want to walk together. Raina was originally supposed to walk with Quinn, so now Quinn doesn't have anyone, so

I volunteered to walk with her. But some girl from T&F was supposed to walk with Gretchen, so I'm sure you guys know each other. That'll be fine, right? Then, like, everyone's got someone?"

"What girl?" I ask, instead of what I want to say, which is *of fucking course it's not fine.*

"It's Jill," Gretchen says, walking over with Raina in tow. "Thank you, thank you, thank you."

Jill Pang is standing behind them, and she makes eye contact with me. We both roll our eyes, so I guess it's fine. As fine as getting ditched at graduation by your supposed best friend can be.

"Are you OK?" Kat asks me while furiously texting.

"Sure." I'd kept waiting for something, but at this point I'm not sure what we still have left to snap us back into place. School is nearly over, and shouldn't something have done it by now? We haven't talked much about prom or even, really, Disneyland, or the simple fact that I can't remember the last time that I was the one Kat was furiously texting. While I miss plenty of things about last year, it's less the lunch table—and maybe even Logan—and more Kat that I miss. I had no idea how you could stand right next to someone and yet have no clue how to get back to them. Though I guess that now it's more that I'm standing behind someone.

"Students, remain in proper formation," Vice Principal Benway says as she makes her way down the aisle. We aren't even moving yet. "Miss Rydell, please put away your phone."

I bite the inside of my cheek to keep from smiling.

"I'm sorry, Ms. Benway," Kat says in her innocent little girl voice.

"Even though we're outside and your graduation is in a few days, we still need everyone to follow the student handbook," Ms. Benway says. Regardless of everything, I make eye contact with Kat because there's no way that statement can escape an eye roll.

"By the way, Miss Rydell," Ms. Benway continues, "I was very impressed with your prom campaign. It's heartening seeing young people fighting for their beliefs."

I regret our mutual eye roll so much now. I regret there's no one here for me to share a new eye roll with. Seriously . . . beliefs? I've never seen someone get so much credit for needing to be the center of attention at any cost.

"Thank you so much, Ms. Benway." Kat actually places her hand over her own heart. "I feel so fortunate I was at a school like Magnolia Park where we were taken seriously."

I glance back at Mariana and Sofia, but they look as enthralled with Kat as Ms. Benway. And, of course, that's why I miss them to begin with. Everything felt so easy then: friendships, boyfriends, the future. But now my feelings are too messy. It's like something has been rotting from within and now there's no way to know when it started.

Kat swings around so that her hip knocks against mine. It suddenly feels like *us*, like James and Kat with no distance, no breakups, no walking separately at graduation. "You're coming to the grad pre-party at Adrian's tonight, right?"

I shrug. "I might not."

"James!" She pulls on her necklaces, the old and new monograms glinting in the sun. "It's our last high school party. By Saturday night we'll be *freshmen* again."

"Oh, god," I say. "Why didn't I think of that?"

"It's terrifying, right? So that solves it. You're coming."

• • •

For all the parties I've managed to avoid this year, I'm not sure why I'm ending the year with one. There was more than a brief moment earlier today when I wanted to just call it off. Even *the idea* of walking with anyone but Kat at graduation, much less *the reality* of it . . . Shouldn't we just admit the friendship had, somehow, run its course? Sure, we might have moments where things feel just like before, but that doesn't erase the long stretches of time when they don't.

So *of course* it might be naive that I'm thinking of tonight's party invite as a potential magic elixir. You have no idea what you'll believe until you have to.

At Adrian Vardanyan's house, I slip past Matty and Co., managing to walk past all of them without any eye contact from Matty, or even from Co. Matty doesn't seem like the center of attention the way he used to, though, and I figure that's because the reigning king of a high school class doesn't do stuff like get hung up for so long on his ex-girlfriend, and definitely doesn't say ugly, shitty things to her. Not Matty Saves the World Evans, at least.

None of my friends seem to be inside, so I text Kat—Are you here yet? I even add a confetti emoji because I know it's the kind of thing she'll like—and head out to the backyard. I spot Hannah, Tobi, and a few others from track, and I step into their circle.

"McCall!" Tobi cheers. She's wearing a sparkly dress and red heart-shaped sunglasses, even though no one else is dressed up and it's nighttime. "We're graduating!"

"She's had, like, a beer and a half already," Hannah tells me.

"I thought her body was a temple," I say.

"Temples have wine and stuff," Tobi tells me.

Hannah and I exchange a look.

"There's soda, too," Hannah says. "And mineral water? You can keep your temple running with Prohibition-era laws."

"Thank god," I say, and luckily a sophomore girl scampers off to get beverages for us. Kat's right; I'll miss being at the top of the food chain. It'll be weird to be the babies again, and I mention this to Hannah.

"Oh, I'm grateful for it," she says, as we accept our

bottles of Topo Chico. "I don't know what I'm doing. Now I can be honest about that again."

I clink my glass bottle against hers. "Also, we can protect each other."

"*Yes*. I'm so glad you changed your mind and accepted—"

"I haven't really said anything to anyone yet," I say.

"You nerd," she says. "Why not? Berkeley's a great school. It was my dream school!"

I make sure Tobi's too tipsy to be paying attention. It's a safe bet. "It's a long story, but I fucked up some of my application deadlines, and then . . . I liked how it sounded to go as far away as possible, so I kept talking about Michigan. It took me a while to sort out what I actually wanted."

Hannah nods. "The whole process makes you not want to say anything to anyone, huh?"

I try not to let it show on my face how true that's been.

"I was so nervous I wouldn't get in," Hannah continues. "And everyone would know I already had this dumb Berkley keychain as a good luck . . . whatever."

"It's all too public," I agree.

"You two have to start beering next year," Tobi says at a very loud volume.

"*Beering*?" I ask.

"Athletes in college manage not to beer, too," Hannah says. "We'll survive."

I feel something in my chest lighten. It was easy to want to believe that when I got to college I'd have to learn to be a bubbly fun girl everyone wanted to party with. I'd have to be like Kat to survive. But Hannah's right; I can stay just James. *Just James* can be enough.

We keep drinking mineral waters while Tobi beers more and loudly outlines her plans for seducing Miguel Carter before graduation. I keep my phone handy but there's still no response from Kat.

It's a little hard to believe that despite how much time I've spent with my track teammates, I've only recently realized I'd have this much fun hanging out with them beyond practices and meets. I wonder how this year—how *high school*—would have felt had I realized it sooner.

And it seems like with school behind us and only graduation ahead, walls are coming down anyway. Everyone's talking to everyone, and it matters less who was a drama kid, who cared only about their grades, or who was basically a clichéd asshole. As more people join our group in the backyard, we end up talking about college, and from time to time it hits me how this is all slipping away. By the end of this weekend, we won't be seniors, and by the end of the summer, most of us won't even live here anymore.

"Wait," I find myself saying. The night's caught up with me and I have no idea how long it's been since I arrived. I check my phone, but there are still no messages. "Have you guys seen Kat?"

Hannah's friend Ryan gestures toward the house, so I take a deep breath and walk inside. I'm assuming he's wrong, because even if it feels like I'm Kat's lowest priority, I don't actually believe that it could be true. What about the magic elixir? And while Kat's more popular and visible than ever, Ryan could be buzzed enough that he spotted someone else with curly hair and not the queen herself.

But when I walk inside, I see Kat sitting backward on the back of the sofa, holding court with admirers all around her. According to my phone I've already been here for nearly two hours. How long has Kat?

"James!" she squeals, and I can tell from her tone and the red Solo cup she gestures with that she's drunk. "I'm so glad you're here."

"Are you?" I ask. "When did you get here?"

"I dunno, awhile? Ago?" She giggles and pats the sofa next to her. "Sit with me! We're all talking about—what do you call it?"

"Lucid dreaming," someone says, which makes Kat nod emphatically. Someone else starts talking about being aware during a dream, which, of course, makes two guys bring up *Inception* because guys at parties love talking about Christopher Nolan movies. Someone squeezes around me, and I watch as Quinn hops up to take the spot on the sofa Kat just offered to me. I don't think Quinn knows it, but Kat knows. But all she does is beam at Quinn and yell at David Levy that his dream about cats doesn't count. I feel like the embodiment of my unanswered text to her.

I back away and make my way toward the front of the house. Matty's crew is still stationed there, louder and drunker and higher than before.

"Hey!" Matty shouts at me. "Where's your friend?"

"I'm not her keeper, Matty."

He stumbles over to me. I've never been a huge fan of Matty Evans, but right now I feel a surge of sympathy for him. He doesn't look fun inebriated, like Kat. He just looks sad.

"She thinks she's hot shit, you know," he slurs.

"I do know."

He moves in even closer. "I made"—he holds up one finger—"one little mistake and she just gets rid of me."

"You slept with another girl," I say. "You didn't forget her birthday or something."

"April second," he says. "See? I haven't forgotten her birthday."

"Good job," I tell him.

"You were my friend then," he says.

"On April second?"

"Before Kat dumped me," he says.

I think about that. Were Matty and I ever really friends? We spent plenty of time together, but I'm not sure I thought about him that way.

"How's your guy?" he asks. "Glasses guy?"

"Logan's fine," I say. "Not that he's my guy anymore."

"That sucks," Matty says, so I shrug. "That guy's a good guy."

Something turns inside of me and all I want to do is cry.

"Man." Matty's still looking into the next room at Kat. "She fuckin' thinks she's something."

I follow his sight line and take in the crowd that surrounds Kat. I watch how her eyes light up and how, even without hearing what she's saying, her gestures tell a story.

"She *is* something," I say.

I don't bother to tell Matty good-bye. I just get out of there.

• • •

I wake up earlier than usual the next morning, since my Habitat for Humanity shift is today. After changing from pajamas into running gear, I take off down the block. Up ahead I see a familiar form, so I break into my fastest sprint.

"Whoa, fancy meeting you here," Logan says.

"You're home for the summer?" I ask.

"Not yet, just home for the weekend," he says, as we match paces like we never stopped. "How are you doing, McCall?"

"This year can suck it."

He cracks up so hard he giggles like a little boy. "Senior

year's overrated. You'll have a way better time off in Michigan."

We run in silence for a few minutes, just the sound of our shoes hitting the sidewalk in almost perfect unison.

"I'm not going to Michigan," I say. "I accepted at Berkeley."

"Hell, *yeah*," Logan says. "I like this news."

"We aren't back together," I say.

"I didn't say we were. It's merely that my plans to make that happen are a lot easier with you only a six-hour drive away."

"Logan . . . there's just no guarantee," I say. "People our age think they're in love, and they make these promises, and then twenty or thirty years later it all falls apart."

"Sure, sometimes," he says. "Not always."

"I don't want it to fall apart with you," I admit.

"So you just threw a grenade into it and ran?" From anyone else that would sound accusatory, but he just laughs. "McCall. C'mon."

"My parents split up," I say. Such a little sentence for something so big.

"Shit, I'm sorry to hear that," he says. "You doing OK?"

I find myself laughing. "Almost, maybe? No, I don't know why I said that. Not really."

He slows down and reaches over to touch my arm. It's been a while since I felt his hands on me.

"Logan, I think . . . I think my world's small right now.

With you in it, without you in it. And I have to make it bigger."

He nods. I wait for whatever he has to say next, but right now, Logan Sidana is speechless. I like how it looks on him.

"I never want to hate you." I expect to think about my parents, but it's Kat's face in my head. I'm sure Kat's still sleeping off her hangover, and I doubt once she's awake that I'll be on her mind at all. Technically there's no reason I couldn't just text her, but right now it feels as fantastical as learning to fly.

"I'm pretty unhateable," Logan says as we resume our run. "E.L.L."

"Everyone Loves Logan?" I ask. "Seriously?"

He cracks up even more. I miss his arms around me, our early morning runs, the way he could still surprise me with a kiss after being together for so long. But his laugh, it turns out, is what I missed most.

"Always and forever." He stops running again and turns to face me, with his arms folded across his chest. "I could never hate you, McCall. Even if you wanted me to."

I step back into a run, and grin when he catches up with me.

● ● ●

"This is *horrible*," Hannah mutters as we walk over to the Habitat for Humanity construction site from my car.

"It's not that early," I say. "I've already been up getting my miles in. When do you train?"

"Certainly not in the middle of the night like you," she says. "Some people don't mind running during daylight hours."

"When exactly do you think the sun comes up?" I laugh and help myself to a cup of coffee. "We're building a house for someone who needs it. I feel like the least we can do is get up early."

Hannah sighs but pours herself a cup of coffee as well. "Thanks for letting me crash your big volunteer project, by the way. If I haven't already thanked you. I'm sure you wanted to be some lone wolf doing good in the world."

I don't know what to say because, while I'd never thought of myself as a wolf, lone or otherwise, I get what she's saying. It probably shouldn't feel so great to hang out with a friend who seems to inherently understand you; it's something I used to take for granted. But I guess there's also something nice about someone new. I'd worry it makes me a hypocrite, if not for the fact that I was the one shoved aside in the first place.

The construction leader goes over our day's schedule, plus safety information. Hannah and I both scribble down notes about protocol, hazards, and expectations. I left this volunteer opportunity for last because it really seemed as if you should build up to it—no pun intended. Still, I'm practically a high school graduate now, but I doubt that makes me ready to construct a home.

I decide to choose the task that'll have the fewest implications for the structural integrity of the house and start carrying materials over from the supply trailer to the lot. As I haul over bags of concrete, I think about my own home and the empty lot it must have been once. Obviously, that was long before Mom and Dad bought it—it was built in 1923—but I have to imagine that everyone goes in with relatively the same hopes and dreams.

"McCall, I'm over there *actually hammering boards together,*" Hannah says, walking alongside me. "You should join me."

"I'm good here," I say, and I realize I am. There's a sense of your own strength in watching this huge stack of items disappear in one place and then reappear in another, thanks in part to your own arms, back, legs. It doesn't necessarily feel like building a house, but it feels like *something.*

We break for lunch, and I sit next to Hannah while we eat sub sandwiches.

"I've never seen you eat carbs before," I tell her, and she laughs.

"I never turn down a free sandwich," she says. "Did you have fun last night?"

The party jolts back into my head, and I see Kat

perched on the back of that couch, gesturing with her stupid cup.

"Not really," I say. "I ran into Logan this morning, though."

"Oh, did you?" she asks, and I register that I actually said it aloud. *Whoops*.

I shrug and try to figure out what to say, because I hadn't really meant to bring him up. It's easier not bringing anything up. I'm still convinced that if one detail comes out, it all might. And Hannah seems to like me and want to be my friend. If I unloaded about my entire year, who knows.

"Yeah, I . . ." I let myself trail off.

"Mmmhmmm."

I laugh even though I absolutely didn't want to. "Stop."

"Can I ask?" Her tone is delicate. "What happened with you guys? You were always sort of my, you know." Hannah shrugs. "My hashtag goals."

I take a few bites of my sandwich. "I don't know. It started to feel silly to me, the more I thought about it."

I don't mention that had been over the course of one afternoon.

"You and Logan?"

I shrug. "Forever starting now. I'm not sure anyone can plan as much as I'd thought you could. I feel ridiculous now. Look at UCLA."

Hannah makes a big show of looking in the direction of Westwood.

"Stop." I do my best to hold back a smile. "Nothing this year went as I thought it would. I'm not sure why I thought I could make it work forever with a boy I met when I was a freshman."

She nods. "That makes sense to me."

I find that I'm waiting for her to jump in with a story of her own, but she doesn't. The moment gets to breathe.

After lunch, Hannah convinces me to join the construction crew, even though I still find it mind-boggling that regular people like us are just *allowed* to do this. Hammering nails into wood feels powerful, though, and unlike my previous volunteer assignments, I think I'm eager to do this again, and keep doing it. Using materials to help someone have a home is so far perhaps the biggest thing I've ever done. Originally, it didn't feel like work if I also enjoyed it, but as I watch the skeleton of a house actually being formed, I wonder how someone *couldn't* enjoy this. Doing good doesn't have to feel . . . well, *bad*. Is it silly that I'm just understanding that now?

The day passes more quickly than I expect, and Hannah and I discuss how long we should allot for driving back to Burbank, getting ready, and arriving at graduation. I see a team walk by us toward the stack of insulation and notice that one guy isn't wearing a mask. This morning the leader warned us not to work with insulation without one, and I almost say something. But I'm brand-new to this, and I'm sure there's a good reason he's doing what he's doing. And I'm not the person who'll shout across a crowd of people. I doubt there's anything I'd notice that's worth calling out.

I focus back on hammering nails, but before too long, I hear someone yell from across the yard. There's a flurry of commotion as people begin clustering around the area. The crew leaders make their way over with authority, which sends a chill through me. There's something about a forced calm demeanor that strikes so much more fear in me than loud chaos. I exchange glances with the crew members around me, as if someone's expression will set me at ease. None do, though.

As the commotion continues, most of us end up putting down our tools and running over to see what's going on. The same guy I saw without a mask earlier is now sitting on the lawn taking deep gulping breaths, and I move in closer without even thinking about it.

"He's fine," the construction leader tells me, as first aid swoops in.

"I'm so sorry," I find myself saying. "I saw him walk by without a mask, but . . . I thought it must be OK if no one else said anything."

"James," she says, looking at my nametag, "communication is key."

Sometimes a moment feels bigger than what it actually is.

● ● ●

As people stumble into seats on graduation night, I feel like a jerk for having assumed our rehearsal yesterday was unnecessary. Apparently walking in a procession and taking an orderly seat *is* way out of the ability levels of a lot of graduating Magnolia Park seniors.

I glance up at Kat as the ceremony begins. Her green eyes are fixed on the stage, so it feels like the wrong time to make fun of our less coordinated classmates. It might be the wrong time even if she wasn't paying such rapt attention. I have no idea what Kat's thinking.

I'm called up for my diploma before she is, because it's alphabetical, and I feel silly at how relieved I am that she cheers so loudly at the sound of my name. I'm still crossing the stage and moving my tassel over when the principal calls *Quinn Morgan*, and I force myself not to measure Kat's cheer in comparison to hers for me. And I cheer my heart out when Kat's name is called, because, no matter what, we did it. We got through four years of high school, and we're all off to see what the rest of the world holds.

Mom and Dad want to take a million photos of me afterward, and I have my second fear of pettiness when I realize how relieved I am that Todd isn't here. I know being a high school graduate isn't actually being an adult, but I'd love to magically feel more mature now that my tassel is on the left side.

"Where's Kat?" Mom asks, as though *now* she suddenly gives a shit about Kat. "We can't have photos without her."

I shrug. "Attending to her legions of fans. And you don't even like her, so does it matter?"

Mom raises an eyebrow. "Everything all right, James? It's strange not seeing you two joined at the hip."

As if on cue, Kat appears with her dad and Diane. I'm glad that Mom can't keep talking about Kat's absence while Kat's there, but I'm also relieved there are already a million photos on my parents' phones of me alone. It feels possible I'll never want to look at myself standing arm in arm with Kat again.

"Are you going to the official grad night thing tonight?" Kat asks me. Magnolia Park throws a late-night party each year for all graduating seniors, though throughout the course of the evening, people tend to head off for smaller celebrations.

"Maybe," I say, because the feeling of being all but ignored by Kat last night is fresh in my head. "Are you?"

"Of course. Then Brandi's. You should come."

"Like I should have come last night?" I ask. "I don't really think that ultimately mattered, did it?"

"Oh my god, I was"—she mouths—"*so drunk* last night."

"I noticed."

"Are you mad?" Kat hugs her arm around my neck. "I'm sorry I'm such a freaking disaster when there's vodka around."

"Kat, we saw your picture in the paper," Mom tells her, and it kills me that *this* is what makes my mother finally respect my best friend. Not the years and years of her being the person who was there for everything I needed. "That must have been so exciting."

"The *Burbank Leader,*" I say. "Does that still count?"

Everyone stops and stares at me, even Kat, who I'm pretty sure said the exact same thing when it was initially announced. Why are her words suddenly so bad when they're out of my mouth?

"Charlie, you must be so proud of this one, huh?" Mom asks.

Kat pretends to look modest while her dad confirms his pride level.

"I never see you around with James anymore," Mom says. For so many different reasons—not even including that I just spotted Logan out of the corner of my eye—I hold my breath. "I'd love to have you over for dinner at the new house."

"What new house?" Kat asks. *Shit.*

Mom cocks her head in confusion, as a cold chill seizes me even underneath the warm sunshine. Why did I think I could outrun this forever?

"Well, James of course told you about the place I got

with Todd in Toluca Lake," Mom says. "I guess it's not *new* new anymore."

Kat drops her arm and steps away from me. I don't know why this is different, but it feels final.

"Sure, of course," Kat says. "It sounds amazing, and I'm so sorry I haven't been over yet. Senior year's intense, you know?"

She lies so well.

"Did you guys get enough pictures?" Kat asks in her tiny sweet voice. "Quinn's parents apparently need me, too."

I don't stick around for an awkward conversation with anyone. But on my way to Logan, I get tackled by Hannah and then Tobi. We take a million photos as well and agree to walk together to grad night later. What if I just try to forget Kat exists for a while? It worked with Logan.

Well, until he started popping up all the time.

"Congrats," he says. "I got you something."

I roll my eyes for effect but smile as he places a tiny ceramic bear figurine in my hands. "What the hell?"

"I'm embarrassed for you, McCall. It's obviously an Oski. Your new mascot up at your slightly inferior UC school."

I squeeze the bear tight in my hands. "How did you even find the time to get this since this morning?"

"Well, between you and me, it's not an *official* Oski. It's just a weird-looking bear. Does the job, though, yeah?"

He looks so proud of himself, and I'm humiliated at how weak that makes me. Why does smugness make Logan so sexy? It's ridiculous. I'm relieved that I don't drink, because I have a flashback of the drunken and desperate texts Matty used to send to Kat, and I can see how with the help of alcohol, I might be doing the same thing.

To Logan, that is. Or maybe I'd have drunken and desperate things to say to my best friend, too. But it's the other way around, sort of, because I'm still out at my celebratory—and mercifully peaceful—dinner with Mom and Dad when my phone starts buzzing.

Your mom moved to Toluca Lake?!

Who even is Todd?!!!

Seriously, what the HECK, J??????

Are you like mad or something that I got drunk last night?

OK so if her house isn't even NEW new then how long ago did this even happen? J I am FREAKING OUT here. This is seriously weird. Please tell me there's a super normal explanation, OK??

"James, come on," Mom says. "You'll be off to school any day now. You can put your phone away for one meal."

There's no point in arguing, so I shove it into my pocket, where it almost immediately buzzes four more times. I'm sure it's not Kat. Why would it be Kat? She's already made her point. I'm sure at this point she didn't hear what I said about her at Jon Kessler's party—not that it was a big deal. It wasn't a deal at all. People can act so thrown by the truth that everyone's already thinking.

"We know this has been a tough year for you," Dad says, with a look to Mom.

"Is that necessary, Jamie?" she asks with a dismissive sigh. I guess it's easy to be over it when you're the one who set it all in motion.

"I just want James to know how proud I am at how maturely she's gotten through it."

I choke back a laugh, even though I want to cry. My list of the ways Kat wronged me feels so right and morally sound. So why do her texts feel like bullets in a well-aimed revolver?

"You should have invited Logan with us to dinner." Mom turns to face me and somehow not look at Dad at the same time. "I haven't seen any of him lately, either."

"James and Logan broke up," Dad says. Before last year, he wouldn't have known anything before Mom did, and I wonder if, given everything, he likes that.

"Honey . . ." Mom reaches across the table, over the bread basket, to touch my arm. "I'm so sorry to hear that."

"It was last year." I pull my arm away and take a piece of bread. "I'm fine."

"Is that why you seemed relieved that you didn't get into UCLA?" she asks.

"No. And I wasn't relieved." I shove most of the piece of bread in my mouth, which ends conversation for a short while at least. And without conversation, you can eat more quickly, so before too long we're saying goodnight to Mom and getting into Dad's car.

I pray the four texts I felt come in are actually from Hannah, coordinating getting to the party tonight. But they aren't.

> OK . . . please tell me there's a misprint in the graduation programs. I just noticed your declared school is Berkeley. What happened to Michigan?

> Seriously, I thought we were both going to be in the Midwest together. Why didn't you

tell me???

J WHAT IS GOING ON!!!

Can you please text back or call me or something? I know I'll see you tonight but please, J.

I don't know what to do or say. More so than usual. So I don't do or say anything. What does it matter at this point?

I go home, change from my graduation dress to jeans and a shimmery blue top Kat picked out for me last year, and head off for Tobi's. I wish I had a non-Kat-related shirt to wear, but that's practically impossible. Kat's objectively good at shopping, and even better at telling me what to wear. There's no getting away from her; her influence bleeds into everything.

"I'll be out late," I tell Dad on my way to the front door.

"Well, I assumed so." He smiles at me. "I really am proud of you, James. Not just for this year, but I know how hard you've worked all through high school."

"I had this whole plan," I say with a shrug. "And who even knows what parts of it still make sense."

I expect Dad to assure me, but he just laughs.

"Yeah, tell me about it."

This probably shouldn't be a revelation, but it's really strange that parents are human, too.

"Maybe you should talk to someone after all," he says. "I've been—and it's been helping me a lot."

Normally I'd immediately push back against even the implied threat of therapy, but maybe it would be good to sort through this year—this life, even—with someone else. My head's felt so heavy, my thoughts so protected, and I think I might be exhausted from all of it. And this is me headed out the door *to a party*.

"OK, I'll talk to someone," I say. "Don't look proud of me. Just look normal. Promise?"

Dad makes a very solemn face and nods. "I'll make some calls. Have a fun night, kiddo."

That seems unlikely, but if he can fake normalcy, I can fake a smile before waving good-bye.

I meet up with Hannah and Tobi, and we walk back to school. Grad night is, like all school events except prom, held in the gym.

"This is going to be dorky as hell," Hannah says as we survey the crowd and the streamer-filled room. "Or maybe it's just me that's a little bit over all the stereotypical high school stuff."

"We literally just graduated," I say. "You are hardly the only one over stereotypical high school stuff."

"You two are party poopers," Tobi says. "Literally."

"Literally?" we ask at the same time. No one wants to dwell on the implications of that statement, so we head off to check out the snack table instead.

I spot Gabriel on my walk over, and even though I'm not dangerous insulation and he doesn't need to wear a mask, suddenly all I can hear in my head is that *communication is key.*

"Hey," I greet him.

"Hey, James," he says.

"Brett Bolton's party? Logan and I had . . . literally just broken up. Not that . . ." I find myself smiling. "Not that there's anything wrong about anything that happened, but if it came across like I blew you off—I'm sorry."

"Girls blow me off all of the time," he says with a smile. "It's fine."

"No, but . . . I could have been clearer."

Gabriel grins. If my heart had only gotten the message that Logan and I were over, I feel how I could have fallen for him and had a very different year.

"You owed me nothing," he says. "And I know where I rank next to Sidana."

I laugh. "Don't believe his hype. You rank fine."

As I walk away it feels like a chapter has finally been closed, and I breathe a literal sigh of relief. Until I reach the snack table.

"Hey!" Quinn's pouring punch into tiny cups as I walk up. From her tone I can tell she has no idea about Kat's texts to me. About anything at all. "I think K was looking for you. Can I get you some punch? From what I hear, it tastes like liquid Skittles, so take that as you will."

"I'll pass," I say.

"This is why you're the smart one," she says, because no matter how hard I try, I can't fully hate Quinn. It would be so much easier if she were horrible.

"Hey." Kat walks up with her hands on her hips. She's changed into a hot pink flowered dress and I'm struck for a moment by how beautiful she is. Something has changed within Kat this year where it's as if I can see the adult she's going to become. Is that part of what's gone wrong? Has she turned into yet another person who I don't know?

"I'm not hearing the most positive reviews on the punch," Quinn tells her, holding out one of the tiny cups. Kat shoots her a little smile before accepting it and walking toward one of the corners of the gym.

I take a deep breath and follow her.

"Seriously," she says, clutching her little cup of red liquid. "I don't understand what's going on."

"Nothing's going on," I say, like an idiot. How can things be so clear in my head and so wrong out of my mouth?

"James, like, even one thing," she says, and I hear the tears in her voice. "College, your mom, someone named Todd?"

"My mom left my dad," I say. "Are you happy?"

"Of *course* I'm not happy! When did it happen? Are you doing OK? Is your dad?"

"I told you one thing," I say. "Like you asked. So please don't follow it up with a thousand questions."

"I'm seriously . . ." She sniffles. "I'm *so confused.* My questions are because I care about you and your family."

"Please don't make this about you right now, OK?"

"I'm not." Her voice breaks on *not.* "But, like, James, I know that you didn't get dumped by Logan. I wasn't going to say anything because I know how hard breakups are, but . . . like, hearing all of this now . . . this whole year really feels like a lie."

I stare at her. Even though I want this conversation to be over, I also wish I magically had the words to make all of this sound fine. If Kat's the one who's made everything so hard this year, why do I have to feel like the bad guy? Why is it possible that I could *be* the bad guy?

"I'm seriously in shock," she says. "Did you not think I'd care about any of this?"

"Uh . . ." I have no idea how to finish the thought. It's so clear how little space I take up in Kat's world anymore.

"I don't know why this was a secret from me. Why freaking *all of this stuff* was a secret from me."

"It wasn't a secret *from you,*" I say. "It wasn't a secret at all. I just didn't want to talk about it. Not everyone wants to discuss every single thing to death, you know."

Her mouth falls open. "Why aren't you telling me anything?"

“What’s there to know?” I ask. “My mom left my dad. Logan and I broke up. I’m going to Berkeley.”

“Right, but, like . . . if I hadn’t seen your mom at graduation and she hadn’t said anything . . . I can’t believe you didn’t tell me about Berkeley.”

“I never said for sure that I was going to Michigan,” I say. “You just assumed that and ran with it because it suited your visions of this perfect college life. Me still at your beck and call only two hours away.”

“That’s not what I wanted. Why would you assume, like, a super crappy thing about me?”

“You could have asked me what was going on in my life,” I say. “When’s the last time you did that? You make everything about yourself.”

It’s hard to explain, but it’s as if saying it aloud makes it true.

“This is *grad night,*” Kat says, as if I’ve interrupted something sacred in a school gymnasium. “Do we have to do this here?”

“We definitely don’t,” I say. “I think we’re pretty much finished.”

I find Hannah and Tobi and fake that I’m having a good time for a while. It’s incredible how I can act like a girl who still has a best friend. The punch does taste like liquid Skittles, and Tobi does manage to hunt down Miguel Carter—even if it’s technically no longer *before* graduating and even if talking to someone doesn’t necessarily count as *seducing.*

But eventually something clicks in me and I can't fake it anymore. I act as if I'm only heading off to the bathroom, but I walk past it down the main corridor and then out the front door.

At first I start walking home, but I don't really feel like being there. I can't think of anywhere I actually want to be. And yet my feet take me down to Catalina Street, right to Logan's door.

"This doesn't mean anything," I say when he opens the front door.

"What doesn't?"

I step into his doorway and kiss him.

CHAPTER FOUR

November of Senior Year

KAT

OK, like, I for sure don't think you're stupid, but . . ." I laugh and shake my head. "I literally don't know another way to explain this."

Quinn dramatically sighs and smashes her face into her calculus book. "I hate this class so much. I feel stupider than I did at the start of the year, solely because of it."

"I don't think a career in calculus is in your future," I tell her. "Sorry, I know that destroys all kinds of your dreams and stuff."

"Wait, is that your pep talk?" She laughs so hard that my bed, which we're studying on, shakes. "You're a terrible tutor."

"Firstly, I am not your tutor, you goober," I say.

"Secondly?"

"It's really not fair that people assume if you get good grades that you understand how to explain something to someone else. That's, like, a whole other skill set!"

"Poor baby." Quinn closes her book and rolls over onto her side next to me. "I'll patiently wait while you finish your homework, while my future gets bleaker and bleaker."

"Oh, shut up." I laugh and close my textbook. "I can do this later. What do you want to do now?"

Quinn is completely still for a moment, maybe the longest I've ever seen her go without moving or saying something.

And then she kisses me.

It's over almost as soon as it starts, and immediately I find I don't know what to do with my body or my face or most especially my lips.

"OK," Quinn says. "That's . . . not how I hoped that would go."

"I just didn't expect you to—I'm not—you're—" I cover my face with my hands, as if that's ever been a cure for not knowing the right thing to say.

"I'm sorry," she says, and I feel her standing up from the bed while my face is still covered. "I'll go."

"What about your calculus?" Oh my god, I'm such a dork.

"Hey, you said it. Calculus is not in my future." She

shoves her books into her backpack and slings it over one shoulder before walking out of my room.

"You don't have to go," I say, following after her.

"Kat, I feel . . ." She shoves her hands through her hair. "Epically stupid right now."

"Please don't feel stupid," I say. "I mean, obviously except about calculus."

"You're *hilarious*." She sighs and looks away. "Look. I know you used to go out with Matty Evans—everyone knows that. But . . ."

"But what?"

"I felt something." Quinn shrugs. "I thought you might, too."

She leaves, and this time I don't stop her. My head's buzzing, and there's no way I'm going to manage finishing my homework right now.

J! Are you busy? Unless you are like ASTRONOMICALLY BUSY WITH AN EMERGENCY I need to hang out RIGHT NOW!

James texts back almost right away.

I'm free. Meet for coffee?

I'll just walk to your place and

we can walk over together, you dork!

It takes her longer to respond this time.

Just meet you there. 5-10 minutes.

She's already sitting inside Simply Coffee when I get there, which doesn't surprise me considering she's a tall athlete whose sport is literally trying to get places faster than her opponents. (I'm pretty sure that's what track-and-field is, at least.)

"Let me buy your drink," I tell her. "Usual?"

She nods, and I dash up to the counter to get her nonfat latte and my iced dirty chai. Everything feels like it's swirling around in my brain, and I wish there was a way to take a snapshot of all of it to show James. A GIF, at least.

"OK, so." I sit down at the tiny wooden table with our beverages. "You know how I'm, like, becoming good friends with Quinn Morgan."

"Yeah," she says, "I've noticed."

"So we were hanging out just now and . . ." I muss my hair so it hides my eyes. "She kisses me."

I expect James to look shocked, but she's just sitting there, listening, like the super dramatic part of my story hasn't even happened yet.

"She *kisses* me!" I repeat like I'm a helpful guide to my own tale. "And, like, of course I was really surprised, and . . . I really did think we were just friends, and . . ."

I take a huge sip of bittersweet chai goodness. "She felt bad about it but I felt bad because I just sat there like a rock, James, like, the worst way to look after someone kisses you." I mime looking like a rock for her.

"It's not the worst way if you don't want to be kissed by someone," James says.

"Maybe." I slurp more chai. "She says she *felt something*."

"And?"

"And . . . how do I know if I did, too?" I shove my hair around some more. Big hair can be a good curtain. "I'd just never even thought about it, like it wasn't an option. Why would it be an option? I like boys."

James nods. "I'm sure she'll understand. And if not . . ." She shrugs. "It's senior year. You don't have to see her around for that much longer, all things considered."

"James, I can't *imagine* not seeing Quinn anymore," I say, as I realize it. Whoa. "She's, like, magically become this big part of my life. Also our college application list is basically the same, remember? We could totally end up at the same school. It would be weird to ignore her all year and then four years more."

James doesn't say anything, just sips her latte.

“I think kissing her might have been OK, if I’d been expecting it,” I say.

“Kat,” James says. “You don’t have to kiss someone you’re not interested in just to keep from hurting their feelings.”

“Obviously, I know. I’m just saying . . . I wish I would have known it was going to happen.” I think about Quinn lying next to me in my bed, how her grayish blue eyes watched me, how she somehow tasted a lot like my favorite sweet spicy beverage. I had to be imagining that last part, though, right?

“I wonder—” I cut myself off when I see a text come in from Quinn.

> Please don’t hate me, K. I will do/say whatever the right thing is. You mean a lot to me and I feel like a dumbass.

“See?” I show James the message. “How can I ignore her for most of a school year and potentially a whole bachelor’s degree?”

James calmly folds her hands together on the table. “Do you like her?”

“Of *course* I like her. She’s an amazing friend.”

She gives me a look. “You know what I mean.”

"I . . . I don't think so. I don't know. I'd know, wouldn't I?"

There's a faraway look in her eyes. "I didn't know right away with Logan."

"James!" I jump up from my chair and crowd in along the booth side of the table next to my best friend. "OMG, I'm terrible! We can talk about all his faults if you need to. Tell me every stupid thing he did."

"I don't want to talk about him," she says. "I don't even want to think about him."

"See, I'm the freaking worst! I'm so sorry to make you have to think about him."

She shakes her head. "It's fine. Moving on."

"It just seems like . . . I mean, I'm seventeen. Wouldn't I know by now if I liked girls?" I try to picture it, *liking Quinn*. It's silly to act like it would mean the same thing as it means now, even if already we spend so much time together. James and I spend plenty of time together, and I'm not in love with her. Liking Quinn would be completely new territory.

Though, would it be? I've liked people before. I've had awkward first kisses and better second ones. I've felt that wave of someone's newness wash over me and wanted to stand there letting it hit me again and again and again.

"I don't know what to do," I say, and find that I've already gone through my entire chai. Would it be financially irresponsible to buy another one? My brain still feels scrambled.

"Do you have to *do* anything?" James asks gently, and then smiles. "I can't believe you drank all that already."

"I know! I feel like a beast." I decide against a second drink and stand up. "I do think I have to do something, though. I'll talk to you later, OK?"

She folds her arms across her chest. "You just got here."

"Duh, it's, like, a very dramatic afternoon. I'll text you full details later."

I wish I was fast like James is, because I'd run over to Quinn's. Instead I walk at my regular pace because this is how people who aren't tall runners get around. I text Quinn once I'm at the path that leads up to her house.

The front door opens, and she stands with her hands on her hips. "Kat, I'm . . ."

"Stop apologizing." I close the distance between us. "Can we just see?"

"See what?"

I reach out and hold her face in my hands, waiting, just a tiny bit, before pulling her closer and covering her mouth with mine. Her arms slide around my waist, and our lips part as the kiss goes from tentative to searching.

And then it's just kissing, period.

Quinn grins at me as we step back from each other. I've never been so close in height to someone I was kissing before.

"What were you seeing, exactly?" she asks.

"Earlier, I was saying becoming friends with you has been magical. And . . ." I hook one of my fingers through one of her belt loops. How am I just noticing Quinn's hips? "Maybe this is the magic."

She groans. "Only you could get away with that line."

"It's not a line! I'm very earnest!" I watch her, scanning for her reaction to all of this. "I'm sorry if I was weird earlier."

"I'm sorry if *I* was weird earlier. It felt like the right time and . . . it turns out I might be terrible at judging the right time for things."

"It wasn't the wrong time," I say. "This is all just . . . new to me."

"It's new to me, too, you know," she says. "*You're* new to me, so, all of this is, too."

"OK, I should . . ." I laugh. "Actually go home and work on calculus now."

"Already?" She smiles, a timid smile I've never seen from her before. I think it might be a question, so I nod, and she kisses me again.

• • •

Dad walks through the front door as I'm finishing my homework. This means I have at least twenty minutes before he yells down the hallway, asking me about dinner.

"Hey," Dad calls, from right outside my bedroom. "Kat. Are you—do you have a second?"

I jump up to open my door. He's standing there holding out a button-down shirt on a hanger.

"Is this . . . OK, you think?" he asks.

"Like in general?"

He sighs and rakes his hand through his hair. "Like for a . . . dinner. With a, y'know. A lady."

My heart feels like it suddenly isn't working at all. I hold my hand to it and pray this passes. It does.

"A date?"

Dad makes a face like he's got heartburn. "Yeah."

"Oh." I try to keep my voice light. "I didn't know you signed up for the thing online. I guess I thought you didn't."

"I don't think online dating is for me," Dad says. "This woman messaged me and asked what kind of music I like. I had a panic attack, replied *Bruce Springsteen*, and deleted my account."

"*Dad.*" I laugh. "So . . . what happened, then?"

"Stacey," Dad says. "She knows this . . . woman. I don't know. I let her talk me into it."

My stomach clenches. A lot of people don't know that cardiac symptoms actually often present as stomach issues in women. It makes me worry no part of my body's safe.

"Oh, I didn't know you still talked to Stacey."

Stacey is—*was* Mom's best friend. The last time I saw Stacey was at Mom's funeral. Back then, I thought that Stacey would want to form some kind of special relationship with me, the only daughter of her very best friend.

But I haven't heard from Stacey since that day when Mom's coffin went into the ground, so I guess I didn't mean anything at all, much less something special.

"Sometimes, yeah." Dad squirms around like he's itchy. "Anyway. This shirt. It's OK?"

"Yeah, Dad," I say. "The green looks nice with your eyes."

"Aw, man." He sighs. "Women care about that kind of stuff, don't they. I have to start caring about all of this."

"Maybe she'll be horrible and you'll never have to see her again," I say.

Dad laughs. "Fingers crossed. Here." He takes out cash from his pocket. "Call and get something delivered. Or have that friend of yours come over and make you another lasagna."

I close my eyes and smile. "Dad? I think I like Quinn."

"Well, sure," he says. "Good kid, great lasagna."

"No . . . *like* like."

"Oh." Now Dad looks even itchier. "Well . . . OK then. I'm gonna change and then—well, we're meeting on the Westside."

"OK." I hug my arms around myself. "Have fun. I mean, good luck. I mean . . . I don't know what I mean."

Dad sort of pats my shoulder and then walks down the hallway to his and Mom's room. He leaves only a few minutes later, and I walk down the hall to make sure everything's still as it was before. Mom's perfume is still on her dresser, and I spray a tiny bit into the air to make myself remember what it was like when she was still in our house. I pass the brand on the shelf whenever I'm at Sephora, but it's only something I want to remember at home, alone.

Dad can't care that much, for real, about this woman Stacey knows if the perfume and the dresser and jewelry (minus her necklace that I haven't taken off since Dad gave it to me after the funeral) are all still here. I slip her rings on my fingers, but they spin around pointlessly on my smaller hands.

It's silly to think something like kissing Quinn can change everything when everything changed anyway, two years ago.

I take one more sniff of Diorissimo before backing out of the room and closing the door.

• • •

MY DAD IS ON A DATE.

James texts back.

Are you OK?

I don't know. He seemed like he didn't really want to go on

dates. I think Stacey convinced him or something. Hopefully this woman will be horrible and he'll get scared off dating for a while longer.

😬

OMG I know I sound awful. Like of course I want him to be happy, J. It's just super weird. I am NOT ready for this!! If he waited ONE FREAKING YEAR I'd be off at college and not having to know about it. Ugh maybe that's worse!

I'm sorry, Kat.

You're so lucky your parents are both still around and in love and all happily ever after.

James doesn't reply, but I know that before Mom was gone I was hardly eager to talk about my parents' love life, either.

Soooooo in other news I kissed Quinn.

Oh?

I don't know if I'm bisexual or if I just like her but I LIKE HER. Is that bananas?

It's not bananas.

J you are the most boring texter!!!

This is just how I text.

I frown at my screen because I don't necessarily think that it is. This feels like huge and major news, and I might as well have told James I got a good-not-great grade on my latest humanities project for all she's reacting.

✵

Exciting enough?

Oh, sure, really great work! You'll have to be this exciting from UCLA next year so I don't miss out on the excitement of that emoji.

I'm likely not going to UCLA.

Wait, what??? Why not? What happened????

I think I should probably get as far away from here as possible.

J! I can't believe you didn't tell me this.

I'm telling you now. And of anyone, you should understand.

??????

You're going as far away as you can too.

Is that how James sees it? How James sees me?

Um, not exactly! I just want to see more of the world! I have legit reasons for picking all the schools on my list, J.

Right. Quinn.

??? I was applying to Oberlin early decision before I even knew Quinn existed. So was she, vice versa.

Sorry, that isn't what I meant. Just that you should understand not wanting to stay in L.A. Sorry if it came out wrong.

It's OK! And I totally DO understand. Where are you going? Do you still want to be pre-med and run track??

Yes. Michigan, probably.

I hear the front door open and close. Dad is home.

Need full report. Five minutes?

I should probably just go to bed.

OMG J my whole life is changing and you're going to sleep??!

. . . It's late?

I make a face at my phone and then creep down the hallway and into the living room. "Hey."

He looks up with a start at me. "Hey, you're up late."

"Dad, it's, like, ten thirty."

"Sorry, guess it is. Is your homework done?"

"Of course," I say. "How was the woman? Terrible?"

Dad sighs and shakes his head. "She's . . . pretty nice."

"Oh," I say like a balloon popping, but then I recover. "That's super great. I'm so glad."

"Well, you should probably get to bed," Dad tells me, as if we haven't just discussed the fact that it's too early for that. But I say good night anyway because if I think about this not terrible woman too much I might burst into tears right in front of him.

I manage to make it to my room before I do.

• • •

Quinn texts in the morning to see if she can walk with me to school. It's not that we haven't walked to school together before—lately almost every single day—but I know it's all different now, sort of. It's also the same because she hasn't stopped being the most exciting person I've met in a long time.

"Ainsley helped me with my homework," she tells me as I walk out of the house. "I think I know what I'm doing now. More, at least."

"Isn't your sister, like, fourteen?" I ask.

"Fifteen, and she's"—Quinn makes air quotes—"'gifted.' Also my sister doesn't wildly distract me with her good looks."

"I don't"—I make air quotes, too—"'wildly distract' anyone."

"Mmmhmm."

I take her hand and lace my fingers through hers, feeling in my fluttery heart how long it's been since someone held my hand for the first time. Matty and I were in the cafeteria and I needed to rush to my geometry class, and even though we'd known each other since middle school, suddenly he was a boy I'd been kissing. And then, just as suddenly, everyone knew.

So I know that Quinn and I might be only hours into whatever this is, and hand-holding is a statement for the rest of the world. But I'm totally ready to make it.

We swing by James's, and I see how her eyes go to our hands and then swiftly away. Should I have texted her that Quinn was walking with us today? Logan was also in walking distance of school, unlike Matty, and so up until he graduated he was always part of our morning routine.

I wonder if it's weird that I miss Logan. I think about texting him, to yell at him for dumping James, to see if he's OK, to ask what college is like and if he misses our weirdly quaint little neighborhood. He's been a huge part of my life, and now he's just gone. I unfollowed him on social media in solidarity for James, but I sort of wish I hadn't.

Also I wish that Quinn and James would become amazing friends, and I can already feel that it's not going to happen. Quinn isn't going to be to James who Logan was to me, and it's strange to know something sad so deep in my heart.

"So humanities class is kinda dorky, right?" I ask, and even though I'm hoping they'll both jump in with examples, they just nod.

"Quinn, did you know that James runs T&F and is, like, super fast?" I ask.

"My friend Gretchen's on the team, so I did know that."

I wait for more, but they're both quiet.

"OMG, James, when Quinn made this lasagna for us, the top got all browned and crispy like you see on famous foodie Instagrams."

James nods. "Yeah. You literally posted that on your Instagram."

I keep throwing out facts as we get closer to school. I'd love to successfully force a friendship on Quinn and James, but I know it's something else, too. I'm obviously choosing to be this visible with Quinn, almost before I even know what's going on with us, but the visibility feels like a bigger thing the closer we get to school. Staying distracted is easier than, well, not.

My fingers automatically find my necklace and pull on it like it might bring Mom a little closer. I wonder what she would think of Quinn, but I don't, *really*, because Mom would like the lasagna and like that I was happy and like that no one would ever describe Quinn as a douchebag.

I think Dad feels that way, too, he just doesn't know how to say things sometimes.

"We don't have to do this," Quinn whispers to me, letting go of my hand as we arrive on campus, and James heads off to her locker.

I grab her hand right back. "We *do* have to do this. I mean, you're out, right?"

"I was never really . . . in." She gestures to herself. "I think people just assume. I'm not well-known enough for it to be a topic of interest, though."

"You're known," I say, which makes her laugh.

"You barely knew me when this year started," she says, but she keeps hold of my hand.

There are eyes on us, for sure. I've sort of had a roller coaster of visibility at school. I guess I've never been invisible, but being in a relationship with Matty made me the most conspicuous I've ever been, especially at the beginning, when I was the girl that made Matty Evans *settle down*.

But, of course, that was nothing compared with having

a very public breakup in a school hallway. Two months ago, it felt like *I* was all anyone could see. Matty was the one who ignored the rules of our relationship—of most relationships—but Kat Rydell was the one people wanted to watch afterward. It was like if you were lucky enough, you might get to see me tear another alleged door off of another alleged locker.

I feel eyes slide past me, and eyes focus on me, and while no one says anything *to* me, I can hear whispers. *Is this because of Matty?* and *Of anyone I wouldn't have guessed Kat Rydell* and *That girl* does *have great hair*.

"I think this is what it's like to be famous," Quinn murmurs to me. "But maybe it's always like this for you."

"It is definitely not always like this for me," I say, though I guess it is, a little. "And I hope you know this—*us*—isn't because of Matty. But, duh, you do have great hair. That rumor is true."

She smiles almost a little smugly. "I'll see you in third period, OK?"

I hug my arms around her tightly. "Why do you always smell like chai, by the way? I've never even seen you drink even, like, generic tea."

Quinn pulls a tube of lip balm out of her pocket and shows me that it's chai-flavored. "Now you know my secret. I don't naturally just smell that way."

"I'll keep pretending you do."

I'm still smiling when Matty intercepts me on my way into AP Lit and Comp.

"What the *fuck*, Kat?"

"I'm really not required to answer your questions anymore," I say. "Actually I was never *required*. They just used to be less rude."

He folds his arms across his broad chest. I can't lie; Matty is pure dreamboat material. There's a reason being his girlfriend brought me so much attention. He's tall and works out just because he thinks it's fun. He's been a vegan since he was fifteen, and he bikes everywhere he can because he doesn't want to rely on fuel. On the surface, Matty is the best person I've ever known.

Also, if it doesn't go without saying, he is gorgeous, in the way old-time movie stars were. He's good at kissing and good in bed and knows exactly how to hold your waist when you're slow-dancing.

"You don't have to do this just because of me and Elise," he says. "Which, by the way, is completely over. It wasn't anything."

"It's not because of Elise," I say. "It's not because of you, either. It's not because of *anything* except that Quinn is . . ." I smile and decide that Matty doesn't deserve the end of the sentence.

"I feel sorry for you, Kat," he says. "It always felt like you needed someone to tell you who to be. You never even thought about the environment or animal rights before me."

I roll my eyes. "Matty, seriously, I thought about *the environment* before you."

"Now, some girl comes along, suddenly you're a lesbian."

"I never said that I was a lesbian," I say. "There are all sorts of ways to be into girls, you know." (I looked up a lot of things on Tumblr last night.)

"Sure. Good luck with this latest incarnation of yourself." He says it like a biting insult, but shouldn't we all be *trying* to be the latest incarnation of ourselves? I've never been happier to feel so little like the girl I was last year.

• • •

Quinn comes over after school. She's done this a lot since we met, but we both know it's different today.

Except that all she does is sit down on my bed and get out her calculus textbook.

"Are you serious?" I nudge it out of her hands and lean in to kiss her. Yesterday I could barely handle even the concept of getting kissed by a girl, and now I'm not sure how I'll ever stop kissing this particular girl.

"Can we—uhhh—" Quinn doesn't move as I try to push her back on the bed. "Sorry."

"No, *I'm* sorry," I say. "You're just really cute and I like your mouth a lot."

She laughs and blushes. "Thank you?"

"You don't actually want to do homework, do you?" I slide my hands up from her waist, but I drop them when I feel how tense she is. "OK, *do* you want to do homework?"

"You went out with Matty Evans," she says. "And Ryan King before that. And I'm sure someone else before him."

"Does it bother you that I went out with boys?" I ask. "I mean, I like boys, too. I think I like all kinds of people. Not now, I mean. Right now just you."

"No! I don't care that you went out with boys. You have . . ." Quinn makes an adorable grimace. "Experience. All I have is a week-and-a-half-long relationship with a girl at camp this summer."

When Matty and I were first together, it wasn't as if I hadn't already kissed plenty of boys. But then we were alone for the first time, in his bedroom, which smelled like sandalwood and lavender and just a little like pot. I could remember hazy details of Ryan timidly approaching my bra, but then Matty's assured hands were on me. And all I could think about then was the fact that Matty Evans had sex with girls, and I'd only had my boobs nervously touched a few times.

I guess I never expected to be the Matty in this kind of situation.

"I feel like I have no idea what I'm doing," Quinn continues.

"You don't kiss like you don't know what you're

doing," I say, and it works because we lean in at the same time. I kiss her lightly, gently, but then her hands are in my hair and her lips are rougher against mine. We alternate, soft, hard, tender, hungry. My lips throb, which just makes me want her more. I had no idea how much I could want.

I definitely had no idea *who* I could want.

"Whoa," Quinn murmurs, right into my ear. I like that there's a toughness in Quinn, in her walk, in the way she holds her jaw. Her voice, though, is sweet and open. "I sort of can't handle what a good kisser you are."

"I was thinking the same thing. You must have gone to, like, a really good camp."

She laughs and slides an arm around me. I lean into her and settle my head into the little crook of her neck and shoulder. I thought I lined up perfectly with Matty, but this is a good fit, too.

Eventually we do get out our homework for real, even though we keep finding ways to still touch each other. We hold hands while reading and I hook my ankle over Quinn's leg while I'm conjugating French verbs and she's fighting calculus.

"Hey, Kat," Dad says, and leans into my room a little. "I was—oh, sorry."

He disappears down the hallway, while I survey the scene to determine just how high the Dad Alarm has been set off. Our kissing didn't progress to the point where any clothes were removed or even askew, but some of my berry lip gloss is stained onto Quinn's lips, and while my hair is often a mess, hers normally isn't. (It is right now.) My ankle's still resting on her legs, and her hand is holding it. None of it is even PG-13 rated, but I don't think dads like seeing their daughters in even chaste romantic scenarios.

"We're just studying," I call down the hallway as I untangle myself from Quinn and our stacks of books. Dad is in the kitchen, scanning the pantry—which I'm pretty sure is still just as unable to provide a full meal as it was the day before and therefore not in need of a serious inspection.

"Hi, Mr. Rydell." Quinn walks into the kitchen with her backpack slung over her shoulder. "I was just heading home."

"Call me later," I tell her, and she nods before letting herself out.

"Think we're gonna have to call in for something," Dad says. "Maybe this weekend we can go to Von's, though."

"I feel like if we don't? We'll die of malnutrition," I say. "Sooo, um, I know that it's maybe weird for you that I'm dating a girl."

"Kat, no, geez." Dad holds up his arms. "That's fine. Good, sure. Quinn's a nice kid. Glad I don't have to worry about you getting pregnant."

"*Dad.*" My voice comes out as shocked as I feel. "Oh my god."

"Make sure she makes us lasagna again," he says while

digging around in our drawer of delivery and takeout menus.

"I think I can make that happen. Dad, you know you can just do this on your phone now, right?" I open up an app and hand it to him while figuratively crossing my fingers Quinn doesn't pick this exact moment to send me any adorable texts. "You can stop living in the twentieth century."

"Hmmm." I can tell that Dad wants to hate it, but before long we've got an order for Chicago-style pizza submitted without the help of any paper menus.

"You're probably doing some party or whatever already," Dad says, "but, just so you know, I'm gonna . . . go out on Saturday night."

I nod and try to look like I'm distracted with moving around all our refrigerator magnets. A bunch are still from Mom's job and say things like, *Watch her as she gets her groove back!* and other super embarrassing go-get-'em-at-a-later-age slogans.

"That's totally great," I say in my very happiest voice.

"It's not a big deal," Dad says, and I just nod because the truer that is, the easier it'll all be.

My dad has another date.

With the same woman?

I think so. OMG J what if they fall in love and get married and have babies?

Hopefully your dad's too old for babies. Aren't you and Luke enough work?

HAR HAR very funny. Though probably that's true. Not Luke, but I'm like a huge disaster nonstop. No one would want two of me.

No comment.

Sooooo J . . . I have to tell you. Quinn is like AMAZING. I like her so much.

There's no response from James.

Like SO MUCH. Like she's basically all I can think about

unless I'm actively trying not to.
And even then!!

💏

That's because studies show love and attraction set off reward pathways in your brain, the same way as if you got addicted to opiates or gambling.

Thanks for that info, J, it's super romantic!!!

And there's no response yet again.

J, is this weird for you or something? It's like totally OK if you think it's weird. I know like 24 hours ago I didn't even know I like girls and by now I basically have a girlfriend, but it all sort of just made instant sense once I sorted it out in my head.

It's not weird.

Well, it's brief, but it's way better than silence. And I know James isn't someone who can fake excitement, even when super necessary, but I guess sometimes I wish she was.

My dad said he was fine with it since at least I couldn't get pregnant!!!

😬

Holy shit. That might be the worst thing ANY of our parents have said, ever?

RIGHT???? He's such a weirdo sometimes. He just likes Quinn because she baked us a lasagna once.

Well, I guess that's more than Matty ever did for him.

Ugh I should go finish my homework. Are you doing OK, J? I know your breakup was like less than a month ago and I know how much it sucks being brokenhearted. I am here for you, OK???

I'm fine. See you tomorrow.

It doesn't seem nice to tell someone she maybe doesn't actually seem fine, so I just send my usual emoji to her, the blue heart and the girl running. My phone buzzes just a moment later with the pink heart and the cheeseburger James has been sending ever since the Matty breakup and my foray back into the world of omnivorous eating. I know this doesn't mean she's instantly not heartbroken or super comfortable with me dating Quinn, but little rituals exist for a reason. My world might actually be changing in almost every way I can imagine, but because of James and four dopey emoji, everything feels safe and right.

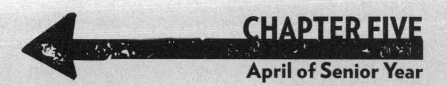

CHAPTER FIVE
April of Senior Year

James

It's going to be a rejection.

"It's going to be a rejection," I whisper to myself, for extra comfort once it happens.

But then I click to see my status, and, amazingly, it now says *ACCEPTED*.

"Yes!" I exclaim with a fist pump, which makes me laugh at myself. It's my standard move for any victory, small or large, in track.

"Is everything all right, James?" Mom asks me from the hallway.

I want to get up and close my door, but I can feel how bratty that would be. The last thing I want is to be seen as the immature one in the household, after everything that's happened to my family.

"I got into Berkeley," I say.

"James! I'm so proud of you."

"I'm sure that it's just because of my track stats," I say. "And it doesn't change UCLA."

"Well, I'm proud of your track stats." She steps nearer my doorway. "And UCLA was wrong. We were going to order Thai for dinner, which isn't particularly celebratory. Still, should I order your usuals or do you want to mix things up?"

I shrug and keep my eyes on my computer. A new message has popped up, and I pray that it's not Logan. He's harder to ignore than I'd like him to be. "I'll just eat something in my room. You don't have to order me anything special."

"James, you know, this is your home, too."

I try my best not to react, even though I want to shake my head emphatically until I'm dizzy. "I know that you think that, or want it to be true, but it isn't. You've only been here a few months—"

"We moved in six months ago." An edge creeps into Mom's tone.

"You moved into the other house sixteen years ago," I say. "The house where I lived since I was two is my home. This is just . . . where you live now and where I have to sometimes stay."

Mom sighs loudly enough that I glance up at her. "I hate that you feel that way, James."

Like I don't?

She stops hovering in my doorway, and I give full attention to whatever new message awaits me. It's only a group text organized by Gretchen and Raina about some kind of prom committee, which I am not interested in enough to even browse the details. Even after spending nearly a full year at their lunch table, I haven't gotten used to how organized and take-charge they are. I miss the days of lunch just being forty-five minutes off from worrying about everything.

Prom doesn't matter anyway. Without Logan, I'm not going. I'm sure that's fine; there are probably many successful, fulfilled people who didn't attend their senior proms. Also, buying a dress when you're tall can be a huge pain.

I text Dad about Berkeley, and he sends back five thumbs-up emoji. Even though, somehow, Kat and I have fallen away from texting at least every hour we're awake or even every day—I know she'll want to see this. So I crop out the Berkeley part and send along with a message.

Dad goes with the unconventional 5-thumbs-up approval.

I realize as I see the three dots on her end how relieved I am that her impending response is almost immediate.

> ha ha ha ha ha OMG does your dad secretly have five hands??! What's the math here??

Next year we'll be at completely different schools in completely different states. It may be normal that our communication has already dipped. Just this hypothesis lifts a weight from my chest I hadn't realized had been parked there.

> I'm walking home right now. You're on the way of course! Want to hang out for a while?

I want to say yes, even though I know I'll probably have to hear a thousand stories built more dramatic than is ultimately necessary or even true. It's possible I hadn't noticed that Kat was always like that until now—when life gave us some actual drama. After all, Mom had noticed, long ago. She hadn't liked Kat even back when I had zero complaints about our friendship. Maybe nothing has really changed, but things just feel more heightened these days.

It's stupid, I realize, but if I could say yes to Kat, maybe something broken could get fixed. But I can't, because I'm not in my home on Fairview. And as far as Kat knows, that's the only home I have. I didn't mean to go this long without telling her, but now it's almost as if it's too long. How do you casually bring up the fact that your world ended six whole months ago?

Sorry, can't. See you tomorrow.

Mom is back in my doorway as I update my college pro/con list now that Berkeley is a reality and not just the far-off possibility it seemed to be when UCLA didn't work out. Now it's just between Berkeley and Michigan. "I know you said not to, but, here." She walks in and sets down a few takeout cartons on my desk. "Panang curry, brown rice, and spring rolls."

"Thanks." I watch as Kat texts back a crying emoji, then three more, then that famous GIF of some actor crying. It's a bit much. "God, this whole year is screwed up."

"Honey, I know you feel that way," Mom says. It's her *understanding* voice. "I promise, when you're older, you'll—"

"Please don't finish that sentence." I search her face, because even though the tone and the expression are familiar, she still feels like a stranger to me. A stranger who showed up in October. "I hope I never understand."

• • •

I should have read the prom committee group text more closely, because I was absolutely not prepared to walk into school the next morning.

"Ohhh my god." Kat giggles and hides her face against Quinn's side. "This is a lot."

There are giant posters flanking the main corridor right inside the main entrance. I remember that last year a couple of Logan's friends had put up a poster campaigning to choose him as prom king. Jace and Nadia had mainly done it as a joke, but Logan wasn't embarrassed, and even though I was a junior and not eligible—and the school *loves* selecting a couple—he won. Jenn Chou, whose boyfriend Joe was a junior like me, was prom queen. It hadn't been a big deal. Logan wore his crown for a while after but then gave it to Joe, and that was that. Logan hadn't actively campaigned ahead of time for such a non-honor. People just *liked* him, and that was enough.

Two posters at the most prime student-poster-allowed location in the school on the very first day posters were allowed up feels . . . I don't know. The first is a very large photo of Kat and Quinn posed in front of the bright blue sky. For some reason, they remind me of realtors on the signs staked into yards of homes for sale. The other poster is a bright glittery purple background with rainbow letters that say LOVE IS LOVE IS LOVE!! ELECT KAT & QUINN AS PROM COUPLE!! Between the glitter, the striped letters, and the exclamation points, it's a lot.

Kat is still playing embarrassed and giggling into Quinn's shoulder. I wonder about the rainbow letters' message, considering Kat's motivations. Does Kat actually care about equality, or is this just a great story so that she still gets to be prom queen?

It made sense when it was Matty, because Matty loved an audience. Why else would he go to such great lengths to make sure that seemingly the entire school knew about his veganism, and his hybrid that he didn't even drive to school, and his eschewing of athletics despite his fitness ability because he found them *barbarian*? But Matty's so far behind Kat now; this must be all her. Quinn seems nothing like this.

"I feel like they went overboard," Quinn says with a sigh.

"You have to go overboard for prom," Kat says with a wave of her hand. "It's, like, required!"

"I mean, it's cool we're eligible but . . ." Quinn sighs and rakes her hand through her hair. "We're not running for Congress."

"You could never run for Congress," Kat says. "You'd cause too much trouble. Someone like James could, though. She's so solid and firm, like an old oak tree."

". . . Thank you?"

Kat laughs. "I love old oak trees! They're beautiful and cast, like, really nice shade. Like you! You're tall!"

Quinn tries to share a look with me, but I don't

want to bond with her over how adorable her girlfriend is.

"I appreciate you," Quinn says to Kat in a sincere tone. "You know that, right? Congress or not."

"Duh," Kat says, even though I think Quinn's trying to have more of a moment than a *duh* creates.

"It's awesome you're so comfortable with this," Quinn continues. "I kind of hate that we have to be so . . . *big* just to ask for the same rights everyone else has. So it's good you don't."

I still want Kat to proclaim these posters over-the-top and ridiculous, though. I want to get rid of this horrible feeling that Kat doesn't care about anything as much as she cares about being prom queen, no matter what Quinn says. Why couldn't Kat feel that conflict the way Quinn does? Does Kat feel conflict in anything?

It doesn't matter, though, because now the crowd is upon them, and Raina starts snapping photos of the two of them in front of the posters. I'm able to fight my way through the approaching swarm to get to my locker. The photo strip from Kat's and my visit to Eagle Rock Plaza is still hung inside, and it's now officially too much. I pull at the edge, but I guess the tape has fused to the metal locker door because the picture tears right in half, straight through our faces.

"Fuck," I mutter, and then wince because Hannah walks up. "Sorry. That was dramatic."

"You know what's dramatic—the light from the sun reflecting off of purple glitter right when I walk into school."

I laugh but feel bad, especially while literally holding a ripped photo of my best friend in my hand. "I actually think it's great the school changed the policy but—"

"Oh, me too! This is probably the first thing to happen in this school that makes us a part of the twenty-first century. That part's exciting and historical, blah blah blah. Anyway, I'm not here to make fun of your friend. Did you hear from Berkeley?"

I nod and try to look neutral. "Did you?"

"Yes," she says. "This is awkward. Say it at the count of three?"

I laugh. "I got in. Did you?"

"I did too! This is great. If you decide to go."

"Yeah, I'm . . . I'm really not sure."

"Well, put me as an item in your pro/con list," Hannah says. "Whichever column you want! See you at practice."

Kat stops by as I close my locker door, and unfortunately I'm still holding the ripped picture.

"Oh my god, what happened?"

"I was trying to move it and the tape was too old or something. Anyway."

"So I know this is all . . ." Kat rolls her eyes, but in her cute way, not her actually annoyed one. "It's all really over the top, but I do need to find a prom dress, you know, prom couple or not. And so do you. Do you want to go over to the Galleria after you're done with practice today?"

I imagine Kat's face and her protests if I say I'm not going to prom. "Sure."

"Great, pick you up at your place at, like, five-thirty?"

I'm unfortunately headed back to Mom's tonight. "You could just get me at a few after five at school. I can take a shower right after practice so I don't smell up any nice dresses."

"Perfect! See you in third period."

• • •

Gretchen catches up with me during our cooldown laps at the end of practice that afternoon. "Sorry you couldn't make the poster-making meeting last night. I know it wasn't much notice."

"It's fine," I say. "I'm not very crafty."

"We're meeting up again on Saturday," she says. "It'll be later in the day, way after our meet, so you'll be able to make it. We were thinking we could get Quinn and Kat some publicity. Tell local papers or blogs about how they're changing history."

"Do you think that local papers would care?" I ask. "It's just prom."

"It's bigger than prom," Gretchen says. "Much. Anyway, I hope you can make it. We'll order good snacks."

Why do all of Quinn's friends have to be so nice and

well-meaning? It knots my stomach even worse. Here they are championing something really important while Kat might just be trying to maintain her prom queen dreams.

I don't say anything about it, though, once Kat and I are in her car on the way to the Galleria. While there's plenty that's probably been better left unsaid, I need to get out of this one now.

"I should just tell you," I say, "that I'm not actually going to prom."

Kat stares at me like I've just confessed to a homicide. "OMG. James. What?"

"It's not a big deal," I say. "I went last year and had fun. But I'm not with anyone this year, and everyone has dates, so . . ."

"Do you need a date? We could totally get you a date," she says. "What about Gabriel Quiroga? You know he'd be in, and he'd look super handsome in your photos for, like, your memories later. You can tell your grandchildren a hottie took you to prom."

"I don't need a date," I say. "And that would definitely send Gabriel the wrong message. Plus those aren't the types of conversations I plan on having with any hypothetical grandchildren."

She giggles. "Fair. But prom is totally not just about dates. It's about your friends and your class and having this, like, beautiful time together before you all go out into the world to do your own stuff. My favorite prom memory from last year is actually when you and me and Sof and Mariana somehow all squished into the photo booth thing at the same time while the photographer guy kept yelling '*ladies, be mindful!!*'"

The memory catches me by surprise and I burst into laughter. "I forgot about that."

"That was way better than anything with Matty," she says. "So you have to come. We have to take that photo again, right?"

"Kat . . . I just don't want to go, OK? It's too hard."

She doesn't say anything.

"I'll still help you find a dress, though," I say.

"Well, duh, you will."

We're quieter than usual during the rest of our drive, and then while we're looking through racks of dresses at Bloomingdale's that we can't afford.

"Imagine actually having nine hundred dollars to buy a bright green floor-length dress," I say, not only to break the silence but also not *not* because of that, either.

"Right? Like, I guess people come here for serious but I cannot imagine it." She reaches out to touch a filmy pink dress that I can tell would be perfect for her. The thing about Kat is that if I had a spare thousand dollars I'd just buy the dress for her. I feel like almost anyone would.

"What's Quinn wearing?" I ask, because there's no way Quinn Morgan is wearing a dress to prom, prom couple or not.

"She won't tell me! I told her she has to tell me *something* so we won't clash, so she said I should tell her instead, and she'll make sure we don't clash. Quinn can be tricky. Oh! Speaking of."

"Quinn's trickiness?"

Kat giggles. "I know that Gretchen's on your team, but since you don't have all the same friends or whatever, feel free to tell your other T&F teammates to vote for me and Quinn for prom couple."

"I'm sure they'll see your posters," I say.

"Yeah, but sometimes you just need, like, that personal touch."

I watch her for a moment. "You *really* want to win."

"No, whatever happens is fine," she says very quickly. "I just want to make sure people know they can help make history if they want to."

We go back to looking at overpriced dresses, as I try to put Kat's words out of my head. Of course, I know that she cares about Quinn, and *of course* this is a matter of equality. But something gives me the feeling that she'd be asking me to talk to my teammates if it were still her and Matty, or her and a different boy. If making history had nothing to do with anything.

"Should we go somewhere you can actually afford to buy something?" I ask, though, instead of any real question I have.

"Probably so. Sometimes it's fun to dream of the stuff

I'd buy if I were rich." Kat's eyes widen and she flies across the section to grab something off of the clearance rack. It's a deep blue dress with very clean and simple lines.

"That doesn't look like you," I say.

"Duh, for you. It's on clearance, and it would be perfect."

"We *literally* just went over this," I say.

"No, I know, but how perfect is this? It's, like, the Jamesiest dress that ever Jamesed." She giggles at her own joke. "Just try it on, right?"

"Even if I was going, I couldn't afford a dress here."

She checks the tag. "It's not *too* bad. Just try it on."

I can't say no with her pleading eyes watching me, so I head into a fitting room and change my jeans and T-shirt for the silky dress. Oh, god. If Mom hadn't left us and if I hadn't had to leave Logan, this would be it. The dress is actually tall enough for me, and I look strong and tough even in this delicate fabric. This is exactly how I would have wanted to look at prom.

"I'm dying to see," Kat says, slipping into the fitting room. "James. OMG."

"It's perfect," I say, trying not to cry.

"It's totally solved, then," she says. "You're going to prom and you're going to look like a freaking bombshell and it's going to be the best night ever."

"I still don't—"

"Here." She pulls something out of her purse and jams it into my hand. I see that it's a few wadded-up twenty-dollar bills. “Dad gave me, like, more than enough. You *have* to get this. Like, it’s imperative.”

Kat might have been shopping for the rich version of herself here, and now I’m wearing a dress for a version of myself who had a different senior year.

And I can’t explain why, but I let myself buy that version of me the dress anyway.

● ● ●

Logan texts me a few days later. Our communication has grown more sporadic, and I don’t have a word for the emotion his name on my phone’s screen makes me feel. Somewhere in between annoyed and relieved and nauseated. Kat would say *all the feels*.

How’s everything? You get into all your dream schools yet?

I don’t have a dream school.

But, yeah. I got into a couple.

UCLA?

No.

Sorry to hear that, McCall.

They don't know what they're missing.

Logan never talks like it's all over; I can tell from his words that I somehow still take up the same place in his heart. I wonder if I still would if he knew what actually happened.

They probably know best, I text, instead of the truth. I'm not sure why it seems less embarrassing.

Nah. While I was an excellent decision the Los Angeles branch of the great University of California system made, they're dead wrong about you.

And then:

McCall, I still don't know what happened, and I really wish you would tell me. Our plan was great.

Our plan wasn't real.

I cry as I type. I can't remember the last time I let myself.

It was immature and impossible. People don't meet in high school and fall in love forever.

You're getting ahead of yourself. Everything was good, wasn't it?

How is the right way to phrase "no" to mean yes? Or is it the other way around?

I leave my phone in my room and walk down the hallway to the kitchen, where Dad's poring over a cookbook. "What are you making?"

"I was thinking about burrito bowls. I roasted some mango to help tell a really interesting taste story."

I grin at him. "Dad."

"People don't think about it, but that's what we all want," he says. "Anyway, you're in training. You need the carbs and protein."

"You always say that."

"Well, it's always the case." Dad watches me. "You OK, kiddo?"

I shrug. "None of us are OK, are we?"

He sighs loudly while taking ingredients out of the refrigerator. "James, I'm not going to pretend things have been going amazingly for me, and . . . it's a hard thing to explain, but I understand your mom's point of view. We were so young when we met, and . . . people can change.

I genuinely want her to be happy. And . . . you know, she wasn't."

"Shouldn't she have tried harder?" I ask. "If something's already been decided, shouldn't you try to stick to that decision?"

"She tried, James," Dad says. "Maybe she should have tried harder. Maybe I should have. But none of that matters now."

I shrugged.

"I know how upset you are. You're allowed to act like it. Get it out of your system."

"My system's fine," I say.

"I probably didn't act the way I should have," he says. "At first. I don't want any of what I went through personally to affect your relationship with your mom."

"I don't need to have a relationship with her," I say. "If her life wasn't enough for her—"

"James," Dad says, and it's the harshest he's spoken to me since I can remember. "That wasn't what she meant. At all. And I think deep down you know that, kiddo."

Do I?

"So . . . can we talk about college?" he asks.

"Uh, sure."

He points toward a colander full of produce waiting in the sink. "Chop the jicama matchstick style."

"Aye aye." I work on peeling it and then grab a serrated knife from the knife block. "Yes?"

"This is hard to say, and I hoped I wouldn't have to. The store is doing well, and it looks like every year we're doing slightly better. But . . ."

"Oh, god," I say. "Are you losing Vino Mag?" Owning a wine shop had been Dad's dream since he got out of college, but it didn't come true until a couple years ago.

"Nothing like that," he says. "But out-of-state tuition would be . . . a lot for me."

"Great, just another thing Mom screwed up for us—"

"Kiddo, no," he says. "We'd just be making this speech together if she hadn't—if she was still—we'd have the same talk. And, look, if Michigan is your top choice, I'll figure out how to make it work. But if it could be Berkeley . . ."

"Dammit." I look down and see I've sliced my finger and not the jicama. Dad rushes over immediately to hold a paper towel around it.

"Just take some time to think about it," he tells me. "I know you're eager to get away, but Northern California's practically another state. Right?"

I laugh. "Sure. I didn't really want to buy an actual winter coat."

"Winter's for chumps," Dad says, and I laugh harder. "Look, you don't have to agree immediately. Your mom and

I will figure it out. Just put it as one of the items in your pro/con lists, OK?"

"Why does everyone assume I have pro/con lists?"

• • •

"James! Wait up!"

I slow my cooldown stride even more, and Hannah and Tobi fall into step on either side of me. "I can cool down as fast as I want, you know."

"We're aware," Hannah says. "You take it pretty seriously."

"Are you doing anything after practice?" Tobi asks. "People are hanging out at Jon Kessler's. His parents are out of town."

"You should come with," Hannah says. "You never do, and it'll be fun. Well, it'll be stupid, but the three of us can not-drink together and gain the upper hand if anyone else does anything stupid."

I've actually always liked that my track teammates aren't really a part of my life, outside of practice and matches. Not everyone needs every part of me.

"I'll probably just go home," I say. "Or see if Kat's up to something."

"You aren't Kat's shadow," Tobi says. A shadow seems like such a dark and invisible thing to be, and so I never would have thought of myself that way. But was I?

"She has, like, a million other friends," Tobi

continues. "You're allowed to hang out with whoever you want."

Hannah shoots Tobi a look, and I can feel how this is something they've already discussed.

"She's my best friend," I say. "I want to hang out with her. It's just that everyone likes her. I'm obviously not the same."

"People like you," Hannah says.

"Well, less than Kat," Tobi says, which makes Hannah and I both burst into laughter. "What? It's true. People love tiny adorable girls."

"Come to this dumb party," Hannah tells me. "We'll have fun."

"For a little while," I say, because it was only last year when I went to parties all the time. Everyone wanted Logan around, and I was part of that package. This year's made me wonder that without him—or without Kat—who would ever think to loop me in? And it turns out that at least Hannah and Tobi will.

It's like any other party anyone at school has, but it's nice to have an excuse to hang out longer with my teammates. If the social order hadn't seemed so set in stone, I guess we'd be hanging out more. Hannah and Tobi don't seem to be drawn to the center of anything, nor does anyone feel the need to draw circles around them.

"Why do people get so excited about cheap beer?" Hannah asks.

"Because their bodies aren't temples like mine is," Tobi says.

"Seriously," Hannah continues, "cheap beer has been around since about the dawn of time. It's at every party. Why do people act as if it's such a novelty?"

"I like that you distinguish cheap beer from other kinds," I say. "As if you're a beer connoisseur."

"Please, you should hear my mom. Being a beer snob is about half of her personality. I can't help what's rubbed off on me."

"You'd think my dad would be like that, because of his shop," I say. "But he takes a weird pride in supporting wine of 'all price points.' It feels like a strange reverse snobbery, though."

Hannah laughs. "Oh, like everyone should admire him for being so nice to consider cheap wines?"

"I can't believe you guys are standing around talking about *your goddamn parents* when there are cute guys everywhere," Tobi says, though she's only looking in the direction of Miguel Carter.

"Go get him," Hannah tells her and shoos her away. We watch, but at the last moment Tobi veers off course to talk to a completely different group of people.

Sofia walks up and joins us. "Hey, James, is Kat here?"

I start to say no, when Hannah speaks up.

"She's not her keeper," she says. "We have no idea if Kat's here."

"Do we know if this is one of her campaign stops or not?" I ask before realizing how bitchy it sounds out of my mouth versus in my head. Sofia and Hannah laugh, though, so it couldn't have been too bad.

"She'll win, of course," Sofia says. "Her and Quinn Morgan are *so cute*. It's good they changed the rules."

"It's definitely good they changed it," I say. "I just wish it was actually for civil rights and equality and not because someone was terrified they might not be prom queen now that they're dating a girl and not a really popular guy."

I don't mean to say it, no matter how true it is, but once I do, I know what to expect. Hannah will laugh—or at least snort—and Sofia will look a little scandalized but laugh anyway. Both of those reactions do occur, but there's more laughter, and I realize the party's crowded enough that other people overheard.

"Or whatever," I add, though I'm not sure it's an effective tactic to erase words said. I'd hate for anyone to misunderstand. All I meant was that Kat needs that crown.

"Well, the good news is equality wins regardless," Hannah says, and I agree very loudly. I know that much is true.

"If it hadn't been someone like Kat, people probably wouldn't have heard about it in the first place," Sofia says, and I realize she's right about that. "I know it's important, but it's also really romantic that the cutest couple will get to win."

"I mean, whatever to romance," Tobi says, rejoining our group. Her gaze is still on Miguel Carter, despite her *whatever*. "You're right, though, that loud people get shit done. The school probably would have ignored it otherwise and been all, *but tradition*!"

Kat texts before long that she's hanging out at Pinocchio's, so I slip out of the party and head over. Sure, Hannah and Tobi just literally called me out for being Kat's keeper or however it seems, but Kat is still my best friend, and so many of my after-practice evenings used to be reserved for her. Friendships can look different from the inside than out, and it used to be so simple and clear-cut when it was just us.

Pinocchio's is an old-school Italian place with cheap red vinyl booths that serves their food cafeteria tray–style. I'm all set to get myself a tray's worth of carbs and protein when I spot them. Matty & Co., lingering by Kat's booth.

"Hi!" she greets me as I walk up.

"Hey." I drop my bags onto the stiff vinyl and push my way past Matty, who's sort of leaning over the table like he's claimed it as his territory. Kat's eating a tiny bowl of gelato and has never looked so small. "Bye, everyone else."

"We were *friends*, James," Matty says to me.

"Not exactly," I say. "Anyway, friends don't cheat on friends' best friends."

Matty rolls his eyes. "That's not a saying."

"I just invented it. Go, OK? Kat doesn't want to talk to you, and I definitely don't, either."

Matty starts to take off but mutters a disgusting word to describe Kat under his breath.

"Sorry," I whisper to Kat before stealing her gelato and throwing it right at Matty.

"What the *fuck*," he says, as everyone in the restaurant turns to look at my extremely mature defense of my best friend.

"You two girls need to get out," a guy behind the counter says. "There's no throwing food at people here."

Kat and I grab our bags and hurry outside. Miraculously, neither Matty nor Co. follow.

"You're my hero," she tells me. "James, be real with me. Was he that horrible before?"

"No," I say without having to think about it. "He was kind of . . . I don't know. A hipster d-bag. But he always seemed sweet to you."

"I know Logan hated him," she says.

"Logan thought you could do better," I say.

"Sorry," she says quickly. "I don't want to make you talk about Logan. Or freaking *defend* Logan."

"It's fine. Logan's annoying, too, but he's no Matty."

"Do you guys still talk?" Kat asks me.

"He texts me still," I say, though I hadn't planned on telling her. "Do you still get drunk Matty texts?"

"Oh my god, I got one on New Year's! I forgot to tell you. Hang on." She takes out her phone and scrolls for a few moments before handing it to me.

> We were gonna spend NYE 2gether

"Two-gether?" I crack up, and everything feels like it used to. I should have thrown gelato at Matty months ago. It worked way better than Disneyland.

"Tonight he said we were destined to be prom king and queen," she says. "Matty didn't give a crap about any of that when we were together."

So it was definitely always her priority.

"Maybe he actually cared," I say anyway. Because I think he probably did. And that's what I want to believe about Kat. "He couldn't act like it and jeopardize his tough vegan rep, though."

She giggles. "Now he's got a dairy product all over him. Great work."

"I didn't even think about the dairy factor." I take a deep breath while watching Kat. "A lot has happened this year."

Suddenly I can just picture them, all the words finally spilling from my mouth. It's been so much to carry around, and while I know that technically it was my choice to do so, it's never felt like one. Until maybe now. And I know it would all come pouring out—the divorce and Mom's new home and the way I felt breaking Logan's heart and how *goddamn stupid* I feel for believing in fairy tales—but then it'd be out there. All of it would be out there. Maybe it could even feel *better*.

"Right? James, do you think it's bad that maybe I don't hate Diane?"

This brief window where it felt safe to tell Kat everything is already closed. Of course it is! How could I presume she'd spend even a single moment that's not about her and nothing but her?

"Of course it's not bad." Kat's mom is gone, and whether her dad dates someone or not won't bring her back. It's not at all like wishing that Todd didn't exist. Diane isn't breaking up something already formed, something already *good.*

"What if she's being erased?" Kat asks. "Her memory. Her stuff in my dad's room is boxed up, and he didn't even ask me if I wanted it. I don't know where it is. And he's really happy and I'm just like . . . I don't know."

"It's good that he's happy," I say. "And that you don't hate her. Think of how much it would suck if you hated her."

"You're right, of course," she says, and since her nose now sounds clogged, I'm pretty sure she's crying. Everything is always such a huge deal to her. "You're always right."

"I was only right about that and throwing the gelato."

"It's enough!"

I'm not sure it actually is.

"Soooo I still haven't found a prom dress, can you believe it?" Kat sighs dramatically. "Raina and I went the other day over to Fashion Square and still nothing seemed right. And you know I don't trust clothes from the internet."

"I can pay you back," I say.

"OMG no, no, no," she says quickly. "That's not what I meant. My dad has no idea what anything costs anyway. He'll give me more if I need it."

Of course he will. Of course Kat would never have to choose between colleges—between futures—because of money. Of course those twenties she shoved into my hand didn't mean what I wanted them to, because there are always more. I guess on the surface I knew that Kat's family had more money than mine, but there's knowing something and then there's *knowing* something. And I'm lucky; plenty of people don't get to go to college at all, or they have to pay their own ways, and that isn't something I have to worry about. But at least it's something I think about. I can't imagine it even crossing Kat's mind what a private university more than halfway across the country will cost.

"Just, like, this is *so important,* you know?"

"I mean, it's prom," I say. "Compared to graduation or—"

"Me and Quinn are getting interviewed for the newspaper," she says.

"Whoa. The *L.A. Times*?"

She snorts. "Not quite. The *Burbank Leader*. Does that still count?"

"You're getting a lot of attention," I say, keeping my

voice level as I wonder how it must feel to seek it out, to love the spotlight, to need even strangers to know what you're doing. Can't anything just be quiet? Why not keep something only for yourself?

Kat shrugs. "Why do people always act like attention is so bad? *Oh, she just wants attention.* So? Attention's great!"

I stare at her.

"What?" She giggles and checks something on her phone. "OMG. You have to see this GIF Quinn just sent me. An otter is eating lettuce, like, super delicately."

"You know I don't share your otter thing, right?"

"Don't you dare call them OCEAN DOGS again, James," she says in her faux-outraged tone. "Look, you're bananas, because there's nothing cuter in the whole world than an otter, except a baby otter."

I just kind of stand there while she texts back. Why am I here and not still at Jon Kessler's party, where I at least feel like people would listen to two sentences in a row from me before getting distracted by otters or girlfriends or anything else?

"I guess I'll head home." I wait for her to stop me.

"Oh, OK! Talk later." She gives me a quick hug and bounds off down the sidewalk without a look back.

● ● ●

"You said this would be exciting."

"I absolutely didn't." I grin at Hannah and then look

back to the pile of canned goods I'm sorting. "But I'm glad you volunteered anyway."

"Sure, sure, sure." She stares at a box of cornbread mix. "I can't even read this expiration date. It's completely worn off."

I point at the discard pile. Unfortunately. Food banks receive so many expired or near-expired donations, and we're here to get rid of the old stuff. It's far from interesting, but if it makes it easier for people to get food that they need, I'm happy to give up a Saturday afternoon.

"Hey, whatever it takes to hang out with the elusive James McCall."

I pretend to glare at her, but eventually I laugh. "You see me all the time."

"We're going to college together . . . hopefully! I'd like to be your actual friend, not the girl from your track team you occasionally walk cooldowns with and who drags you along to parties."

I open my mouth to point out other times we've hung out, but notice that she's closed her eyes while she's shaking her head.

"What?"

"I sound like such a sincere weirdo," she says, and even though Hannah isn't Kat, at all, it sounds like something Kat would say. Maybe there are things about Kat that are also about Hannah, the things I miss, at least. Not the things that have kept me from even mentioning my volunteer work to Kat in the first place. I try to imagine Kat quietly working toward good in the world, and I literally can't. Everyone would have to know.

"Sincerity isn't weird," I tell Hannah. "And we *are* friends, aren't we?"

We work silently for a while, which is good because a coordinator from the local food bank peeks in to see how our work is going. I never want to be a teenage stereotype, so the last thing I'd want is for someone to catch me chatting instead of working.

"I am here to help," she says. "I'm not just scamming my way into a friendship via volunteer work."

"Likely story," I say, and I'm relieved she laughs because my sarcastic voice often sounds eerily similar to my regular voice. We keep working, and I like the silence punctuated with only the sound of boxes and cans of food being sorted into piles. This is where it's different, I feel. This is where it's not Kat, not at all.

I know that, originally, I wanted to prove something to Mom by volunteering. Of course, I care about the world and also about my own future. Sitting here making sure that people who are hungry have food to eat, though, I feel ridiculous that I'd ever thought that this was about me. What a relief that, really, it never was.

CHAPTER SIX
January of Senior Year

KAT

"Did you know that what you're doing at midnight is supposed to be, like, symbolic of how you spend your whole year?"

Quinn's standing right behind me with her arms around my waist, so when she laughs, it's right into me. "That sounds OK."

"Only OK?" I turn around to kiss her, but her serious face gives me literal pause.

"I like you," she says.

"Duh." I laugh and kiss her. "I like you, too. Like, a huge amount."

"Earlier was . . ." She gazes away into the distance as a grin slides across her face. "It was pretty great."

"It was amazing," I say. "We could go back to your house and—"

"Kat, trust me. When it turned 12:01, my parents said good night to their friends and immediately Ubered home."

"My dad probably didn't even stay out until then! He was probably all, *OK, Diane, let's be home at a reasonable hour.*"

Ugh, I'm somehow sneakily alone with my amazing girlfriend at a party and it's only moments into the New Year and my brain decides to fixate on my dad and his love life. Super awesome.

"Want more beer?" Quinn asks me, and I nod and follow her back to the crowd. She navigates through the room easily and has nonkeg beer for us almost immediately. I look around for James, but I think she's still on the roof. I only said the symbolic midnight thing because at midnight exactly I was mid-extremely-dreamy-kiss with extremely dreamy Quinn, but I genuinely hope it isn't too real. Otherwise, it means something that my best friend was up on the roof, a place I was afraid to climb to.

And, like, symbolically? That sounds pretty bad.

• • •

Logan is ahead of me in line when I walk into Simply Coffee a couple days later, and I'm not sure what the correct best friend protocol is. I decide that ignoring him is proper and not harmful to him or to James.

"Hey," he greets me. "How've you been?"

"Pretty good," I say, immediately. Oh no. I'd be terrible in wartime; I'd give my secrets over to an enemy as soon as they asked. Forget being a spy! Not that I ever considered work in the spy industry, but it's never fun to learn a new shortcoming.

"It's OK," he says, and I wonder if my thought process is that obvious on my face right now. "You can go ahead and feel as sad as you want for poor pathetic brokenhearted Logan."

"What?"

He turns around to order his cold brew, and then he's back to facing me. "Rydell, I'm not a proud guy. I am a sad broken shell, hoping my ex-girlfriend reconsiders whatever she's thinking, and texts me."

"But I—" I stop myself, pleased at my restraint. "She broke up with you."

"Don't remind me." He sighs and turns back to the counter, as it registers I've had this whole thing wrong, and James has never bothered to correct me. "And whatever my friend Kat is getting, on me."

"No, Logan, I—" But I can't resist Logan, who's the

nicest guy I've ever known. Nicer than my own brother! "An iced dirty chai."

He orders it for me, and even though I guess I don't really know what's going on, I feel somehow so *settled* at seeing him. He's a calming presence, just like James. Even if, right at this moment, I don't even know what's going on with James. Is that normal? Maybe best friends don't have to have every detail logged. Maybe this is just growing up.

But it doesn't feel like growing up, not really. It feels like lying.

"So how's UCLA?" I ask. "Are you still on winter break?"

"I am, and it's good. I feel less smart now, 'cause there are some certified *geniuses* in my classes. But I probably need the humbling."

I grin. "You probably do."

"What about you? Where are you off to next year? You still think you need to flee the state?"

"I'm not *fleeing*! But, yeah. I just want to see what else is out there. I've barely left LA. And Mom always said—" My voice gets hung up on the words and I stop.

Logan touches my arm. "Any advice your mom gave you was probably pretty awesome."

"She wanted me to see the world," I say. "And, like, I know she's gone but—"

"Hey, I get it. I'm just giving you shit because I can.

And I've missed a few months of doing it. Making up for lost time."

"Is it weird that I've missed you?" I cover my face with my hands. "Sorry, I'm such a dork."

"It would be weird if you didn't," Logan says. "I'm cool as hell."

I laugh. "Uh huh."

"What's your college list?" he asks.

"I applied early decision for Oberlin," I tell him. "And I have, like, a whole list of other liberal arts schools I'll try for if I don't get in. Kenyon, Wellesley, Smith, Vassar, Wesleyan, et cetera. Someone has to want me, right?"

"Someone definitely will," he says. "I'm not worried about you."

"Oh, thank god! Since you're a college expert and all now."

"Oh yeah, just living that college life, nothin' else!" He takes my beverage from the barista and hands it to me. "You didn't get back together with that vegan asshole, did you?"

"Oh my god, no." I push a straw into the cup and take a long sweet-spicy sip. "Actually I'm dating someone else now. Someone freaking amazing. I think you would like her."

Logan's eyebrows go up. "Her?"

I grin. "Yep."

"No wonder you're trying to get into all of those women's colleges."

I can't help but laugh. "That is *not* why. Those were on my list anyway."

"Maybe it was a sign." He tinkers a bunch with his cold brew: half and half, simple syrup, a lot of stirring and testing.

"You should refollow me," I tell him, even though I'm the one who unfollowed him, everywhere I could, out of best friend solidarity. But, like, what even is that now? She broke up with the nicest guy I've ever known and then lied about it? What's solidarity for?

"Look, I'm just trying to figure out her rules and abide by them," he says. "So, I don't know, Kat."

"I'll refollow you, then," I say, and he grins.

"You're hard to turn down," he says.

"Duh! That's my charm."

He surprises me by giving me a very sweet hug. "Take care, Rydell. Hopefully see you via the magic of social media soon."

I add Logan back as I walk home. And I barely feel guilty at all.

Luke is in the living room reading a thick novel when I get back to the house. Dad and I have basically quit using this room altogether since Luke left in August, and I'd almost forgotten people could be in here.

"You should go out and do fun stuff while you're here," I say. Luke glances up from his book, which is probably something about dragons or quests. "You're on break! You can't hang out with George R. R. Martin all the time!"

"Firstly, this book is not by—never mind, I know you don't actually care. And I have plans for later. Keith's having some of us over to hang out in his garage."

I'm pretty sure Luke spent some portion of every weekend of grade school, middle school, and high school in his friend Keith's garage. "That doesn't seem very exciting."

Luke shrugs. "There'll be beer. That's exciting enough. And Delia will be there."

"Oh my god!" I hop up and down. Delia was Luke's crush throughout most of high school. And I'm pretty sure if he wasn't so slow-moving with girls that she'd be his girlfriend already. "Have you talked to her lately?"

"We text sometimes—"

"Ooh!" I exclaim.

"Kat." He gives me an exhausted look. "Anyway. I saw her on New Year's, but I don't know what she thinks. She probably met some cool guy at Emerson."

"If she flirted with *you* all through high school, she's probably not looking for a cool guy." I laugh and sit down next to him. "I'm kidding! A little. Not really."

He marks his place in his book. "How do I figure out if she's got a boyfriend at school?"

"Luke, oh my god, you just *ask her*. You don't have to be all sneaky and artful about it. Just treat her like a human you're having a normal conversation with."

Luke sighs and messes up his hair. It's thick and straight like Dad's, nothing at all like mine. "You get that we're pretty different people, right? You're the one everyone likes and who goes out with whoever you want."

"That is not at all how I would describe myself," I say, though there's something about Luke being back that makes me reconsider our family dynamic. I've always thought of him as somehow *more* than me. Stable and smart and thoughtful and reliable. The stereotypical perfect big brother. But I guess at the end of the day he is a guy who likes to hang out in a friend's garage or read books alone when he could be out with friends. There's nothing wrong with that, but he's right that we aren't the same.

Somehow, we still feel like the same to me, though. Maybe that's what family is.

"Hey, guys." Dad steps into the room, looking as surprised as I feel to be using it again. "I wanted to talk to you while you were both here. Since Luke's around for another week, I thought maybe . . . we could have dinner with Diane."

I glance at Luke, who shrugs and nods. "Sure."

I shrug and nod, too, even though I'm only pantomiming what casual people look like. Inside my chest my heart thuds and I try to count beats like a metronome. Maybe I should own a metronome. You can't worry about skipped beats when you can line them all up like that.

Once I'm alone in my room, I start to text James. It's

just my auto-reaction to anything happening, but now there's this lie hanging out there, and I'm not sure what to do with it. Regardless, though, there's a more urgent matter at hand.

I have to meet my dad's girlfriend. I was sorta hoping I'd never have to???

Sorry. Hopefully she'll be cool.

Ugh I don't even know if I want her to be cool? Is that bad?

I don't know if it's bad. But I do think you should hope you like her.

James you're so mature!!! I feel like a little baby. What if I accidentally yell at her YOU'RE NOT MY MOM!

You won't. You'll be fine.

Everyone loves you.

Why is everyone saying that???
Plenty of people do NOT
love me.

Name one.

I actually have no idea who to type. Why does it feel like something horrible to be . . . I don't know, *popular* or something? Not that it hasn't always been like this, but it's definitely intensified. I know that there's something people want to like about Quinn and me as a couple. It's a good story that Matty Evans' ex-girlfriend fell in love with a girl. But being popular doesn't mean what it means to be loved by James, by Luke, maybe by Logan still. And if I can see that difference so clearly, I don't know why other people can't.

Ugh, Logan. Should I tell James about our conversation? I need her to be there for me while I'm figuring all of this out with my dad. Potentially pushing her away right now is almost literally the very last thing I need. Sure, I'm dying to ask, but I'm not an idiot. Our texts are not what they used to be. My side of the screen is always so much heavier these days.

And, anyway, breakups are hard. Maybe it felt like getting dumped, the way I technically broke up with Matty but he's the one who did something unforgivable. Not that I can see James or Logan doing anything horrible. Not only to each other, but at all.

• • •

Even though I have homework and even though it might not be the most ethically sound thing to use someone for distraction, I go to Quinn's after school our second day back from winter break. The night I'm supposed to meet Diane.

"Can you help me with my calculus homework?" Quinn asks once we're in her bedroom with the door closed and I've already stepped out of my shoes.

I sit back on her bed and pull her toward me. "Um, I can, but does it have to be now?"

Quinn and I have only had sex once, on New Year's Eve. It's not that we haven't wanted to since; it's that logistics have been super annoying. Luke is almost always at my house while he's home on break, and when he's not, my dad is. Quinn's sister is nearly always home here. Today is a rare occasion that we have a house to ourselves, and I thought we were both well aware that we needed to take advantage of this situation.

She leans over to kiss me. It is not a sex-starting kiss; it's way too polite.

"You should talk to James sometime," I say. "She's way better at explaining math stuff than I am, and unlike your sister she's actually taking the same classes you are."

Quinn shrugs. "I don't really think James wants to help me. We're not friends, you know."

"No, I know, but, like, you're not *not* friends, either."

"I don't think we're going to be friends," she says in her most gentle voice, like it's a consolation. "James doesn't like me, K."

"No, totally not true," I say as quickly as I can. "James is just, you know, all stoic and quiet. She's a tough nut to crack, but those are always worth it 'cause they're the most delicious nuts."

"Sure," Quinn says, and there's one tiny ribbon of hope laced through the word. Unfortunately, there are way more ribbons of reality in there, and so I know she doesn't really believe it, no matter how good it would be if she did.

"Also, I don't think that's true about nuts."

I pretend to gasp. "Do you doubt my nut knowledge?"

She cracks up and I take advantage of the moment to tackle her back on the bed. She slips right out of it, though.

"Not homework," I say. "That can't be what you want to do right now."

"Of course it's not. But I also want to graduate with a decent GPA and get into a good school and have a future to look forward to. Calculus is jeopardizing all of that."

"You dork, we're early decision. Oberlin has probably already made its mind up about us." I grimace when I realize that's true. "Whoa. We'll know within a few weeks if it's happening or not. How weird is that?"

Quinn sighs and looks away from me. "I . . . should tell you something."

It is never good when people start sentences that way.

"K, I didn't apply early decision," she says.

It feels like someone just threw cold water all over me with no freaking warning at all. "What are you talking about? Did you mess up the deadline? I feel like they completely changed since I wrote them down last year."

"No, I didn't mess up the deadline. I just didn't apply."

"Quinn, what is going on?"

"I'm sorry I didn't say something." She runs her hands through her hair. "It just wasn't right for me, and I didn't think you'd understand."

I search her face for some change, something I could have seen in her eyes. But that's never where you see important things, and I have no idea why I bother to check anyway. "Why didn't you even *tell me*? You could have given me a chance to understand! Do you not want to go to school with me anymore?"

"No. It's not that at all," Quinn says. "It's . . . you treat me like I'm perfect."

I don't know what I'm expecting her to say, but it's not that.

"But you are perfect!" I tackle her back on her bed and mess up her hair. "You're, like, amazing and magical and—"

Quinn sighs and squirms away from me. "Kat. You get that you think that because you're my girlfriend, right? You have a pretty biased take."

"Are you mad at me?"

"No," she says, though her voice sounds potentially the

opposite. "I just wish I could make you see reality a little more clearly. You had really good reason to apply early. My grades aren't as good as yours, and I'm positive I won't write nearly as good of an essay as you did. We aren't the same."

"I don't think we're the same," I say. "I just think you have, like, tons of value that you pretend isn't there."

She just sighs.

"Is it because you have to commit?" I ask, because if you apply early decision to Oberlin and get in, you are going to Oberlin. Which means right now that I could be signed, sealed, and delivered to a school my girlfriend has rejected.

"We hadn't even been together two months at the deadline," Quinn says, which is technically true, but why are we just counting from the afternoon she kissed me? Why can't we count from the night we met, when suddenly there was this new person I couldn't get out of my brain? Why do we even count time when it means nothing? Mom's been gone for years now but I still occasionally have mornings when I have to remember that she's gone. How many days do I have to log with Quinn for it to be real?

"No, like, I totally get that," I say anyway, because I do, even if I also hate it. "I just thought we—"

"We are! I promise I'm applying for regular decision," she says. "And all my backup schools, which have plenty of overlap with yours, if Oberlin doesn't work out. Early decision was just too much. OK?"

I inch my way over to her, trying to close this gap that seems to have opened up out of nowhere and threatens to swallow everything. I wish she'd told me sooner, but she did tell me, which isn't at all like James and Logan's breakup, still out there with its truth unsaid. I mean, it would be way better if it wasn't a thing at all, but at least Quinn told me.

Eventually.

"Are you mad at me?" I ask again, because that, I'm sure, I can fix. I can be a better girlfriend. I can try even harder and be the best girlfriend who's ever lived.

"Of course I'm not," Quinn says, though, again, her tone doesn't totally match her words. "You have to promise me something."

"Possibly," I say, as my stomach drops again. Today Quinn seems full of scary possibilities. "What is it?"

"If I don't get in, you have to go anyway."

"I might not get in either!"

"If you do."

"If I do, I have to go. You know that. That was why we were doing this together."

She's quiet.

"But I might not," I say, because at the moment it's a less heartbreaking scenario than the one where I do but Quinn doesn't even try, and next year she's—what? Just some girl I remember? I don't want to have to *just remember* anyone.

"And, like, I'll still apply regular decision then," I say.

"Then it still depends where else we get in. Oberlin isn't, like, my dream school. I don't *have* a dream school. I want to be somewhere cool and liberal artsy and hopefully where my girlfriend is, too."

Quinn makes a scoffy noise.

"Why are you being like this?" I cozy up behind her and wrap my arms around her shoulders. My bare toes are cold against the backs of her still laced-up boots. "Please talk to me."

"I'm talking! I just think I could end up getting in nowhere, and going to PCC next year, and that's fine, but I don't want your future screwed up when you have more choices. I worked out this whole plan where getting into a computer science program at a liberal arts school is my best chance, but there's no guarantee, K. We haven't been together that long, and you shouldn't rearrange your whole life for me."

I feel that I'm about to cry and try to distract myself by looking at the soft blonde hair at the nape of Quinn's neck.

"You're quiet back there," she says, and her voice sounds soft again, the voice that I know is just for me, for moments like this when we're lying in her bed. "I'm just nervous."

"Well, duh, me too." I bury my face against her shoulder and hope she can't tell I am crying, just a little. "I don't feel like I'm rearranging my life."

My life got completely rearranged the day Mom died. Trying to be at the same school as Quinn next year doesn't feel anything like that at all. And I'd say it, but it's so freaking depressing. I don't want to be the crying grief girl, when I can be the girl snuggled up against my girlfriend and her soft hair and the back of her neck with all my tears hidden.

"I feel like I screwed this whole afternoon up," Quinn says. "I just wanted help with my homework and to have sex with you. Which would have been a much better use of our time."

I reach into her pocket to take out her phone and check the clock. "I definitely don't have to be home for a while longer."

"Oh thank god."

• • •

Diane is waiting in the lobby of Firefly when the three of us walk in. I don't know what I expected her to look like—I just hoped that it would be nothing like Mom. And she doesn't. Mom was fair and blonde, and even though she was a tough businesswoman, she had this sort of carefree quality about her. Diane has dark curly hair, dark brown skin, and a perfectly put-together outfit of expensive-looking jeans, gray boots, and a cashmere sweater layered over a soft-looking T-shirt. It's good Dad asked me about the shirt for his first date with her, because Diane's style is perfect. The restaurant is dim and sophisticated, and so I assume she chose this as our meeting spot.

"This is Kat, and this is Luke," Dad says to her, even

though it's probably not necessary. I pull on my monogram necklace as Diane shakes Luke's hand and try to look friendly when it's my turn.

"I've heard so much about you both," she says. Her voice is warm and husky, like a lady who'd be on NPR.

"I'm not that exciting," Luke says with a smile. "Kat, on the other hand . . ."

"Oh my god, I'm super boring, too," I say. "Trust me."

Dad sighs loudly. "Don't be weird, guys."

For some reason that breaks the tension and we all laugh. Diane's laugh is warm like her voice, and I already don't hate her. Already I hope she thinks my outfit is cute and that my hair is well-styled. Her curls seem in much better control than mine.

"Luke, Charlie tells me you're a freshman at Purdue," Diane says once we're seated and looking at menus.

"Yeah, I'm in the engineering program," Luke says. "My plan is to specialize in civil engineering, get into urban planning."

"Luke is, like, a genius," I say.

"You do OK," Dad says with a grin, and I feel it, how proud he is of us. I don't totally understand how that works, being a parent. Luke got into a great college and has these big and real goals to make cities better. I'm still not sure what my future's going to look like. Is there much to be proud of me for—yet, anyway?

"Your dad says you applied early decision for Oberlin?"

Diane asks, and I nod, while a lump tightens in my throat. I'm not sure that I want it as much without Quinn, and I don't know that I like feeling that way. But is it wrong to feel that Quinn's so *right*? It's not like I was making college plans with Matty. I don't fall the same way for everyone.

"I did," I say. "I haven't heard back yet. It's OK if I don't get in. I can go somewhere else."

"What do you want to study?" she asks, and she looks so eager for my response that I feel even worse that I don't really have one.

"I'm still figuring that out," I say. "I just want to be somewhere where I can learn a lot and be surrounded by interesting people."

"That's more than enough right now," she says. I'm sure she's trying her best to seem nice to us in front of Dad, or maybe she's just flat-out being nice to us. So she might not mean it. She might have had her plans all lined up at seventeen. But I am so glad to hear it anyway.

"Diane's a social worker," Dad tells us, and I like that. It sounds like an important job, that she has to be responsible and look out for people. I sneak a look at her and see the way she's looking at Dad, and then it's sort of too much for me, even though I wish it wasn't. I want to feel the way Luke looks, calm and accepting and mature. Instead I sneak a look at my watch and count my heartbeats.

Luckily a waiter pops up at our table to get our drink order, so there are a few moments I don't have to think too hard about what to say next. Diane orders a beer, just like Dad, and suddenly I can't remember what Mom's drink was, if Mom even had a drink.

It's not Dad going out with Diane that's erasing Mom, I realize. It's time and distance and death.

Luke elbows me. I try to evaluate what my expression is because apparently it's not the best right now. My heart could choke me, I think, and then I wonder if that's literally possible. For now, I can still breathe, so I focus on that.

"You OK?" he asks, but quietly, and I nod.

It's just a dinner, I realize, even if it's also a big scary deal. I eat pasta and make conversation, and before I know it, we're saying good night to Diane and getting into Dad's car. We all survived.

"Diane's cool," Luke says, almost like an afterthought. He's so chill it just rolls off his tongue.

"Diane's super cool," I say. "Her job sounds awesome, too."

"You don't have to do that, you know," Luke says, and I glance back at him from my regular spot in the front seat. Mom's old spot. "You can just be normal. Nonperfect."

I wince as if I've actually been stung. It's true I'm not chill and I've probably never had a casual afterthought. It's true I want to be perfect and that I wish that was my normal. With Dad and Luke and Diane—and Quinn, I realize. Before Mom was gone, Dad and Luke felt as safe as James still does to me. But we've lost too much; I can't let them down.

"Guys, come on," Dad says, and the rest of the ride home is quiet. Luke slinks off to his room once we're back at the house, but I hang around the shared spaces like Dad will suddenly be the kind of guy who has the right thing to say to me.

"Hey, kid?"

I look over to Dad, my heart pounding. My hands clasp my chest, just in case.

"You good on cash for lunch and whatever?"

I nod. And remember something I've forgotten.

"What was Mom's drink?" I ask. "Did she have, like, a regular drink?"

He looks off in the distance like she's only actually that far away. "Vodka and soda, and she wasn't picky about what kind of vodka. Said it all tasted the same to her."

We laugh together at that.

"Kid . . ." Dad sort of sighs. "Thanks for coming tonight."

"Did I have a choice?" I mean it as a joke, but I don't think it comes out like one.

"You should get some sleep," he says. "Or do your homework, if you've still got homework."

"Good night, Dad." I want to hug him, but then maybe everything would seem too big and serious, so I just kind of wave before heading off to my bedroom.

I take the tiny gift box out of my dresser drawer and examine the KRE monogram necklace. The letters feel so unfamiliar compared to the loops of JLA, which maybe is silly. After all, these letters are mine.

I take off Mom's necklace, slide the new charm off its chain, and add it to Mom's. It's slightly heavier when I refasten it around my neck, but the weight actually feels comforting.

My phone buzzes, and I scoop it up when I see Quinn's name.

Are we OK, K?

Are we?

I wish you would have just told me.

ME TOO. Trust me.

I start typing about my evening, but think better of it, delete it, and pull up a new text to James.

She's actually great.

The girlfriend?

Yes. She's nice and smart and pretty and I did not hate her even a little.

That's great.

Just for freaking once I wish James would use more words than the bare minimum. Because even though everyone in my general circle of friends knows that my mom died, it's not a continuing conversation with any of them, besides James.

Quinn didn't apply early decision.

Oh?

JAMES THERE IS NO MAXIMUM ON HOW MANY WORDS YOU'RE ALLOWED TO TYPE YOU KNOW.

She's probably worried that she won't get in.

OBVIOUSLY that's what's going on! But I don't get it! Why wouldn't she get in?

Well, you probably have a higher GPA and come from the same high school, so she could lose the spot to you. Also, early decision applicants are often higher academic achievers, and I'd hardly call someone who accesses free tutoring sessions a higher academic achiever.

Great work at sounding just like an admissions website, James!

You literally just asked why she wouldn't get in. There are some probable reasons.

OMG now I'm terrified she won't get in. Do you seriously think she won't even get in during regular admissions?

I see dots that she's typing for quite a while, but then there's no dots, and nothing from her. Is the news that bad?

And am I so horrible to talk to?

How bad of a sign is it if your girlfriend says she's applying early decision with you but then doesn't?

I look at the message for a while before hitting send. Logan responds almost right away.

It's not good, Rydell! I might be a depressing case study though.

My phone buzzes again, but it's not more from Logan, and it's definitely not more from James. I feel like I only get conversations with James these days when I pick the right topics, and no one gave me a guide to what those topics even are.

Good night, K, Quinn texts. I send all the appropriate emoji (hearts, girls holding hands, girls kissing) in return. And then it's easy to put my phone away and not let Quinn think I'm a tortured sad girl when, after all, with her, I'm not that girl. I'm light and easy and I'll do nothing to make her not apply for Oberlin at all.

Quinn's in front of the house when I walk outside the next morning. She's holding coffee cups, and I can see how this is her extended apology or explanation or whatever she thinks it is that I need.

"This is the most dramatic thing I've ever done for a girl," she says, which makes me laugh.

"Maybe don't admit that to anyone," I say. "Not anyone who's used to big, sweeping gestures at least."

She kisses me, tasting like hot cocoa and her chai lip balm. I love whenever the brim of her baseball cap knocks lightly against my forehead. It's our prelude to kissing.

"I had to get up at six A.M. That's pretty huge for me."

I can feel how much she cares about me, but I can't stop thinking about her lying. It was lying, wasn't it? Did I make her feel like she had to lie? Were Luke's words accurate?

I realize that maybe more than a tiny part of me thought that being with a girl would be so much easier than being with a boy. Now that seems so stupid! Quinn felt easy to me, but I guess the truth is that none of us are.

• • •

I get in to Oberlin, which I know would feel better if not for only a million factors. It's just the latest in probably a never-ending list of things I can't share with Mom. I'm not sure when I should tell Quinn, and how I should do it. And maybe it's not fair and maybe I don't actually have any proof, but a gross feeling in my stomach tells me James isn't overly interested in any of this anyway.

So I text Luke and Logan. When both responses

contain multiple exclamation points, it starts to hit me that this is real and actually happening. The school whose campus I sat on last year will be *my* school.

So I text James anyway. Whether or not she cares, it's a big deal.

I got in! Ohio's close to Michigan, right?

I realize you're terrible at geography, but for once you're right. Congrats!

I smile at how much James sounds just like she used to. Responsive, full sentences, no detected boredom!

I no longer have to care about my geography abilities! Oberlin wants me! Are you doing anything now? Can we go out to celebrate or something? I feel weird asking Quinn to celebrate this right now.

Sorry, I'm busy. I can't be your Quinn backup right now.

J OMG that is totally not what I meant!

She doesn't respond.

J I feel like a big jerk. It came out bad. You're my best friend and I want to celebrate with you!

I said I was busy. Congrats again.

It might have come out wrong, but it's like it didn't even matter that I tried to make it right. College was this thing we've been working toward for so long, and I'm not sure James even cares that much about my dreams coming true.

I decide to text Quinn, even though I seriously have no idea how she might react. And . . . she doesn't. There's no response at all, even though as far as I know she doesn't have plans tonight.

I hear the front door open, and I try not to rush Dad as he walks inside.

"What's up?" he asks. I see the little furrow of worry between his eyebrows. I wonder if I'm always so transparent with every little concern in my head and heart. Is it all right there on my face, no matter how hard I've been trying to keep that stuff to myself?

"I got in." I try to say it calmly, but it comes out fast and bright. It's my first time saying it aloud, I realize.

"Oberlin?" Dad asks, and I nod. "Kid, that's great. Really proud of you. OK if your old dad takes you out to celebrate?"

"You're not *that* old," I say, which makes him laugh. I'm pretty sure when Mom was still around that his laugh came easier.

Didn't everything, though?

The doorbell rings, and I make Dad get it because we're not expecting anyone and so an adult should deal with whoever stops by. Except suddenly Dad's letting Quinn inside, and she's holding out a plant.

"I wanted to get you flowers," she says, "but Handy Market was out. So this is your congratulatory basil."

"Oh my god, *Quinn*." I throw my arms around her. "Like, I totally cannot handle how freaking cute you are."

"I'm gonna . . ." Dad gestures toward the doorway, but I shake my head.

"We'll go outside," I say. "It's super nice today. I mean, it's totally global warming and actually really depressing, but it's beautiful right now."

Quinn follows me out, and we sit together on the front porch. I look down at our feet, my ballet flats and her Converse. I always liked feeling dainty next to Matty, but I like that Quinn and I are about the same size. I like how my fingers feel laced through hers. I like how I can kiss her without being on my tiptoes. None of it means anything, but we still somehow feel matched perfectly.

"If I don't get in, this is still great," she says.

I shrug.

"K, come on." She nudges me with her elbow. "You should see how happy you look. I want this for you. Honestly, I want it more for you than I want it for me."

"I want it for you," I say, and sort of grab her elbow as it's still touching me. Two girls holding elbows and basil. "OK?"

"Sure," she says.

"I still think you're perfect."

Quinn sighs deeply.

"How are we arguing over this?" I ask. "Just accept you're—"

"Oh my god." Quinn sounds exhausted, but then she laughs. I could list a thousand reasons that I like her—like how her laugh always sounds open and not mocking, or how she does things like bring me a little juice box because I just happened to mention I occasionally miss drinking them, or of course the way her lips feel on mine and on the rest of me. I also like the realization that I can see in her eyes the things she'd list for me.

And so if all of that's true—which it just wasn't for Matty and me—I don't know how it can still feel hard right now. It was always so easy with Matty.

"Hey, kid." Dad leans out the front door. "Does Quinn want to go out with us?"

"Yes," I say. "Thanks, Dad."

"I actually have to check with my parents," Quinn says.

"Well, check! I want to celebrate with my girlfriend."

"I need some more information first," she says, and glances back at Dad. "Where are we going, exactly?"

Dad laughs. Is it weird that one thing I love about Quinn is how much Dad loves her? "Wherever you girls want."

Quinn's parents say it's OK, so Dad ends up taking us to the Smoke House, which is super old-fashioned with weird burgundy vinyl booths and wood paneling and old people everywhere. The steaks are so big that Quinn and I split one, and it feels absurd to me that we're eating off one plate with our feet touching under the table and somewhere in the back of my brain I still can't relax. Something's maybe still off, and I can feel how something's off with James, too, and even though my dad might just be the best dad ever, it's never just simple there, either. Especially not now.

I'm tired of feeling a little bit sad, no matter how I try to make everything perfect.

CHAPTER SEVEN

February of Senior Year

James

It's funny that while I run all year—even when Burbank heat hovers in the triple digits—it doesn't feel completely *right* until I'm circling the Magnolia Park track surrounded by my teammates.

It feels even more right when I'm in the lead.

This is my first year running track without Logan here. Well, *there,* at least. The boys' team shares the track with us, but they get only half of the lanes and the half of the field we don't use for drills. At first, he was a guy I caught glimpses of, not my boyfriend—not even on my radar in that way. In high school, I've been part of or at least peripheral to a certain social circle, though the older I get the more I realize that's about my friendship with Kat and nothing I could sustain on my own. But I didn't realize that as a freshman, so at first I didn't question that perfect Logan Sidana talked to me. Plenty of people talked to me, or at least to Kat when I was nearby.

It made Logan laugh to realize how clueless I'd been to all of it. I quicken my pace to drive the memory out of my head. His laugh was so silly that the first time I heard it, I thought he was doing a bit. But, no, he radiated this easy confidence that guaranteed a goofy laugh could never bring him down.

Shit. I need to run even faster if these Logan memories are going to clear out any time soon.

"Good work out there," Hannah says to me while we're stretching. "Almost like that wasn't supposed to be an easy warm-up mile."

I grin. "Sorry. I can't really help it."

"Are you planning on running next year?" she asks, and I nod. "Oh, thank god. People keep telling me track isn't something worth doing in college."

"I'm hoping track is one of the things that gets me into college in the first place," I say. "Plenty of people have good grades. It's something to set us apart. Sorry that people have been weird, though. I'm not planning on being a professional runner, but that doesn't mean I want to just *stop*."

"Seriously!" She turns her head from side to side,

surveying the new team, and smiles. "It's good being a senior."

"Is it?" I ask without thinking. It's just a coincidence that this is the year everything's gone to hell, and not because I've reached a specific point in high school. But, no. It isn't good being a senior. I had no idea how good I'd had it before.

"Yoo," she says, and elbows me. The only teammate I've really gotten close to in my three full years running was, obviously, Logan, and so even though I guess Hannah would come in second, I wouldn't call her a friend. I respect her, though.

"I'm glad to be doing this again," I say.

"Me too. Though I feel rusty and all . . ." She gestures to her feet. "Bound to earth? I'm not great at training all year."

It's true that Hannah rarely beats my numbers, but she's almost always right behind me. Her modesty doesn't annoy me, though.

"Let's run some 8x300s, guys," Coach Singer yells, once the distance runners have been sent off around the neighborhood. We take off at his whistle, and I focus on covering 300 meters as quickly as I can. We'll have to run that much eight times, every three minutes, so the quicker you are, the more you can rest in between. I like the rest, but I like the challenge more. Starting the second day of practice, one of the fastest kids will get to wear Coach's stopwatch and be in charge of the time. I prefer when that's me.

"Isn't it weird how all of the stuff we do here seems like a math problem?" Tobi Ortiz asks me during the brief window after finishing 8x300s and as Coach is explaining 10 Minutes of Hell to the freshmen. Tobi adjusts her bleached platinum-blond ponytail, because she's one of those people who manages to look glamorous no matter what. "Run one minute! Rest three minutes! Run one minute! Rest two minutes!"

"This all seemed so terrifying three years ago," Hannah says, and I nod.

"It *was* terrifying three years ago," I say. It had been a big deal for me to show up, even though I ran for fun all the time. The idea of putting an official number on it scared the hell out of me. But then we circled the track as a group and almost right away I felt like I'd finally tightened some loose part of me.

I have texts from Kat when practice is over that she's doing homework at the coffee shop, so I walk over to join her. She's immersed in her calculus textbook with a nearly finished dirty chai and a purchased-elsewhere bag of chips, and I sit down across from her, still in my running gear.

"Am I stupid for still trying?" she asks me, not even looking up. "I've already been accepted at Oberlin, and I'm going no matter what."

"Kat, are you actually able to not try?" I ask, and she cracks up. "Exactly."

"Ugh, I know! I'm such a nerd. Maybe in college I can become, like, a super chill slacker. I would *kill* to be chill."

"I'm pretty sure the killing negates the chilling," I say, and she laughs harder. It's so easy to make your best friend laugh, but I don't mind—especially now. I'll take easy laughs where I can get them.

"What are you doing tomorrow?" she asks. "I thought maybe we could go to the downtown library to find books for our humanities projects."

"I definitely can, but we'd have to go after practice lets out," I say.

"Ugh," Kat says. "My least favorite time of year! T&F gets so much of you."

"Don't call it T&F," I say, which makes her giggle.

"Are you going to Sofia's party on Friday?" she asks, after eating handful after handful of Doritos.

"I hadn't planned on it," I say, which isn't a lie because you can't plan to do something you didn't even know about. Sofia—and Mariana, too—were such a big part of high school before we switched tables this year. Why is Kat still included when it's like, if I'm not seen, I'm forgotten?

"You should come! I'm sure Sofia will be super happy to see you. It'll be—well, it'll be like every single other party, but aren't you the one who wants to soak in and savor senior year like a big weirdo?"

“Ha ha,” I say. “I don’t know. I have early morning stuff on Saturday, so I’ll probably sit it out. But text me if anything exciting happens.”

I realize it’s fully my choice to stay home on Friday, but when everyone’s photos and stories pop up on Instagram I still feel a tug of resentment that I’m not included. I wonder if people ask Kat about me when I’m not around the way they ask me about her. But I’m afraid I’m the one who blends into the background when she’s there, or when Logan was. Maybe I’m easy to forget.

• • •

After my run on Saturday morning, I head to Griffith Park for my volunteer day with Tree People. Technically, it’s a volunteer day for all of Magnolia Park, but I drove myself and manage to keep to myself even when I see a small crowd of kids—they look like freshmen and sophomores—wearing our blue and gold. Yes, of course I’m here to do something good for the environment, but I’m doing it for my own reasons.

There are signs featuring the leafy Tree People logo near the check-in area for people to take selfies with, but even though I was hoping I’d have an easy way to document the work I’m trying to do this year, a selfie isn’t what I had in mind. It reminds me too much of what Kat would do if she were here.

A woman who doesn’t look too much older than any of

us—well, not including the freshmen—introduces herself as Darien, our team leader, and walks through what we'll be doing this morning. I honestly expected to just plant trees, but Darien lets us know that at this point in the season, all the trees have already been planted. We're here to take care of them.

"James?"

Before I can make myself look less visible, a girl from track wanders over to me. I push myself to say hello and look friendly though distant.

"You're friends with Kat Rydell, right?" she asks me.

I guess I didn't fully pull off *distant*. "Why?"

"Oh, she's just really cool," she says with a shrug.

"Yeah," I say. "I am friends with her."

"That's awesome. Oh, we have a bunch of Vitamin-waters," she tells me. "If you want to work with our team. It'll be super fun."

Since Darien told us we have to work in groups of three or four, I guess I have to agree to this. Last month, I cleaned up litter in Johnny Carson Park, which let me accomplish something while working on my own, headphones in, nonrunning playlist pounding in my ears. Then I felt guilty because I spent half a sunny day surrounded by greenery listening to Chance the Rapper's latest mixtape, and it hardly felt like giving back. So the next weekend I stood at the midpoint of a 5K run to hold out little cups of water to runners who needed them. Their runners' high was contagious, though, and I left feeling great again and also eager to start signing up to run non-school affiliated races. Last weekend I ended up sitting alone while assembling purses full of supplies for a women's shelter. It was quiet work and gave me plenty of time to think: about the women who needed these supplies, about how I didn't know what on earth my future would hold now that my fifteen-year plan was trash, about how there must be something I could do to make my life feel the same as it used to.

It could be a good thing to not be left alone with my own thoughts right now.

We haul buckets of mulch from one side of the park to another, which is a fairly easy assignment. I had no idea that so many actions you could take to help were *simple*. But it turns out that something like carrying a bucket is one small part of helping the planet, and I feel almost guilty that none of this had ever occurred to me before.

Once the new mulch is in place, we have to scrape off the old mulch from the newly growing little trees. I assume we'll use shovels, but instead it's our hands, and before long there are lots of shrieks from anyone who makes contact with a bug. Somehow, I manage to contain myself, even though it's a bit more nature than I expected to encounter.

"What are we supposed to do again?" the track sophomore—I'm fairly sure her name is Olivia—asks me, and even though I'm just as new to this as she is, I recite back Darien's words about rebuilding the berm around the growing tree. Before today I didn't know that a berm was basically a donut made of soil, but I find that I'm able to explain to Olivia how it'll help bring water toward the tree's roots. Being a senior is like this all the time. It's hard for me to think of anything else besides my future I'm expected to figure out, but underclassmen look to seniors as wizened elders with so much to pass down. If I keep talking about berm and mulch, maybe no one will realize I might not actually know anything about life.

We work until Darien dismisses us just a little after noon, and I notice as I walk to the car that my sweatpants are covered in dust and soil. Is it possible to take off your pants to drive home and have no one notice? I'm not sure on that, so I choose trashing the driver's seat over potential public pantslessness.

By the time I'm home, showered, and in dirt-free clothes, there are five texts from Kat asking me to join her to go on some art walk somewhere on the Eastside. (She can be astoundingly vague for someone who uses so many words.) Dad's at the shop, so I text him that I'm going and walk over to Kat's house. I know, of course, that one reason I feel Kat's absence more on the weekends is that, last year, we were both in relationships and so I spent plenty of time with Logan. I didn't miss her so much when she was with Matty. But I'm still convinced she didn't give quite so much of her time up to him, the way she seems to disappear into Quinn.

Mr. Rydell lets me in. “Hey, James. They’re all in Kat’s room.”

I try not to sigh until I’ve thanked him and am headed down the hallway toward the sound of conversation. Of course Quinn’s here, and Raina and Gretchen are, too.

“Yay!” Kat jumps up from her bed and hugs me. “Did you just get up? Why are you freshly showered? Were you doing running stuff?”

“Why are you so nosy?” I ask, and then smile really widely so that it doesn’t sound like I’m snapping at her. But good lord.

“I care about your life!” she says with a giggle. “OK, who’s driving? My car’s too tiny.”

Kat, who doesn’t even need a car to get to school and has never needed to get to a job or a volunteer gig, has a tiny, bright blue Mini Cooper that Mr. Rydell gave her on her sixteenth birthday. It mostly sits in the driveway. Kat once confided in me that it was practically too small to have sex with Matty in it, which was far too much information for me. We tell each other a lot, but often broad strokes, not the specific mechanics of things. To me, sex is so private—too private even for best friends. But I guess entire TV shows have been based around the premise that, for a lot of people, it isn’t. It’s strange to think you could grow up right alongside someone and be one category of person when it turns out they’re another entirely.

Raina has her mom’s SUV, so we pile in. I was here

because I wanted a Saturday with Kat like we used to have all the time, but as everyone talks about bands I don't listen to and TV shows I don't watch, I wish I was back home.

"James, you should go with us," Raina tells me, and I try to hold my face neutrally so that no one knows I haven't been paying attention. "It'll be—"

"—the most fun thing we do in March," she and Gretchen end up saying together, before bursting into laughter. Oh, god.

"James is too cool to listen to pop music and eat ice cream," Kat says. "All the songs she likes have, like, strong language and adult situations in them."

I laugh against my will. "Sorry about your delicate ears."

"Remember when Luke tried to tell us some gross joke and I burst into tears?" Kat rolls her eyes. "I'm such a nerd."

"She got scared during *Finding Nemo*," Quinn says. "Which I didn't know was possible."

"OMG, Quinn, don't mock me. The shark parts are intense."

It seems as if there's nothing else that only Kat and I share anymore.

The art walk is only a few exits down the 5 Freeway but in Los Angeles proper, which anyone would agree is inherently cooler than hanging around Burbank. When we get there, I drop behind everyone, as I assume the two couples will want to pair off, but it stays less divided than that. Quinn's chatting with Raina, while Kat shows a cute dog video on Instagram to Gretchen and me.

"Does anyone want an iced coffee?" Raina asks, as we near a tiny coffee shop.

"I'll help," Quinn says, as soon as everyone says yes.

"Gretchen?" Raina asks, and Gretchen nods and heads off with them as well, and so I'm alone with Kat.

"You didn't have to include me," I say.

"I do! Best friend bylaws or whatever!"

"Did you think about the fact that it would be awkward for me to be the fifth wheel with two couples?"

"Raina and Gretchen aren't a couple," she tells me. "Though, *please,* they clearly want to be, right?"

We share a look.

"Mmmhmmm. People think their feelings are allllll locked away, but, like, duh."

I smile at her and realize that maybe things do feel more the same than they do different. Friendships don't fall apart over *nothing,* and certainly not so soon. It was literally only a year ago when we, along with Logan and Matty, skipped a Friday's worth of school to escape to Disneyland for the day. Logan and Matty are both gone from my life, but it's still one of my favorite memories, and that's all Kat.

"Remember how much fun Disneyland was last year?" I ask, and her eyes do everything but literally light up.

"*Yes*. OMG, James, we should totally do that again. I can get away with skipping. Can you again?"

"Sure," I say. "It's so much better to go during the week, considering how bad crowds get on the weekends."

"Exactly. Yay! This is totally what I need right now. You are a genius."

"No boys this trip," I say, which makes her giggle.

"Seriously, like, no boys at all. We'll have so much fun."

She's already turned around because the other girls are back with iced coffees. Already I don't resent their presence quite as much. Kat and I are still intact, after all. Also, obviously, it's a relief to know I'm not tagging along on a double date. And maybe it's just the caffeine, or having my hands in the literal dirt earlier, but today doesn't feel like this shitty senior year I've resented. Today feels much closer to the one I thought I'd have.

My phone buzzes while we're walking around, and even though it should make me furious, I feel a smile cross my lips when I see Logan's name.

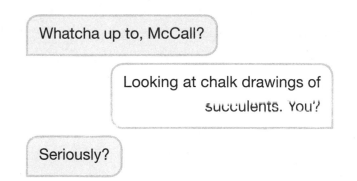

Whatcha up to, McCall?

Looking at chalk drawings of succulents. You?

Seriously?

Seriously. K & Team dragged me to some art walk.

You? Walk when you could run? Art when you could science?

“Ooh, who’s texting you?” Kat asks me, and I look up with a start.

“No one,” I say.

“Really? Because you’re smiling like there’s a boy involved.”

“I just saw something funny on Instagram,” I say, and I wish I could explain it to her. But I can’t explain Logan even to myself right now. If he’s supposed to be gone, why isn’t it worse that he doesn’t seem to want to actually stay away?

• • •

I’m pretty sure my parents no longer talk at all anymore, and so it’s easy to let Dad think that Mom arranged a doctor’s appointment for me the next week. He’s great about nearly everything, but even whispering the word “gynecologist” will lead to a very quickly changed subject. He calls school for me without another word, and I try to get into my car without any Disney-inspired glee on my face. I doubt anyone has ever looked that happy to go to the gynecologist, after all.

When I pull up to Kat's house, she's standing outside already wearing mouse ears—real subtle, Kat—next to Quinn. I hope that Quinn's just here to bid Kat good-bye since she's going all the way to Anaheim, but then I realize Quinn's also walking to the car and that she isn't wearing a Dodgers cap today but one with the old-fashioned Disney character Oswald on the front.

"Hey!" Kat sits down in the front seat and immediately switches my stereo input to Bluetooth so she can play something from her phone. "Can we stop at Starbucks even though Quinn is morally opposed?"

"I'm not *morally opposed,*" she says from the back seat. "I only said their regular coffee tastes burnt. I enjoy a Frappuccino like any reasonably minded person."

"Quinn's coming," I say and manage not to make it a question, though just barely.

"I know, right? Yay! She escaped her parents without any questioning this morning." Kat waves her hand dismissively. "I swear I could leave for school, like, two hours later than usual, and even if my dad was home he'd be fine as long as I told him the rules changed or something."

"Your dad is great," Quinn says.

"He is," I agree.

"Duh. I'm just saying. His grasp on my schedule and life is, like, tenuous at best. And now he's all extra distracted with Diane, so. It's all fine."

"Everything's OK there?" I ask because I'm pretty

sure that the last time Kat brought up Diane, tears were involved.

"Of course, why wouldn't it be? No, don't go to this Starbucks, the one on Alameda is way better, and then we're right by the 5."

"They're all the same," Quinn tells her.

"They aren't! This one doesn't have friendly baristas."

I sigh but head toward one of the other billion Starbucks locations in Burbank, as Kat and Quinn debate the merits of barista friendliness. We somehow miraculously manage not to hit much rush hour traffic, and we're parking at Disneyland while there's still coffee left in our cups.

"We should make a plan of what rides we have to go on, and anything extra we'd like to work in." I get out my phone and tap to my notes app. "I can make a list."

"Churros first," Kat says, dragging Quinn along behind her. I'm grateful—I guess—that I walk quickly enough to catch up. Kat and Quinn split a churro while I'm left ordering one on my own. This too-big churro feels like the dumbest metaphor for my life.

We start making a list, but Quinn and Kat keep agreeing with each other, so I finally just tell them to point me wherever they want to go. I'm going to get outvoted no matter what; at least this will ultimately save time. Also, to be fair, I like nearly every ride at Disneyland.

"Where are you going?" Kat asks me as we walk up to the Indiana Jones ride.

"Single rider line," I say while pointing. "We'll get through faster." The annoying thing about Disneyland is that even when you pick a random Friday morning in February, the park can still be packed.

"Aw, but I have to ride with Quinn," she says. "I'll get scared of the boulder alone!"

"How can you get scared of it when you already know of its existence?" Quinn asks, but she's smiling, and they drift together into the regular line.

"You can get into the other line if you want," Kat tells me in the voice I know she thinks is extra sweet.

"It's fine."

Kat gets out her phone and starts to take a selfie of all of us.

"Don't post this," Quinn says quickly. "Not today at least."

"Your parents aren't going to look at my Instagram," she says.

"You don't know that," Quinn says.

"Fine, fine, fine. Can't I just save pics for myself? Yes, I can. Take off your hat, there's a weird shadow on your face."

Quinn sighs but does so. I lean in, but I can see from the camera's screen how fake my smile looks. Was it that much to hope this would just be the parts of last year that still exist? Kat and me, me and Kat.

Kat swaps Quinn's hat for her ears. "Look, you're cute with ears!"

"I *have ears already*," she says, as she and Kat collapse into giggles.

"Not mouse ears. James! You aren't being festive at all!" She hops up to try to place the hat on my head, but there are benefits to being nearly six feet tall.

"I'm festive without headgear," I say.

"I disagree, but I know you're stubborn as heck."

Kat gets out her phone to take more selfies of her and Quinn in their switched hats, which at least means that I'm off the hook for a while.

The three of us end up in one row in the fake Jeep, with Kat in the middle. She clings to Quinn the entire time, and screams just *in anticipation* of the boulder. I try to remember if she was quite this annoying last year, but all I remember about this ride then is Logan sitting behind me (we were both big believers in the single rider line) and trying to tap me at the scariest points. It never worked because Logan would scream even louder than Kat is now. He was such a baby.

I guess that he still is. Or maybe college has changed him. It shouldn't be my concern anymore.

"Haunted Mansion next," Kat says as we exit the ride. "Right?"

"Sure," Quinn and I say together. Of course, when we get there I remember that the little buggies only seat two, and so I'm left alone in one. I can hear Kat and Quinn giggling behind me in that very specific way I know is associated with making out. It's not as if I've never made out in the Haunted Mansion, but I'm almost startled at how lonely I suddenly feel.

It goes like this for the rest of the morning and early afternoon. I'm either next to a giggly couple on the verge of PDA or immediately in front of or behind them—including now, in line to get Dole Whip floats.

"We could just get ice cream on the way home," Quinn says as the line in front of the Tiki Room for pineapple soft serve slowly inches forward. "Isn't there a place at the Glendale Galleria that has these?"

"Quinn, you of all people who cares about real food and the honor of a recipe should know that place, like, completely pales in comparison to the real deal."

"The true glory of the Dole Whip?" Quinn asks with a grin.

"Exactly."

I can tell from how they're angling the conversation toward me that I'm supposed to feel included, but people need more than angles. I get out my phone and hope that they can see they're off the hook. Kat and Quinn keep debating the merits of nonregulation Dole Whip, so I check my messages and then scroll down through Instagram. Kat must be pretty confident about skipping school today, because she's posted several times already. (She was at least thoughtful enough to leave Quinn and me out of it.) I keep scrolling, but something lodges there in my brain, so I scroll up a little and see it, on a selfie of Kat and her mouse ears. *You look great as a rodent, Rydell.*

I click on Kat's profile and then tap through her photos. logan_af didn't only comment on this selfie. Somehow I haven't noticed that logan_af comments all the time, or, at least—weirdly—has been commenting plenty since last month.

"Are you and Logan friends?" I ask.

Kat looks to me with what I can clearly see is a start. "Friends, like, how?"

"He commented on your photo," I say. "He's commented on *lots* of your photos."

"We don't, like, hang out," she says. "We were friends—are friends, though, I guess."

"I'm really surprised you'd"—I cut myself off to find the word. "*After—*" What after what? I hate that I can't end the sentence. I can't even *middle* the sentence.

"I totally know it's, like, a best friend violation," she says, and then we're at the front of the line. Quinn steps up to the register and orders for everyone, as Kat and I continue to watch each other.

"So if you knew that—"

"We were friends, too," Kat says. "I missed him. Also sometimes I need . . ." She nods to Quinn and drops her voice. "Girl advice."

"You're friends with literally everyone at school," I say. "There's no one else?"

CHAPTER EIGHT

March of Senior Year

KAT

"I brought you something."

James jumps as she approaches her locker.

"Did I scare you?"

"How much shit will you give me if I say yes?" She smiles slightly and takes the travel mug from me. "Coffee?"

"Amazing homemade cocoa," I say. "Life-changing! I didn't make it."

"You can barely operate a Keurig," she says. "So, I figured."

We're silent for a few moments. I wordlessly hold the mug for her while she unpacks her bag into her locker. The dumb photo booth picture we took at Eagle Rock Plaza

"Um . . ." Quinn is somehow balancing all three Dole Whip floats in her hands. "Should we eat these in the Tiki Room? Or just sit out here?"

"You can't not eat these in the Tiki Room," Kat says. "I can only enjoy pineapple soft serve when I'm being serenaded by animatronic parrots."

"I'll wait out here," I say, and I can see how Kat doesn't even hesitate to walk in without me. Quinn dashes out a second later to give me my float, and then, with an apologetic look, heads back in. I guess that it's apologetic. Who even knows what Kat's said to her about me?

They're out in fifteen minutes, and we wordlessly walk away together.

"I should find something for Ainsley," Quinn says, and then glances at me. "My sister has a *Little Mermaid* obsession."

I nod and we both watch as Quinn disappears into a gift shop.

"I just wanted to have fun today," I say.

"Well, duh, me too."

"You're almost eighteen," I say. "Maybe you should cut out the whole *duh* thing."

Kat steps back as if I've slapped her.

"I'm trying to help," I say.

"Help what?" She blinks her eyes a bunch, clearly drawing attention to her tears. I'm not going to let her force me into feeling sorry for her, when there's nothing about today that doesn't feel like a betrayal. "Maybe we should just go home."

Suddenly the moment is like a wave that's swept me out to sea before I could even see what was happening. I don't want to be manipulated, but I didn't want to give up on this so soon.

"Only if you want to," I say.

"Of *course* I don't want to! I wanted to have a super fun day, and I thought *we were,*" she says. "Yes, I'm, like, social media friends or whatever with Logan. I didn't know if I had to tell you or not, but, like, the last thing I wanted to do was make you think more about your breakup, *which you still haven't even told me a single thing about, you know,* so I didn't."

"I'm fine about my breakup," I say. "What's there to say? No one should realistically expect a high school relationship to last."

Quinn emerges from the gift shop holding a bag. "Where to next?"

"I think we should probably go home," Kat says.

"I didn't—"

Kat cuts me off with a look. "My head hurts and we should probably try to beat rush hour traffic."

Last year, we were here until the park closed. I remember that Logan drove home and that in the middle of a conversation on our way back north on the 5, Kat fell asleep against Matty's shoulder. For some reason at that

point, Logan had been wearing Kat's mouse ears, and I kept a photo I took of him driving as my lockscreen for months.

The ride back up is quiet, besides the playlist Kat plays over my stereo. She's staring straight ahead every time I sneak a glance over at her, and I wonder how she can be so clueless about today. Why would I want Quinn here if the whole point of today was to try to recapture something we still had last year? Of course, now that seems stupid. Last year's already gone, and trying to hang on to it is like grasping a glass of water after it's been poured into your hands.

still hangs there, and it's always a relief to see our smiling faces.

"Can you hang out later?" I ask. "After T&F?"

"Uh . . ." She seems to be actually mentally scanning her schedule and not just looking for an excuse. I hope so, at least. We haven't made plans *just us* since the day that Disneyland became the saddest place on earth.

Though I guess that wasn't technically *just us*.

"Yeah, I think so," she finally says.

"Yay! Can we, like, drive somewhere? Sometimes I feel so sick of our neighborhood. We could pick something super fun we never get to do."

She agrees to that and picks me up after her T&F practice. I settle into this seat I've spent so much time in and watch out the window as our neighborhood gives way to greater Burbank, and then Glendale, and finally Los Angeles proper.

"Do you think you'll still live here someday?" I ask, even though of course James knows. She has a whole plan. James is ready for adult life, while I'm still doing my best as it comes.

"I don't know." She sighs. I wait for the follow-up, but that's it.

"I feel like I'll totally be back," I say. "I'm even afraid, like, that someday when I have babies I'll literally be back in the same neighborhood. And they'll go to Magnolia Park and I'll turn into my dad or something."

"You talk way too much to turn into your dad," she says.

I'm grateful I get a text I can focus on because that seems like a sign I should probably be quiet for a while.

James parks by the overpriced ice cream place in Silver Lake, and I treat us to ice cream cones since she drove. We walk over to the dog park and watch through the fence as a bunch of little dogs fight over balls and rope toys. James and I are laughing at the same dog drama, and it feels nice and safe. Maybe I can make it even better.

"So, um, Disney and everything," I try. "I'm sorry I didn't say anything about Logan."

I'm still not even sure if I did something wrong by staying friends with him, but I guess I'm not totally stupid enough to think I'm one hundred percent innocent. I'd hate it if James and Matty were still friends, but it's not a fair comparison.

"OK," she says, staring at a pug dog.

"I mean, I don't know what happened," I say. "Maybe I *should* hate him. If you tell me to hate him, I can try to hate him."

"I just said that it was fine."

"I know, but, like, we can talk about it, and I can—"

"I don't know how else I can say it's fine," she says. "Disney was a stupid idea. This isn't last year."

"It wasn't a stupid idea." I have a feeling I'm supposed to apologize for bringing Quinn, but last year was literally us and our boyfriends? Why was I supposed to leave out my girlfriend? "I should have told you and I don't blame you for calling me out and I'm also sorry if I should have said something about Quinn, but "

"I feel like we're now having a conversation about a conversation," James says. "A conversation we literally just had."

"James, I just want to fix whatever happened! Just tell me and I'll fix it! I'll go in and wrestle that pug dog if I have to!"

"You don't have to say *pug dog,*" she says. "It's not as if there are pug hamsters or something."

"OMG but imagine if there were!"

I can tell she doesn't want to laugh.

"Fine. That would be extremely cute."

"Duh," I say, though I regret it. It didn't seem very long ago that I wasn't afraid to be myself around James. Now it's like a whole new person is there judging me and no matter how freaking hard I try, I come up short. And I don't even know how to try with James! I never used to have to try with her at all. I'll keep trying, though, because the alternative is way too terrible to consider.

• • •

Dad's standing in the kitchen when I walk out of my room on Friday night on my way to a party at a junior's. I mean, free beers are free beers. I did my best to get James to join us, but I guess I'm not that surprised she wasn't interested.

Hopefully I at least seem like a caring friend who won't ever screw up again.

"Do you have a date?" I ask him, because he's wearing a shirt I think is new, and he smells like aftershave.

"Diane's friends are having some *thing*," he says. "I'll have to make conversation with a bunch of people in the South Bay."

"OMG, be nice, Dad," I say, because Dad's often said he doesn't understand why anyone would live so close to the ocean.

"I'll do what I can," he says. "You going out with Quinn?"

"Well, we're going to a party. It's always, like, the same people, but hopefully it won't suck. If it does, we'll just go get tacos or something."

"Always a good backup plan." He pats my shoulder. "Be safe. Don't drink and drive."

"We're just walking," I say. "We'll be careful. Haven't you noticed that Quinn's, like, a very smart and careful person?"

"She's a lot better than that joker you went out with before," he says. "That's for sure."

"Dad, can't you like her not just in comparison to Matty?"

The doorbell rings, and Dad gets it. "Come on in, Quinn."

She walks in and grins at me. Her hair looks extra

tall and swoopy, and she's wearing a black leather jacket over her flannel, like an old-timey heartthrob. I clench my hands into tiny fists so that I don't accidentally start running my fingers through her hair in front of my dad.

"Have fun, girls," Dad says. "Quinn, you're careful when you're out with my daughter, right?"

"*Dad.*"

"Yes, sir, of course," Quinn says, like my dad's not being weird when he super clearly is.

I grab her hand and say good night to Dad before dragging Quinn outside. "Hi."

"Hey." She leans in and kisses me, slow and hot and intense. She can just do that, out of nowhere. My breath feels gone.

"My dad's about to leave." I slip my hands around her waist, under her jacket, over her warm soft flannel. "We could sneak back in."

"Is it really sneaking if you have a key?" she asks me, but I know that it's a *yes*. We hide out around the back and wait until Dad's Subaru leaves the driveway, turns left on Clark, and disappears into the night. Of course, I have a key and this is my freaking home, but I feel myself heating up over the idea of sneaking in with Quinn. It's like we're getting away with something, when in truth I always feel like we are. How can it (mostly) be so (mostly) perfect?

It's a rush to get to my room, to manage to not pull each other's clothes off before they can be safely discarded on my bedroom floor. But then it's slow, as Quinn holds me and practically dares me with just a look to take my time. And I know I seriously just yelled at Dad for comparing her to Matty, but considering that I've only had sex with two people, sometimes it's impossible for me not to. And it was good with Matty, like, *good.*

I didn't know how incredible it could feel to just be *seen* though.

(It's pretty incredible to have someone's lips and fingertips all over you, too, of course.)

This is the first time we haven't had to hurry off immediately—I could barely care less about some junior's party, and if we hadn't told Gretchen and Raina we'd be there, I wouldn't worry about it at all—and so I stay under my covers with Quinn, our clothes still all piled on my floor.

"Did you have sex with that math camp girl?" I ask Quinn.

"It was coding camp," she says. "And, *no*. Why are you just asking me now?"

"I dunno. I guess I didn't care if you had, I was just curious. I'm curious about, like, every single thing about you."

Sometimes Quinn makes a face like I unexpectedly shot her with a confetti cannon and even though it's pretty and fun it's way too much all at once. Like right now.

"Am I overdoing something or—"

"No," she says quickly. "I like that you say everything."

I wonder what she'd think if she knew how much I don't say. I mean, I say all the Quinn things. I just keep plenty more to myself.

"Do you think we're too serious or something?" I ask, and then it's a regretted question because it makes us sound like an illness, and also, what if she says yes?

"No," she says, quickly again. "We just don't know what's going to happen next year. And you think I'm your experienced hero, when in reality I may be a college reject who up until last summer was too nervous to make it under a girl's shirt."

"You *are* my experienced hero," I say.

"Kat," she says, but I hear her tone shift, and then I put my knowledge of her most ticklish spots to good use.

We eventually walk over to the party and find a group of our friends in the backyard, sipping out of red Solo cups. I think I still just want to be alone with Quinn, but I also like being in a group with her, feeling how much bigger my life seems now that she's a part of it.

And I'm sure that all the parts that maybe are still somehow unsteady will right themselves perfectly once we know about Oberlin and can start thinking for real about next year.

Sofia and Mariana find me and pull me away, though, to another spot in the yard, and even though Matty isn't there, it sort of feels like last year in this moment. I still like everyone in this circle, of course, but it's sort of funny how

I don't necessarily miss how things were then, when they were my daily group. Mariana's so funny and Sofia's pure sweetness, but it's like I can already see all our separate paths after high school.

"Did you hear Matty's hooking up with Ashby Grant?" Mariana asks.

"Mar!" Sofia grabs my arm. "I'm sorry if that's how you had to find out."

"It's super fine," I say, for real. "It would be the grossest if he was still, like, hung up on me."

"I'm pretty sure he still is," Mariana says. "Sorry to be the bearer of the grossest news."

I roll my eyes. "Whatever. It's been months and it was his fault anyway. He can pine away for me until we're all old and withered."

"Do you miss him, though?" Sofia asks. "I really thought you guys were true love, meant to be, all of it."

"I really, really don't," I say, and thanks to the beer I don't really have any filter to keep me from giggling at her crestfallen expression. "What? We weren't going to last forever, trust me. I know that now. And in retrospect there were some gross things about Matty that I just seriously don't miss, like him being way more of a stoner than I wanted to admit. Also that natural crystal deodorant was *not* strong enough."

"So, are you just totally gay now?" Sofia asks, and I

see Mariana try to subtly punch her arm. "What? I can ask that, right?"

"You can ask it," I say. "But, like, I don't really know how to answer it. I mean, like, I *can*; I identify as bi. I like girls and boys and people who identify as both or neither, you know? But also right now I like Quinn and that's all that matters."

"Is it because Quinn's like a boy?" Mariana asks.

I glance across the yard at Quinn, who's deep in discussion with a bunch of boys right now. I get what Mariana's asking, and I guess I think about it for a second, despite that I know it's of course not why I like her. Quinn does have tall hair like a boyband member and wear baseball shirts and boy jeans, and sometimes cashiers and baristas mistakenly call her *young man*, but also, Quinn *isn't* a boy.

"It's totally not because of that," I say. "It's just because she's her. She's like the best person I know."

They let out a collective *awww!* "You have everything totally figured out," Sofia says, and now I feel like such a fraud and a liar that my heart speeds up. I take a couple deep breaths, but it's like my heart has a mind of its own. I know that doesn't make any sense, but also it feels truer than medical science could ever explain.

"I guess," I say, and throw my hands up like I'm the wacky neighbor in an old-fashioned sitcom, for dramatic effect. They laugh, so it works, but the lie tastes gross in my mouth.

Or it's this beer. I hope it's this beer.

• • •

Luke texts me the next week about an amazing internship he's been offered, and even though I don't understand the details, I know it's a big deal.

> I'm surprised you're this excited.

> 🚿

> WHY WOULDN'T I BE?

> Because I won't be home for most of the summer?

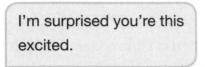

I make a face at my phone. Why didn't I think about that?

> But you're getting an amazing opportunity! And everyone at your genius school is clearly like, LUKE RYDELL IS A GENIUS! That is so awesome!

★★★★★★★★★★

Seriously, you could just react like a person and not a cheering squad. And worry less about me thinking you're fine with everything and more about figuring out your own shit.

I text frantically.

What do you mean? My stuff is figured out! I got into Oberlin! I'm set!

Also, I'm not trying to be a cheering squad; I'm just me. The most supportive version of me possible, but isn't that a good thing?

Are you still undeclared? Do you even know what you want to do?

Oh, no. Everyone keeps acting like it's fine, but of course I knew deep down it probably isn't. People like Sofia and Mariana might see me in the best possible light, but Luke, one of the people who knows me best, isn't fooled at all.

I just want to have a good life and be a good person, I reply, and regret it immediately. It's what a little kid would say, not someone nearly ready to go off to school. Luke just sends back the shrugging emoji guy, which sort of feels like he thinks I'm like a little kid, too.

We actually used to fight all the time, even though I looked up to him so much and always thought he could solve any problem, like a grown-up. But then Mom died and it didn't feel like there was room in our family for any of that anymore.

The doorbell rings, and I'm thrilled for a distraction. Any distraction, like, even if it's some shady character up to no good. But when I open the door, it's no shady character. It's Quinn, wearing an Oberlin baseball cap and a huge grin.

"You got in!" I shriek, and I throw my arms around her before she can answer. "Heck *yeah*."

She laughs and leans in to kiss me. The Oberlin brim smacks me and it's like a little high five. "If anything deserves a *hell yeah* . . ."

I punch her shoulder like we're athletes who just won the big game. I feel like we *did* just win the big game. "See? I told you."

"K, this is a big deal," she says as the corners of her mouth turn down. Oh, no. "There was no guarantee I was getting in. I'm a hopeful computer science major struggling with calculus, *an advanced math class*, and it's like you can't even see it."

"No, I know," I say quickly.

"You don't! You're always like, *of* course *you'll get in, Quinn,* and there was no *of course*! It was really scary for me and you refused to see it. You couldn't see that I'm a person standing here, not some perfect girlfriend you conjured up."

"But you are perfect," I say, which makes her eyebrows furrow. "Quinn, to me you are. Why is that bad?"

"I'm *real,*" she says.

"Duh, what else would you be? Of course you're real!"

"Things are hard for me, and I don't succeed at everything," she says, and it makes no sense to me, because I can't think of a way Quinn hasn't drastically improved everything. I think back to the night we met, how confidently she took charge of the kitchen, how I felt taking the first bite of the lasagna she made for me. Technically I didn't even know Quinn was going to be an option for me until months later, but I also think I fell in love with her that night, this amazing girl who just knew exactly what I needed.

"But, like, you *are* succeeding."

"I give up," she says, and turns around.

"Quinn!" I call, but she doesn't turn around. I start to race after her but her movement is so determined. And out of nowhere, even though I'm still not sure what I did wrong, I feel like Matty on my lawn begging me to take him back. And of course I never want to feel like Matty, so instead of dragging Quinn back to me, I watch her walk away.

• • •

"Hey, kid."

I look up from my physics homework, though I'm only pretending to pay attention to it. My eyes are blurred with tears, and my brain can picture only the back of Quinn getting farther and farther away from me. The incredible shrinking Quinn Morgan.

"Diane's, uh, over for dinner," he says. "Thought you might want to come out and eat with us."

"Why didn't you tell me she was coming over?" I close my textbook and notebook and jump up from the bed. I turn to glare at Dad for the lack of warning, but he's already headed back toward the kitchen. My mirror confirms I look like I've been crying big horrible tears for a couple hours, and I wonder if dusting on a bunch of powder will actually hide anything or only make me look like a sad, powdered sugar donut hole. I change my jeans and sweater for a dress, carefully fluff my hair, and walk down the hallway in as carefree a manner as I can muster.

"Hi, Kat," Diane greets me. She's standing at the counter drinking a glass of wine while Dad is serving salmon with veggies. I can't remember the last time that he made this dish, but I'm positive Mom was still alive. It's one of the only meals he's good at that doesn't involve delivery.

"Hi," I say, and smile the biggest smile I can manage. "Dad, do you need help? Can I do something?"

He mumbles something that sounds a lot like *set the table*, so I gather plates and silverware and our one set of cloth napkins. Diane quietly joins me and helps me line everything up perfectly.

"Everything OK?" she asks me, and I'm prepared to lie but a stupid tear betrays me and courses a track down my cheek.

"I'm sorry," I say quickly, before I go full beast. Dad's girlfriend shouldn't have to see or hear my snot.

"Don't be." Diane takes everything from me and finishes setting the table while I try my best to stop crying.

"I had this . . . I don't know. It wasn't a fight, exactly? My girlfriend's really mad at me, and I don't know what I did or said. I texted her that I was sorry but she hasn't responded, and I just . . . I wish I knew the right thing to say so I could just fix it and—"

Diane somehow interrupts me with a look. I realize not only that everything *had* felt like it was spinning, but that—suddenly—it doesn't.

"Would you like my advice?" she asks. "For whatever that's worth?"

"Of course! I love advice!"

"When you don't know the right thing to say, maybe it's time to listen instead."

"I, uh . . ." Dad gently pushes his way past us with a serving plate. "We're ready to eat. I guess."

"Oh, you guess?" A peal of laughter bursts from Diane, and she rubs my shoulder gently before sitting down at the table. I take my seat and try not to think about my phone in my room, or that Diane chose the spot Luke used to sit—which is obviously much better than if she'd taken Mom's.

"You OK?" Dad asks, and I realize he's looking at me. I'd hate for Diane to see him made itchy and awkward by his daughter's girl problems, so I quickly nod.

"She's going to be fine, right?" Diane asks, with a smile to me.

"Yes," I say super emphatically. "Maybe, at least. Hopefully?"

"Hmm, so around ninety percent?" she asks, and I laugh.

"That sounds right." I wonder what the chances are that my dad would meet someone who has smart advice and a cool radio voice and isn't hateable at, like, any level. Definitely not ninety percent.

After we eat, they tell me they'll handle dishes and I can go finish my homework. As I leave the room, I try not to look too excited that I'll get to be near my phone again. Unfortunately, my only text is a question from James about our humanities homework, and then the next morning Quinn isn't outside waiting for me. I'm trying to follow Diane's advice because it seems grown-up and right, but giving Quinn a chance to tell me what she's thinking feels like it's taking *forever*.

"Hey."

I look around my locker door and see Raina standing facing me. "Hi. What's up?"

She grins. "I'm sure you know all about best friend duty, right? Well, I'm doing mine right now. Go talk to her. She's sulking around and it's extremely annoying."

"I screwed up or something," I say. "And I don't want to make it worse."

"Oh, god." She grabs me by the wrist and marches me down the hallway.

Raina parks me in front of Ms. Kennington's classroom, and I realize that Quinn's walking up to it from the opposite direction. "Be nice, girls."

I watch Quinn's face for a reaction as Raina leaves, but it's as blank as I've ever seen it.

"Hi," I say, even though I'm supposed to be listening.

"Hi."

I reach out for her hand. "I'm sorry if I hurt your feelings."

"It's not that . . . exactly."

I can see the tenseness in her jaw, but instead of offering a hundred more apologies, I keep my mouth shut.

"I need you to see me for me," she says. "Not for who you want me to be."

"I know that you think that—" I say quickly, and then pretend I didn't stop listening to her.

"Let's not do this in front of my American lit class," she says.

"OK." We're still holding hands, so I squeeze hers. Hard. I'm not really used to this. Matty was my first serious relationship, but we didn't have issues to sort out or genuine talks about us. Everything was OK, until it wasn't.

"See you in third period," she says, and disappears into Ms. Lin's classroom.

We sit together at lunch like usual, and I try to gauge, while eating fries and Sour Patch Kids, how things feel. I would not say *normal* because she's still holding herself stiffly and I don't think she's mentioned to anyone else that she was accepted. What if she's already decided she isn't going? Of course, it's her right, but considering Oberlin was at the top of her list before we were together, does that mean something?

"Ugh," Gretchen says while flipping through our school paper. "It's almost time for people to campaign for prom king and queen."

It seems like everyone at the table, even James, whose boyfriend was prom king last year, makes a similar *ugh* sound. Not me, though, because suddenly all I can picture is how I, once upon a time, thought the year would go. Up until the first week of school, it was all but a given that Matty and I would take the titles and the crowns. Last year, they'd been cheap plastic, but in my daydreams the crowns sparkle like they're encrusted with real diamonds.

"It's so heteronormative they still do that," Raina says.

"What's heteronormative?" James asks from her spot behind me.

"I told you you should go on Tumblr more," I say, and I realize it might be the first time we've spoken today. I probably should have texted back last night about humanities or not been late to class because I was trying to find ways to be nice to Quinn as we walked over together.

"It's like when being straight is seen as the default option instead of just one option of many," I explain.

"Like when people tease little girls about having boyfriends when they grow up," Quinn says.

"Remember when my mom said you'd make a good wife someday because you're such a good cook?" Raina asks Quinn, who laughs.

"You *will* make a good wife," I say. "Just for, like, a lady who can't cook."

Quinn blushes really hard, and it's the cutest thing I've maybe ever seen. The cutest non-otter-related thing, at least.

"You two are so goddamn cute," Gretchen says. "I wish you could be prom king and queen."

"Honestly, that should happen," Raina says. "It shouldn't be king and queen anymore. Just . . . a couple or whatever."

"It's not a requirement it's a couple," James says. "Last year it was . . ."

We all just let her trail off because it's way too sad forcing James to talk about Logan. Even if maybe Logan being gone was her decision. Sometimes your own decisions are the saddest.

"Still," Raina says. "Why can't it be two people of any gender? The way we do it now is so outdated."

Gretchen nods emphatically. "We should—"

"—start a petition," she and Raina say together.

"I feel like almost everyone in the school would agree," Gretchen says.

"It's a really good idea," Raina says. "You two would totally be prom couple if it was changed to that."

"I doubt that," Quinn says. "No one knows who I am."

"People know who you are, dork," I say, though I regret it right away, because are we back on firm enough ground for me to be making fun of her like it's any other day? Prom could only help, though. I'm sure of it!

Raina already has a notebook open and is drafting up the petition, as Gretchen leans over her shoulder. Conversation between other people quiets, and the whole table directs their attention toward Raina's notebook.

I know it'll probably come to nothing, but I'm already

picturing it, Quinn and me crowned in front of the entire junior and senior classes. Our crowns sparkle while we're dancing to something amazingly cheesy. The night is *ours*.

I mean, you shouldn't have to give up something because you fell in love with someone *objectively better*. You shouldn't be seen as the most deserving of something only if you go out with a boy. Gretchen and Raina are right.

"We'll start the petition," Gretchen tells Quinn. "You two don't have to do anything."

"I agree with you morally," Quinn says, "though I still don't think anyone will care about me personally."

"People care about Kat, though," James says, though she doesn't say it like that's a positive thing. I would understand if being popular was still like how it seems in old movies, where it's all jocks and cheerleaders bullying smart sensitive kids, but at least at Magnolia Park that's totally not how it is anymore. And, anyway, I can't control who likes me and who talks about me. That kind of stuff has a whole life of its own.

"It'd be fun," I say, "if it happened."

"Lots of things would be fun if they happened," Quinn says, and I laugh even though she sounds grumpy. The sides of her eyes look crinkly, and so I feel right. This will totally get us back on track.

• • •

Quinn comes over after school, though we stay outside on my porch because we both have a stupid amount of homework to get through. Also, maybe we feel weird about having sex right now, or at least I do. There's this specific kind of intimacy with Quinn that I never had with Matty. When you have sex with a boy, there isn't always a lot of discussion about what's going to happen. With Matty and me, at least, we knew what we were going to do.

With Quinn, I talk a lot. We whisper under the sheets. We check in. I've discussed my body and her body and talked about what I liked with words I never thought I'd say aloud. Honestly, if I was ever with a boy again, I wouldn't assume foregone conclusions; I'd talk more with him. But right now, I have no dreams of any boys, or of anyone else. I just want things to be perfect again with Quinn.

"Did you nail your essay?" I ask her. "That's totally how I saw it going. You always win people over with the way you talk about things. People *love* you."

She shrugs.

"You did! You freaking *nailed it*!" I lean my head on her shoulder. "I'm really proud of you, OK?"

"OK," she says. She doesn't stop working on her calculus assignment, so I get back to mine. It stays like that, quiet and productive, and somehow in sync. I get a text from James, but it feels like the wrong moment to pay attention to someone else, so I turn my phone upside down and get back to work.

"Did you see that Dave Bell got stuck to his locker with that weird scarf he's been wearing lately?" I ask, looking up from my physics homework.

"No, but I'm not surprised. That scarf is clearly a danger."

"Yeah, a fashion danger," I say, which makes us both laugh. "It's not like it's cold out."

"Maybe he has a delicate neck," Quinn says. "So, the prom thing is weird. I'm sorry if they're taking it too far."

"I think it's awesome, actually. The school is being super old-fashioned, and we could be the ones to fix it."

She watches me for a few moments before leaning in and brushing her lips over mine.

"I love that you think that way," she says, and I smile as the warmth of her words fans out over me. We get back to work again.

"K?"

I look up from my notebook. "Yeah?"

Quinn grins. "I did nail my essay."

CHAPTER NINE

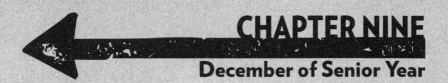

December of Senior Year

James

"Don't forget about tonight."

I glare at Dad, even though he has a smoothie ready for me. Dad without Mom gets up much earlier and has what seems like half a day's worth of accomplishments completed before I'm even out the door. I want to tell him that I know how he feels, that without Logan and without Mom, my life feels more open. I'd stuff anything into it so that on the surface it feels almost the same, if I could come up with anything other than a half of a beer and a few kisses with a boy I have no feelings for.

"You're not eighteen yet," Dad says. "We can treat this as casually as we want, but if you completely refuse to go to your mother's, legally she could do something about it. Let's just keep that from being a possibility, OK, kiddo?"

"I just don't want to spend the night there," I say. "I haven't *completely refused* to go there. I ate stupid dinner with stupid Todd. I went over on Thanksgiving for half the day."

Dad smiles. "I believe it was an hour and a half."

"Close enough. I ate some of Todd's terrible turkey."

"I wish we could change tradition on that," Dad says with a heavy sigh. "It's not an easy bird to master, but on Thanksgiving anyone thinks they can just throw it in the oven with a little butter and it'll turn out fine."

"What do you wish it was?" I ask. "Thanksgiving steaks? Well, actually, that sounds great."

He grins, but it quickly fades. "Go to school. I can't have you turn into a truant."

I expect to see a bunch of texts from Kat wondering why I wasn't outside on time, but my guilt dissolves upon seeing my blank phone screen. Is it horrible to hope she's been struck with a horrible illness? But, no, she's sitting in humanities third period, without any immediate comments about not seeing me this morning. I wonder if, now that she's dating Quinn, she'd even notice if I disappeared altogether.

After taking roll, Mr. Wellerstein announces something about group projects. Almost immediately, Gabriel turns around and smiles directly at me.

"Want to work together on this?"

"I, uh—"

"Sorry," Kat says in her candy-sweet voice. "BFF rules. She has to work with me. You should work with Quinn."

Quinn and Gabriel both give her looks. I'm not sure this was the easiest way I could have let Gabriel down once again.

"Thanks for getting me out of that," I tell Kat when we're at her house after school to work on the project. "That night's still a little fuzzy, but I know I couldn't have kissed him any more than seven times."

She giggles so hard she snorts. "Precise as heck! Even after consuming a third of a cup of beer."

"That was a lot for me."

"Snacks!" she says. "Hang on."

I wait while she dashes out of the room and returns with a whole pack of pepperoni sticks and a tub of cold marinara sauce. ". . . Wow."

"It's like eating pizza," she says, even though it is, emphatically, *not*.

"Do you miss being a vegan at all?" I ask her. "Wasn't that important to you . . . ethically? Not just because of Matty?"

She dunks a stick into the sauce. "I dunno. I still like some vegan stuff."

"Right, but . . . your beliefs?"

She shrugs. "I still eat vegan sometimes. It didn't feel

like something I had to keep doing constantly. OK, let's get this thing started."

"Do you think we should start this on the micro level and zoom out, or macro and zoom in?" I ask Kat as I set up the PowerPoint.

"Either or, they both sound good. Let's just do it one way and we can always switch it later," she says. "Start micro. We can use a cool photo from a march downtown and be like, *This Is What It Means to Be Los Angeles!*"

"That's a terrible title, but it's overall not a bad idea," I say.

I open a new tab on Kat's computer to pull up Wikipedia, and a screen full of otter GIFs appears. "Whoa. What's up with this?"

"OMG." Kat seems to let each letter linger on her tongue, like melting chocolate. "It's literally, like, the cutest, right? If you reload it, you get all new otters. Quinn did it when I was away from my computer, because she found out otters are my favorite animal. She's like this coding genius, did you know?"

"I didn't know." I hope Quinn's coding skills extend further than bursts of otters. "I mean, she's pretty bad at math."

Kat grimaces. "Don't mention that in front of her. She's so freaking stressed about it, but, like, you don't *have* to be a math genius to create amazing websites."

"You don't?"

"Totally not," Kat says, as if she's now an expert on coding and websites. "She's fine. More than fine."

Kat's phone buzzes, and she makes a groaning sound that sounds like *blargh*.

"Quinn?" I ask.

"My dad. He's going out straight from work and wanted to make sure I could handle feeding myself."

"So, it's . . ." I try to choose the right word so as not to make things sound scarier than they probably already are to her. "Serious?"

That was probably not the right word.

"I think it is." Kat makes a face. "He's so *happy*. And I want to be, like, super happy about that and for him, but I hate how it makes me feel and then I hate that I'm a person who hates how it makes me feel. And I just . . ."

Kat bursts into tears and I might just be the worst friend in the world.

"I'm sorry I brought it up." I abandon my research and turn toward her. "We can talk about anything else."

"It's not you." She throws her arms around me and sniffles onto my shoulder. Kat crying is always a full production. "Oh my god, James, it's never you. I just miss my mom so much."

"I do, too," I say. *Shit*. "I mean—"

"Duh, you dork, you're allowed to miss my mom," Kat says, and I breathe a sigh of relief I was so generously misinterpreted. "My mom was freaking awesome."

"I always remember how she'd give you those little fancy boxes of chocolate, and one time she brought one for me since I was staying with you guys for the weekend."

"Do you know that she told me she did that because she knew you'd actually appreciate it?" Kat laughs while wiping her eyes. "She said Luke wasn't allowed to have fancy chocolate because he didn't savor it enough. He ate it just like a Hershey bar."

"It sucks that she's gone," I say, and immediately shake my head. "God, I'm sorry. I feel like I'm saying the dumbest, most insensitive things right now."

"Why are you so hard on yourself?" Kat asks. "You're, like, the best friend in the world to me and I *know* you're always thinking the right thing so why would I ever worry?"

"Not always." I come up with beginnings of sentences, *I know this is a little shocking* or *I hate to tell you this* or even *Everything's gone so wrong and maybe there's no way out of it* but it's so much. I can't imagine telling Kat just about Mom, or just about having to say good-bye to Logan, without all of it spilling out. And it's so much, maybe too much to throw at someone, even your best friend. It'll come up over time, I'm sure, when it's right, when I'm ready, when I'm not feeling so barely together.

"I'll take over on this stupid project," Kat says. "Even though this is all so you don't have to give more false awkward hope to Gabriel Quiroga."

"His face when you said he should work with Quinn."

We burst into laughter and imitate his disappointment.

"He's honestly lucky," Kat says with a smirk. "Quinn's way better at designing presentations than you are. She'll do all the work."

"Sorry you're stuck with me." I try to say it like a joke, but it would be a lie to say I'm not hoping for some assurance. Kat and Quinn have only been dating for a month, and it's already assumed Kat will do everything with her and not me? But Kat just starts reformatting our slideshow, after reloading swimming otters a few times.

• • •

Mom opens the door to her new house and sighs when she sees me.

"You could look slightly less disappointed," I say.

"James, what are you talking about?" She hugs me tightly, and I picture a giant snake slowly constricting an innocent animal in its path. Just like the last few times I've seen her, she's wearing a dress and stylish boots, as if this is her new uniform. It's bad enough that I have to stand in an unfamiliar doorway and act like it's normal, but it's worse that my mom looks like a stranger.

"I gave you a key, didn't I?" she asks. "You really don't have to knock. This is your home, too."

"Um." I shake my head. "It's not. But I'm here."

"I'm so glad," she says in a voice that sounds sincere. When I was younger, everyone thought I was brave because I could run as fast as any boy and was constantly covered in scrapes and bruises from what I called *my adventures*. I liked how adults spoke of my strength, so I kept it secret that, on most days, all I wanted to do was get back home and hug my mom. Now that that's never going to be possible again, I might as well be five years old with scraped-up knees right now.

The house is not like mine. It's newer, and I think Mom and Todd paid someone to decorate it. Everything, from the furniture to the wall hangings to the little bowls and vases on nearly every flat surface, complements each other, and I can imagine it being the backdrop for a home catalog or something else generic.

Mom and Dad had explained to me, years ago, that when they bought their house, it was just about literally all they could afford. There was the house, and then there was food, and there was me. So we lived with furniture hand-me-downs that I know now clashed in color, style, and material. But at the time, it was all just our stuff, so I loved it. I actually remember crying when they were able to afford to switch out our overstuffed sofa for something sleek and modern. There'd been something so comforting about the mauve and sage stripes, even if now I can see through almost-adult eyes how ugly that thing must have been. One step at a time, my parents built their home into something they were proud of. And now Mom and Todd think they can fake it all at once.

"We're just about finished with dinner," Mom says. "I'm so glad you finished up your project in time to eat with us."

I leave my things in the front room and follow Mom into the kitchen. Todd is tossing together one of those premade salads Trader Joe's sells in bags, and I think of the time that Dad shoved a fresh sprig of dill at me and insisted I taste it. *Whole ingredients, James,* he'd said. *That's what makes flavor.*

"Hey, James," Todd greets me.

I admit I might have held out some hope that for a woman to leave her home, husband, and only child, the man involved must be thoroughly amazing. There had to be a chance that once I met Todd, everything would come into sharp focus. But Todd is just a middle-aged guy with glasses, some kind of boring office job, and the inability to cook from whole ingredients. Mom burned down her life for nobody.

"What kind of project was it?" Todd asks, and I stare at my phone until I realize he's talking to me.

"Just for humanities," I say. "It's boring."

"You guys have such interesting classes nowadays," he says. "Back in my day, it was really just the basics. Math, science, English, history. I took French because I thought it would make me more interesting, if you can believe it."

No, I can believe that, Todd.

"I should finish the rest of my homework," I say. "I have calculus and statistics to get through tonight."

"We'll let you know when dinner's ready," Mom says.

I walk down the hallway to the room here that's been designated as mine. It's decorated like a hip hotel we stayed at the other year when we traveled to Dallas for Dad's cousin's wedding. I sit down at the desk and get out my textbooks, and I figure, between homework and dinner, before I know it I'll be tired and then before I know it it'll be morning. And I can go to school and forget all about this pretend home.

Mom calls me down for dinner before long, and I stay as silent as possible while Mom and Todd discuss local businesses they patronized two days after Thanksgiving to support Small Business Saturday. They talk like it must be new information for me, so I let them know that Kat and a bunch of her friends—though I say *our* friends just to keep Mom from frowning—organized a whole shopping trip that they documented on Instagram. I also manage to not mention that I didn't actually join them.

Mom might be right about me needing to do more with my life, though, which is the actual worst part. If Mom's world being small is why she's given up her whole life for someone as boring as Todd, then maybe she's not wrong about me. Or, at least, I can't risk that she's not.

So I make an appointment first thing the next morning

with Ms. Malkasian, my guidance counselor, and slip out of my first period class to meet with her.

"James," she says when I walk in. "Ready to talk colleges? It's a little later than I'd recommend, but with your grades and test scores, you've still—"

"I'm actually pretty good there, I think," I say. "But I had the idea that for my senior year, I'd like to take on some kind of big project, some way to broaden my world."

"Sure, that'll look great on your applications," she says.

"It's really not about that." Why does it seem that right now everything's supposed to be? It's as if once you enter senior year, your life's in limbo until college? What's this year supposed to be, then? "I turned in most of my applications already anyway."

"Which schools?" she asks.

"Berkeley and Michigan," I say.

"Great choices. I thought I had UCLA down as your top choice, though."

I almost submitted my UCLA application once, twice, so many times, when my cursor hovered over that *Submit* button. It felt so big, though; UCLA had been the goal for so long—but in another lifetime. How could I just walk past Logan on campus like he was any other student?

"Oh, sure, UCLA too," I say, even though what actually happened was that I enacted my nearly nightly ritual of *nearly* applying and finding that I couldn't. It was December, the November 30 deadline was behind me, and I'd let time slip away. It was always a huge possibility that I wouldn't get into UCLA, but at least then I could tell people how hard I'd tried for what I wanted. Even if I didn't want it anymore. Even if I didn't have any idea what I actually wanted now. Instead I'd gotten too freaked out to even try.

"We can definitely look at some volunteer options," Ms. Malkasian says. "In the meantime, why don't I sign you up for the tutoring lab? You might enjoy helping other students, and I know you're more than capable."

It's not even close to what I had in mind, but I agree and stay after school the next afternoon for my first scheduled shift. It's pretty quiet, so I work on my own homework while I wait to see if someone's going to need my help. I'm not even sure how qualified I am to do this. Plus, nothing could feel less experience-broadening than sitting in the library of my own school.

"Miss McCall?"

I look up to see the tutoring lab advisor, Mr. Charles, and—*really?*—Quinn Morgan standing in front of me.

"Miss Morgan has a few questions about her calculus assignment tonight," Mr. Charles says. "Miss McCall will be happy to help you."

Quinn takes a seat at my table and sighs heavily as she takes out her textbook from her backpack. "This is so weird and formal. I seriously don't remember the last time anyone referred to me as *Miss Morgan*."

"I can ask if someone else can help you," I say. "If this is awkward."

"Of *course* this is awkward," Quinn says. "But I really need to understand this assignment so I can do well on next week's test, and you have the best grades in our class. And my sister has cello lessons tonight, so she can't help me."

I flip to today's assignment and walk her through it, and it's impossible not to notice how tense her posture is. Her shoulders seem about six inches higher than where they should be.

"This isn't life and death," I tell her. "It's just calculus."

"It *is* life and death," she says. "I need to make sure my math and science grades are all as high as possible for my college apps."

"Well, sure," I say. "So, do you want to try the first problem?"

She sighs but looks down at her book. Her shoulders get even higher and I can tell that it's impossible for her to accomplish anything right now.

"Did you ever play sports?" I ask her.

"Why?"

"Because I played softball in middle school, and one thing I learned is how you'll never connect with the ball if you're carrying that much tension in you."

"I *wish* I'd played softball," Quinn says. "I'm really uncoordinated. But I love watching baseball, so I get your metaphor."

"It's not a metaphor," I say. "You should literally try to loosen up."

She gives me an even weirder look.

"You're not stupid, and you know what you're doing," I say. "You're choking because you're scared."

Quinn messes her hair around while staring at her textbook. I let her work silently for a while, and even get out my statistics assignment so that I'm not staring at her. But I glance up every so often to make sure she's loosened up somewhat.

"OK," Quinn says, finally. "Can you check this over? And clear the way for me to go run into traffic if I still screwed it all up?"

"There's not exactly a lot of traffic out here," I say, which makes her laugh. And, miraculously, her work is mostly right, and I feel a little smug that I figured out her problem so easily. Though, seriously, tutoring is not going to make my senior year any bigger or better than it currently is.

"Are you leaving now?" Quinn asks, as she gathers up her things. "Kat and I were going to take a walk as soon as it gets dark to check out all the houses that go really overboard putting up Christmas lights. I'm making hot cocoa."

"That sounds like a couple thing," I say. "But have fun."

"It's really not. Join us. I'm great at cocoa."

I shake my head. "Thanks, though."

She slings her backpack over her shoulder and pulls a

baseball cap onto her head. Hats aren't allowed at school but I guess after-school tutoring sessions have fewer rules. "Thanks for your help, James."

"Well, I have to," I say. "Tutoring lab."

She nods, and her expression is as if she's seeing something for the first time. I hope that she's internalizing something about sports and calculus and believing in yourself, but the truth is that I rarely can guess what's going on in someone else's head.

Dad's in the kitchen when I get home, with a pot or pan on every burner on the stovetop. "James! I'm glad you're here. Can you start chopping the tomatoes?"

"Is someone coming over?"

"Who'd be coming over?" He chuckles. "No, I just thought it'd been too long since we had a good meal. Just because your mom's taken off doesn't mean we can't eat how we're supposed to, right?"

I'm honestly not sure, but I like seeing Dad in this state of cooking frenzy again. So I chop tomatoes and handle as much of the rest of the salad as he'll allow. We debate how much fresh mint to use, even though I know that it's not really up to me.

"So . . . how're you doing, kiddo?" he asks once we're at the table eating beef bourguignon with garlic chive potatoes. It's nice to pretend for even a moment that it's a few months ago, and Mom's working late or out with one of her friends. But it comes right back, how maybe *working late* or *out with a friend* were all probably code words for *Todd.*

"Fine," I say.

"You don't have to be," Dad says. "I'm sure not. If you want to talk to someone—"

"Like a therapist?" I ask.

"Something like that, yeah."

"I definitely don't need a therapist," I say. "I just need this year to be over, and to be away at school."

"There's no shame in it," he says. "I'm seeing one. It's probably the only thing keeping me tethered to sanity right now."

"Dad, don't joke around like that."

"I'm so proud of you," he says, in a voice bursting with earnestness and, maybe, held-in tears.

"Dad." I try to convey that this line of conversation is over, and not only because I might not be great at raw earnestness. Why be proud of someone who couldn't even get the application in to her dream school in time? Why be proud of someone who isn't even sure she *has* a dream school anymore?

"You always cook great dinners," I finally say. "And there's no new reason to be proud of me."

He opens his mouth as if he's about to argue, but then it's as if he thinks better of it. So I concentrate on eating and then escape to my room. Kat's posted a million photos of Christmas lights and overly decked-out houses to her Instagram, and even though I don't follow Quinn, I check hers to find more of the same, plus a selfie of her, Kat, Raina, Gretchen, and a few of their other friends I don't know as well. I guess it wasn't a couple thing, but it doesn't matter now, and it's not like I'm looking forward to Christmas this year anyway. I can't imagine looking forward to one again, now that I have no idea what my life's going to be like and that there's the huge possibility I've already veered too far off course to recover.

• • •

Ms. Malkasian has me paged into her office the next week. I wonder if my project request came off to her as more urgent than it actually is. Or should it be urgent? It's hard to know objectively how urgent your own life is.

"I don't think tutoring is for me," I say, before I've even sat down. "It's not broadening my world. It's literally in my own school with the same people I have to see every day helping with the same homework I'm getting."

"That's absolutely fine," she says. "I did put together some other ideas for you."

She's printed out a bunch of websites, which seems like a waste of paper, but I flip through them. Reading to kids, talking to the elderly, handing out fliers for various causes, collecting canned food, collecting used backpacks, collecting reclaimed water, and so on.

"Could I do all of it?" I ask.

Ms. Malkasian cocks her head at me and raises an eyebrow. "*All* of it?"

"Yeah, all of it."

"OK," Ms. Malkasian says. "Well, this will still certainly look good to any schools you plan on applying to."

I sigh. "Why can't I just want to do something good? Why does it have to be about college? Why is *everything* about college now?"

She lets out a heavy sigh but promises to help me coordinate with the organizations' leaders. I think about how excited I was to be a senior, and it's strange just how much everyone wants you to worry about next year instead. Yes, I personally would love this year to be over, but my bad year isn't what most seniors are going through. I don't understand why we're so encouraged to stop living in the moment.

Gabriel's in the hallway when I walk out of the guidance center, and I give him a little wave.

"Oh, hi," says a tiny girl who somehow pops up in between us. I assume she's a freshman because she barely looks old enough to be here. "Sorry to bother you."

"There are stairwells at both ends of the hallway," I tell her, because for some reason no freshman class has ever figured this out and they always clog the one at the north end of the building.

"Oh, I wasn't going to ask that, but—well, I didn't actually know." She laughs in what I guess is a nervous manner, and then I know what's actually coming. "Are you friends with Kat Rydell?"

I nod, as Gabriel watches me with a smirk somehow all the way across his face.

"She's just . . . really cool. Her and that girl are so cute together." The girl waves and walks away down the hallway toward the north stairwell, as Gabriel laughs.

"Hey," he says. "Is that a thing?"

"You have no idea."

He gestures toward the counseling offices. "College stuff?"

"Oh, god!" I shake my head when I realize I sound angrier than I am. "Sorry. I'm just noticing how no one wants to talk about anything but college with us. It's only December. Our second semester hasn't even started."

He grins at me. "I'm ready to get out of here."

"Well, sure, me too. It's the principle of it." I look away from him. It's easy to fix my gaze on a row of student-made posters promoting the winter choir concert. I don't actually have to tell him nothing's going to happen between us, do I? That fact couldn't seem more apparent. "I should get back to class."

He nods. "See you, James."

• • •

For some reason, I'm not included in the discussion between Dad and Mom about my plans for Christmas, and so even though I feel like I've more than already fulfilled my December obligations to her, I'm expected at Mom and Todd's for Christmas Eve. I text her that I already have daytime plans and also that I'd like to bring a cake from Porto's, so that gets me out of a big chunk of the day but also, hopefully, makes me look thoughtful.

"You really don't have to do this," I tell Kat while we're standing in the seemingly miles-long line for cakes, even though we go to Porto's together every Christmas Eve. "Don't you want to go hang out with Quinn or something?"

"Duh, no, I always hang out with you on Christmas Eve, and you know it, dork. And Quinn had to go down to Orange County for some family thing anyway."

"Yikes," I say, which makes Kat laugh.

"I know. Part of her family is, like, super uptight and conservative, and they're always like, *you look like a boy! You're never going to get a boyfriend like that!* Like, uh, do you think she's trying to get a boyfriend? It's like they refuse to see her for who she is."

"That sucks," I say. "I like guys and I'd still be angry if someone said I had to dress differently to get one."

"Right? And Quinn's so freaking nice, she just sort of deals with it, I guess. I would boycott going or show up looking, like, as gay as possible."

I really wouldn't have imagined that someone as out as Quinn would have to deal with family members like that. "Is she OK?"

"Oh, yeah, she's totally fine. Quinn handles everything, like, super amazingly, you know?"

Actually, what I know is that even *math* physically stresses Quinn out, but Kat seems to have some alternate Quinn she's dating who isn't afraid of anything.

"Why didn't you preorder your cake?" Kat asks me.

"I forgot. Aren't you having fun in this line?"

She giggles. "I like hanging out with you no matter what, you goober. So I feel like this is a trick question."

I notice a ring shimmering on Kat's index finger, right below her top knuckle. "Is that new?"

"Quinn got it for me for Christmas," she says. "I think I mentioned once I wanted one of these midi rings, and she found, like, the best one. Plus a little stuffed otter, and she made us, like, a vat of tiramisu. My dad's totally obsessed with her because of all the food she's made us, or helped me make."

"That's good," I say. "Considering he clearly hated Matty."

"Sometimes I think he's just way more comfortable with me dating a girl and not, like, having some boy steal me away, which I freaking hate," she says. "You're so lucky your dad's not like that."

I shrug. "I guess."

"My dad asked my help so he could buy a present for . . ." Kat sighs. "His girlfriend, I guess, is what I have to call her? Diane. He was going to buy her this really fancy candle, which just seemed weird, right?"

"Well, how fancy?"

We both laugh and debate the merits of expensive candles until I finally reach the front of the counter and ask for a Tres Leches cake.

At Kat's house, I get out my gift for her and she hands me a tiny gift bag overstuffed with sparkly tissue paper.

"Kat, if this is a fancy candle . . ."

She bursts into giggles. "OMG, I wish."

Wrapped inside the sparkly tissue paper is a sleek pair of blue leather gloves.

"They're 'cause it gets cold in Michigan," she tells me. "And that's one of the Michigan colors!"

"I might not get in," I tell her. "But, thank you."

I actually got her jewelry, too, but seeing the sleek little ring on her finger makes me hate my gift so much. It feels so young and in the past now.

"OMG," Kat says, though, in an excited tone. "My emoji! Where did you find these?"

I shrug. "The internet. It's amazing what people on Etsy will make."

She immediately fastens the emoji earrings and takes a selfie for Instagram. It's stupid to feel some sort of relief being tagged in her photo, but I do anyway.

Kat stays over until Dad's home from the shop, then she heads home. We've promised to hang out first thing on the twenty-sixth as per tradition. Before we could drive, we'd force one of our parents to drive us to the Americana so we could spend our gift cards. Now the thought of the mall seems pretty horrible, but traditions are traditions.

"So I know that you don't want me to say this, but . . ." Dad gives me a fairly serious look.

"But what?" I ask.

"Don't you think it's time that you headed over to your mom's?"

"Oh." I shrug. "I can feel that you're about to make me."

"Good guess."

I take my time packing an overnight bag and remember to grab the Tres Leches cake on my way to the door. Dad hasn't moved, and he gives me what I think *he* thinks is a genuine smile. But his eyes are sad, and it hits me that I'm saying good-bye to my own dad on Christmas Eve. I hug him as quickly as possible, and make it to my car, out the driveway, and then all the way down Riverside Drive before bursting into tears.

● ● ●

I get up early on Christmas Day, change into my running clothes, and take off from the house. Instinctively, I keep an eye out for Logan, who must be home on break. But of course I'm not dashing through the tiny streets of Magnolia Park, so there's no chance I'll run into him. Which is for the best. I think.

Mom (and technically Todd) gave me new running shoes for Christmas last night, and I have to admit they're lighter on my feet, and I'm looking forward to training in them in the upcoming track season. It'll be my first without Logan and—seriously, could I stop thinking about Logan for five minutes, even?

The house smells like cinnamon and coffee when I walk back in, exactly like a house should on Christmas morning. Mom's alone in the kitchen, wearing her fuzzy blue robe that she's had forever. I can almost pretend nothing's changed.

"How are the shoes?" she asks.

"Really good. Thanks." I pour myself a mug of coffee. "The season starts soon."

"You must be excited."

I shrug. "It's always good to be out there again. I can't really explain it."

"You don't have to," she says. "I can see it on your face when you run."

"Oh, god! My face gives me away!" I start to laugh, but it collapses in my mouth as Todd walks into the room. He's not my family. He's barely more than a stranger. And I'm definitely not home, no matter how this house smells.

"I should head out," I say, and while I'm prepared for

an argument, Mom just nods. Outside I gulp in the fresh air before speeding back, but when I walk inside and it's only Dad and me, it hits me so hard I could literally fall over. This home is gone, too.

We do our best. Dad's gone overboard with the fanciest tablet he could have bought—*for college,* he says—and a huge batch of his homemade cinnamon rolls that are reportedly so labor-intensive that we only have them for Christmas and my birthday. I'm pretty sure my gift pales in comparison—a selection of unusual or hard-to-find spices—but Dad promises he'll use each of them to make me a special dinner in January.

"Doesn't that actually make it a gift for me?" I ask. "*Another* gift?"

"You've had a rough year," Dad says. "You deserve it."

"You've had a rough year, too," I say, and then we say nothing because what is there to say? We clean up discarded wrapping paper, put away our gifts, and are back in the living room with nothing else to do. I can't fully blame the lull on Mom's absence, though it's not helping. The last couple of years, I'd send Logan a text as things were winding down for the three of us, and suddenly he'd show up in an ugly Christmas sweater, holding a foil-wrapped plate of food and a present his parents insisted he bring for mine. And eventually we'd figure out a way to sneak off and make out.

"We could go see a movie," Dad suggests. "Isn't there a new one with that Isaac guy you like so much?"

"Dad." I have no idea how he latched on to the idea that I have a crush on Oscar Isaac, but it's not something I feel we need to bond over. Can't I just innocently find an actor attractive? Oscar Isaac is not going to be my rebound fling.

My phone buzzes, and I promise myself that if it's Logan outside in an ugly sweater and holding a plateful of food that I won't even glance out the window. But it's Kat.

> I know it's Christmas (duh) but can I please come over? I'm having like the worst day ever.

> Of course.

"Dad?"

"What's up, kiddo?"

"Kat's having a bad day and . . ." I shrug. "I told her she could come over. I'm sure she won't be here for hours and hours. We can see the movie later, right?"

"Of course," he says. "I'll check the listings at all the AMCs."

There are, inexplicably, three movie theaters within a few blocks of each other over by the mall. It's like no one thought to ask anyone at their own company if they were building a movie theater in our town, much less where.

The doorbell rings only a few minutes later, and a jolt goes through me. Our house is so clearly lacking Mom. She might not have liked Kat much, but she was still always *around*. I don't feel like having The Talk with Kat today, especially if it's already a bad one for her. But maybe we could have this one horrible day together, and then it could all be past us? It might even feel like a relief.

"Hi." Kat throws her arms around me before I even really see her. I try hugging back as hard as she is, but I have to force myself. It's embarrassing enough when I cry when I'm alone; I can't even imagine having so much emotion that it's crashing against and then over my inner walls.

"Let's go to my room." I lead her down the hallway. "Do you want something? Water or cocoa or juice? God, sorry, why do I keep offering beverages?"

Kat snorts a big, snotty laugh. Her face is red and wet and streaked with mascara and her no-longer-perfect eyeliner. "I don't need any beverages."

"What happened?"

She flops down on my bed. "Maybe I will have cocoa, if you really don't mind."

I leave her in my room and find Dad in the kitchen. "Kat wants cocoa. I know you don't approve of mixes, but do we have any?"

He gives me a look as if I suggested painting our house neon green. "I'll make actual cocoa and bring it to your room. Don't worry, I'll knock on your door and leave it outside so you can keep talking privately with Kat."

"Dad, you don't have to go that far," I say, but he waves me off, and I explain to Kat why I'm returning empty-handed.

"No, that's good," she says. "Now that I've had Quinn's cocoa I probably can't go back to a mix."

I decide to let that go.

Kat shoves a little box in my direction. "My dad got me this."

"Should I open it?" I ask.

"Duh, yes."

I take off the lid to see a sparkling gold necklace, just like the one Kat wears every day. For a moment, I'm confused that her dad gifted her with something she already owns, but I realize that not only is Kat already wearing her necklace but that this one has different letters.

"Your initials," I say.

"I think he wants me to stop wearing this one," she says. "And it's, like, *all I have*."

I don't know what to say because while it can't actually be all that Kat has, it's something big. Jennifer wore that necklace every time I saw her, including the last time, at her funeral. I missed almost the entire eulogy that

Jennifer's friend Stacey gave because I was concentrating so hard trying to remember the actual last time I saw Jennifer and what she was wearing. The truth was that I'd spent the night at Kat's and left early to run, and Jennifer had waved good-bye while wearing pajama pants and a ragged promotional T-shirt from her company. It didn't seem right that the last time you could say good-bye to someone they'd have on a shirt featuring a cartoon outline of a menopausal woman getting her groove back.

"Her stuff was all there," Kat says. "And then it wasn't. Like, at all. I don't know where it went. Like, thank freaking god I already had the necklace or he would have gotten rid of that, too."

"Maybe he just put it in storage," I say, but I don't know if that sounds any better.

"He's erasing her." Kat starts to cry more. "Because of freaking *Diane*. What kind of name even is Diane?"

I shrug because it's so much better than *Todd*.

"It's only been two years, and—Hang on." Kat stops talking and glances down at her phone before tapping the green *Accept* button and holding it up to her ear.

"*Hi*," she says into the phone. "Merry Christmas! Officially!"

The tears are instantly gone from her voice, and each word sounds dipped in sugar.

"Yeah, it was fine. Nothing exciting. I'm super glad you survived the OC." She giggles. "Totally. So I'm at James's right now but—oh my god, don't even. I like hearing your cute voice, you dork. I'll call you later."

I try to look distracted by my own bedroom as Kat says good-bye to Quinn.

"Is everything OK?" I ask. "With Quinn and Orange County?"

"Oh, totally, I'm sure she's fine or she would have said something," Kat says.

Dad knocks on the door, and when I open it, he's already disappeared and left only a tray containing mugs of cocoa topped with gourmet marshmallows.

"It feels like we have a butler," Kat says as I bring in the tray.

"Remember Lana Schwartz's party?" I ask, and Kat practically shrieks. In sixth grade, a girl who's since moved away invited us all over for her twelfth birthday, where maids cleaned up behind us and a man we were pretty sure was a butler opened the door for every guest.

"That was, like, the first time I understood that there were rich people." Kat sips her cocoa. "I'm not wearing that stupid necklace."

"I don't blame you," I say, even though maybe Kat's dad just wanted her to have her own initials on something beautiful. But after all these years, I don't think I could guess what her dad would really want. He's not like Jennifer was, and not like Kat.

I'm not sure which of my parents I'm not like. Obviously, my fingers are figuratively crossed for one outcome there, though.

"Kat—"

"I know," she says, and I wonder if she *does* know. "My dad means super well, blah blah blah."

Nope.

"That's what mature people like you would think, James. Meanwhile I'm completely terrible for wishing nothing changed with him even if he wouldn't be as happy."

"I'm . . . I'm really not that mature."

She makes a scoffing noise. "Please. You're like the most freaking together person I know."

"I'm genuinely sad to hear that."

She laughs again, though it fades fast. "I guess I should go home. I just sort of took off."

"I'll walk you out."

"Aw!" She hugs me again once we're at the front door. "Thank you, thank you, thank you for everything. You're the best friend seriously ever."

I notice something out of the corner of my eye as I say good-bye to Kat. Once she's walking away down the street, I lean over to see a carefully wrapped plate.

Merry Christmas, McCall reads the note taped to the Press'n Seal. Inside I peel back the wrap and inhale the fragrant scent of Mrs. Sidana's samosas. They're a big deal; apparently, they're as labor-intensive as Dad's cinnamon rolls, so Logan's mom only makes them once a year, too. The first year that we were together, I was at the Sidanas' while she was assembling them, and I heard her whisper to Logan, *Are you sure it's serious?* I didn't hear his answer, and so for hours I worried that he'd said anything but *yes*. Then a huge plate showed up later, and so I knew.

"Whoa," Dad says as I walk inside. "I didn't expect to see those this year."

Me neither.

"You can have them," I say, because suddenly the aroma isn't delicious. It's Logan's snowflake sweater and the Sidanas' kitchen, it's kissing outside by the glow of Christmas lights and gearing up to count down to the new year. It's my fifteen-year plan and just how on board he was. "Can we go to the movie now? Whatever movie?"

It isn't until we're sitting in the dark (in the biggest of the AMC Theatres) watching Oscar Isaac and others on a very large screen that I realize Kat didn't even notice that Mom and all her things were gone. Kat didn't ask about my holiday at all.

• • •

There are at least three different New Year's parties happening, but I'm relieved Kat also thinks Jose Vasquez's annual My Parents Are at Big Bear Party is the right call. His house isn't quite as centrally located as ours, but

I'm actually happy for the long walk over in the crisp Los Angeles winter air.

Mariana waves as soon as I walk in, and I'm happy that neither she nor Sofia brings up the fact I've abandoned their lunch table and therefore haven't seen much of them this year. I'm always prepared to say, "Well . . . Kat and Matty . . ." and leave it at that. But I think people understand breakups. You don't have to fill in every blank space.

"Are you still planning on UCLA?" Sofia asks me.

I shake my head and pop open a Sanpellegrino blood orange soda. It's always a relief when there's anything nonalcoholic at parties besides tap water. "I need to get far away," I find myself saying. It even sounds believable. "As far as possible, honestly. Probably Michigan, as long as I get in. I can run track and it'll be fine for pre-med."

"I can't imagine going somewhere cold on purpose," Mariana says. "You're going to freeze. Our blood's too thin for it."

"I'm sure I can build up my blood." I like the sound of it, becoming more powerful from deep inside. I'm starting to believe this lie, too, that Michigan *is* my dream now. I can picture myself on campus next fall. I've Googled it, and it's easy to picture myself standing there among the changing leaves in the crisp autumn air. I can even picture me forgetting what was supposed to happen. Maybe, if I'm lucky, I'll forget even sooner.

More people crowd into our circle, and it feels like

nothing has gone off course. It's even fine that Kat's not here yet, because something about her would ruin this grand illusion. Though I guess it's weird that Kat isn't here yet. We coordinated only what party to attend, not what time. And I've barely seen her this break anyway. For some reason, I want Kat's absence to be something big and meaningful, but I have to remind myself that before Quinn was taking up all of Kat's time, Logan was taking up plenty of mine and Matty hers. And Mom was still around, and my life felt . . . fuller.

"Hey there." Gabriel Quiroga pops up over Sofia's shoulder. "Happy New Year, James."

"It's still December," Mariana says, and glances at Sofia and me like we should all laugh at him. But they don't know what happened with Gabriel the other month, and even if they did, I feel like I've lost the ability to share a private joke with two friends I've barely talked to lately. The actual shared moment is the knowledge between Gabriel and me.

"Happy New Year," I decide to say in return. I can at least be kind. "How are you?"

"I'm good," he says, and I see a smile somehow start in his eyes. "What about you? Right in the here and now? Enjoying your whole senior year before even acknowledging college?"

It catches me off guard and I laugh a little. "Like I said, it's just the principle of it. Obviously, I care about college, too."

"James!" Kat runs over to me, and I check my phone to see that it's already after eleven. "Oh my god, I'm sorry. We . . ." She giggles. "We lost track of time."

"It's fine," I say, waving to Gabriel as I feel I'm about to get dragged off.

"Come with me to get a drink." She steers me by the arm over to the keg. I'm pretty sure Kat picked up her keg skills from Matty, because she's as adept as a frat boy. "Soooo."

I open up another Sanpellegrino. "Yeah?"

Kat pulls me away again, this time to a quieter spot in a corner of the dining room. "I just had sex with Quinn."

"Oh," I say. It's not like when she told me about Matty. There had been such a buildup to that. She'd made me shop for lacy underwear with her and give her the contact info for my gynecologist. I had to help make a pro/con list because I was *so good at them*. This, though, wasn't something I even knew that she was considering.

"For the first time," she clarifies.

"I got that." Then I wonder. "You were ready? Quinn didn't—"

"James! Of course I was. And like Quinn would be like that? Quinn's *perfect*."

I see how expectant her face is, and I realize that she needs this to be like when she told me about Matty, after all. "Was it OK? Was it . . ." I don't mean to, but I laugh. ". . . really awkward?"

She giggles, too. "It was more than OK. And you know how it is when you really like someone. It doesn't matter that it's awkward."

I think back to last year, Logan's bedroom while his parents were at a party. Awkward didn't begin to cover it, but, no, that didn't matter at all.

"I just wanted to tell you," she says. "Don't look at Quinn like you know, though. She can be really shy about stuff. She's shy about this, I think."

"I won't." I examine Kat's face like something has changed tonight. "Do you think you're—"

"Oh, yeah, I'm definitely bi," she says, like it's old news. "It's not just Quinn. I mean, of course it's just Quinn right now. But, no. It's more."

I nod.

"Is it weird now?" she asks. "I haven't been secretly in love with you or anything."

A laugh bursts out of me. "Oh, god, Kat. I didn't think that at all."

She cracks up. "No offense."

"Oh, shut the hell up," I say, and she laughs harder. Quinn walks into the room, holding three bottles of an expensive-looking beer.

"Hey," she greets me.

"James doesn't drink." Kat discards her keg beer for the sleek bottle. "But you're super sweet."

"I'm just good at stealing beer," she says.

I watch her, this girl who's changed my best friend's life. Kat says *magic* so much regarding Quinn, but she's just a normal girl. Everyone could see how special Logan was. *Is*. He's not dead, after all. I could even understand Matty. There's something about Matty, a certain presence, that even when he's being an asshole is pretty undeniable. Quinn, though, has no magic as far as I can see.

Gabriel might have a little, if I'm being completely honest. But even if Kat could go from being in love with one person back in September and someone completely different now, I can't imagine my feelings cycling through that quickly.

"People are going up on the roof to watch fireworks," Quinn says. "There's still space."

"Kat's afraid of heights," I say. "It's not that far up, though. Can you try?"

Kat shakes her head emphatically. "What if I just tip over? What if someone else does? What if, like, I drop my beer and it picks up speed and kills a little squirrel or something?"

"The probability of any of that happening is incredibly low," I tell her.

"Yeah, are you sure?" Quinn asks her.

"I'll look out a window," Kat says. "I'm not, like, afraid of fireworks."

"What about windows?" Quinn asks, and Kat laughs and winds her arms around her.

"Not windows, either. Hardly anything at all except heights."

"I'll protect you," Quinn tells her, and I feel how suddenly this isn't about me anymore.

I climb up to the roof and end up sitting with Mariana and Sofia. I guess it's just like last year, but without Logan, and without Kat, it doesn't feel like it at all.

"This'll be the year *we graduate,*" Sofia says.

"The year we all move away," Mariana says.

I feel that I'm supposed to have a third thing, but this coming year feels so unknowable and foreign still. So I stay quiet, sip my bubbly water, and get ready to count down to midnight.

CHAPTER TEN

May of Senior Year

KAT

Magnolia Park High's Prom Changes with the Times

by Allison Chen for the *Burbank Leader*

At the beginning of this school year, many students already considered Magnolia Park High School senior Kat Rydell a lock for prom queen. Rydell certainly fits the title: pretty, popular, and at the time dating someone considered by many to be the most popular boy in school.

However, that relationship ended, and Rydell, who identifies as bisexual, began dating Quinn Morgan, another girl in her senior class.

"Prom was definitely not on my mind all year," says Rydell. "But when announcements were made for the prom king and queen nomination period, it hit my friends and I that the whole system was super hetero-normative."

"It was not at all important to me to be on the prom court," Morgan says. "Then I realized that only boy/girl couples could even qualify, and that fact really bothered me."

Morgan and Rydell, along with a group of friends, organized a petition to change the prom court rules, ultimately collecting signatures from sixty percent of the student body.

"When we saw how important this was to so many of our students, we knew we had to reconsider the way we did things," said Principal Juan Ochoa. "We never want MPHS to lag behind the times, and we're proud to make this change."

As of this school year, thanks to Morgan and Rydell's petition, there are no longer any gender requirements for what Magnolia Park High School is now calling prom couple.

"It's important to us that, in the future, kids like us feel like they're just as much a part of the school as anyone else," Morgan says.

"I know that prom isn't, like, hugely important, in the whole scheme of things," Rydell says, "but it's a big deal at our school, and it's so cool that two girls—or two people of any gender—together could be a symbol of it."

Principal Ochoa agrees. "No matter who wins the crowns, these girls have made history, and they prove just how commendable MPHS students can be."

• • •

After school, the day our issue of the *Burbank Leader* goes out, Raina and Gretchen convince us to drive around collecting as many extra issues as we can so that we can hand them out at school tomorrow. Quinn sighs and mutters a bunch about it, but I also keep catching her staring at our names printed right there in black and white.

"We're famous," I murmur to her, and she laughs and rolls her eyes all at once.

"Who even reads this paper?" she asks.

"Well, us now," I say. "And, like, pillars of the community."

"You guys are definitely going to win," Gretchen says, and I reply, "We'd better!" right as Quinn says that it doesn't matter. I pretend I was only kidding. I mean, I basically was.

A car I don't recognize is in the driveway when Gretchen drops me off, and when I walk inside I see Diane sitting with Dad at the kitchen table. I guess that seeing her is becoming almost completely normal for Dad, and so it should be for me, too.

"Kat, Charlie just showed me the paper," Diane greets me. "It's really amazing."

"Oh, thanks. I mean . . . it's just prom, I guess." I didn't even know that Dad had seen it. Of course, I texted him when I saw that it was out this morning, but he didn't respond. Dad is not great at texting. Once I sent him a cute GIF of a puppy to cheer him up, and he just wanted to know whose dog it was and where I had gone instead of school.

"It's definitely bigger than that," she says. "You broke ground for equality."

"Oh my god," I say with a laugh. "It's, like, at least one step less than that? That sounds so huge and serious. I think people are just excited to get to do something new."

"And people like you," she says.

"She's real popular," Dad says. "And she's nice, not like the popular kids when I was in school. They were a real bunch of assholes."

"*Dad,*" I say, but I like knowing that's how he sees me.

"What's your dress like?" Diane asks. Diane somehow always says the exact right thing.

"I don't actually have one yet—"

"*Kat,*" she says in a tone like I just super casually said I murdered someone. Then she bursts into laughter. "I'm sorry. I didn't think I'd react so strongly."

"I know, I know. I just haven't seen anything I like a lot, and I don't have that much to spend—"

Dad sighs heavily. "You should have said something. I don't know what dresses cost!"

"No, it's not that. There was, like, this super perfect dress for James at Bloomingdale's, so I gave her some of my cash, and—and it really doesn't matter. I can find something."

"I might be overstepping but . . . I'm great at finding dresses," Diane says.

"Please!" I say without thinking about it. Then I feel my brain trying to catch up, so it's like I set off running from it. "I totally need help. I'm gonna, like, look at these photos when I'm old, and it'll be so sad if I don't have the perfect dress."

This is how I end up at The Grove after school the next day with my dad's girlfriend. I don't think anything about getting to know Diane is hurting Mom's memory, but sometimes I still think about it. If Mom could see me flipping through racks of clothing with this woman when obviously ideally it would be with her . . . I don't know how she would feel.

I guess I don't totally know how I feel, either. It's a lot of emotions all at once and so I'm trying to focus on the ones that are good.

"Thanks for letting me take you." Diane piles another dress on top of the stack in my arms. It sort of seems like I don't have much of a say over what I'm trying on today, but that might be for the best. I need the best dress I've ever worn in my life, and Diane is pretty much the best-dressed grown-up I've ever met.

"What did you wear to prom?" I ask her.

"Kat, I don't mind telling you that it was pretty spectacular." Diane laughs. "It was black satin but it had a large—and also shiny—white bow around my shoulders, centered in front. My dad said, 'you look like a present' and he did *not* mean that as a compliment. Though I felt ridiculously sophisticated."

"Oh my god, it sounds totally amazing," I say, even though I find that I can't remember what Mom's prom dress looked like. I focus on picturing Diane's instead. "Was your date super dreamy?"

She laughs even harder. "Oh, I thought so at the time. I bet your photos with Quinn will age better than mine did, though."

She takes her phone out of her bag and checks the screen. "Your dad's nervous about how this is going."

"He's, like, *always* nervous about something, I swear. Please tell him everything is great and he has nothing to worry about at all."

She smiles at me. "Charlie's lucky to have a daughter who worries so much."

"I don't worry! I'm pretty chill," I say. Ugh, you pretty much cancel out being chill by saying you're chill, don't you? How can I convince Diane I'm not some kind of stressed-out high-maintenance nightmare?

J, what is the secret to being so calm and cool as a cucumber?

I text her, even though it's started to feel weird just randomly reaching out to her. I don't have to scroll up *that* much to see how it used to be, practically a nonstop conversation with no start or stop, just pauses for sleep and, occasionally, school. Once we messaged only in GIFs for nearly forty-eight hours before I cracked and asked her for help with our trig homework. And even then it was only because I couldn't find GIFs that represented the hypotenuse clearly.

?? Not sure what you mean.

I frown at my phone. James! Of course you know what I mean. Why are we being this way and acting like we don't have a million things to say to each other? Maybe I'm the worst one, because normally I say everything, and yet now I'm holding back, too.

"Everything all right?" Diane asks me.

I shove my phone back into my bag. "Totally. Of course. Should I try on some of these three dozen dresses you've picked out?"

"Let's not exaggerate, Kat, I'm sure there's no more than a dozen," she says, with a smile. "A baker's dozen at most."

I head into a fitting room and slip the first dress over my head. It's a really beautiful shade of yellow but somehow on me it looks like a banana. In a sparkly dress, I feel like a disco ball and, somehow, not in a good way. In black, all I can see is how I looked at Mom's funeral, and it hits me that maybe I haven't even worn a black dress since. Who wants to look like one of the worst days of your life?

"How's it going?" Diane asks from the other side of the door. "You're quiet in there."

"So far everything's stupid," I say.

"I was actually hoping you'd say that," she says, and slides a hanger over the door. "I know that it's not up to me, but I'm pretty sure this one's exactly the right dress."

It's a shimmery and vibrant shade of pink, and when I slip it on I'm not a banana or in mourning. I feel like a girl who could make history.

I step out to let Diane see, and her face lights up. I feel such a huge urge to have Mom there that I can't stop it.

I'm crying in freaking Nordstrom.

"Hey." Diane really gently rubs my shoulder. "Can I do anything?"

I shake my head, though it sends tears and snot flying in all directions. Even wearing the most beautiful dress I've ever seen, I'm so freaking gross. "I hope this isn't, like, a really offensive thing to say, but . . ."

"You miss your mom? Honey, of *course* you do," she says.

"I mean, you have way better taste in dresses, I think?" I laugh through my snot and tears. "But, like, I wish I could feel this for, like, the last freaking time. Every new thing it's like it all starts again."

We're quiet for a few moments.

"This is the dress, though . . . right?" Diane asks, and I burst into shocked laughter.

"Oh my god, *obviously*!" I throw my arms around her without even thinking about it. "Thank you for finding it."

She hugs me back in such a genuine real way. It's funny to feel so lucky and so unlucky at the same time.

Once I'm back in my regular clothes, I check my phone to see no follow-up from James but a GIF of two otters holding hands from Quinn.

While I'm replying to Quinn (OMG the cutest!!!!), Diane's carrying the dress away from me. "What are you doing?"

"I'm the one who forced the overpriced dress upon you," she says. "Therefore, the overpriced dress is my responsibility."

"Is that like a law or something?" My phone buzzes again but it's still not James.

Get it? It's us. If we were otters.

Yes, Quinn, all cute animals in

> couples are us, ESPECIALLY OTTERS! You're such a dork.

I glance up at Diane. Maybe I should put my phone away if she's being so amazing as to buy this perfect, perfect dress for me. "Can I ask, like, a weird question?"

"As weird as you want."

"Is seventeen too young to think you love someone? Because sometimes I . . ." I cover my face with my hands. "Oh my god, sorry. I'm such a goober sometimes."

"Of course it isn't too young," she says. "And you should hear your dad rave about Quinn. She sounds pretty special."

I can't imagine Dad being so open with someone, especially someone new. At least the someone new is Diane. "It's only because she baked us lasagna once!"

"It's definitely not just that," she says. "Though he has brought up the lasagna quite a bit."

• • •

I invite James over on Friday night, like old days, like everything's fine. Maybe everything *is* fine. People sometimes say I'm dramatic. This could be what they mean, the way it's easy to take a small kernel of something and imagine the whole popped cob. A kernel can be a kernel sometimes.

"I found a dress," I tell her once she's arrived and we're sipping fruit-flavored seltzers I bought in an attempt at festivity. "Do you want to see it?"

She says yes, so we head down the hallway. It's weird to see James at my house, in my room, and then it hits me that it's weird that it's weird to see James at my house. There were weeks when we were little that she was probably at my house more than she was at her own.

"Wow," James says when I unzip the dress from its bag, and she sounds sincere. "It's pretty great."

"Right? It ended up being, like, this whole thing because I got all weird and missed my mom *so much* out of nowhere, but Diane is sort of amazing actually? She didn't let it seem awkward at all, even though I was crying in Nordstrom like a freak. And I think she didn't say anything to Dad, thank god, because you know he'd be all awkward about it."

"It's good that you like Diane and that she seems great," James says.

"Duh, I know. I can like Diane and still be allowed to have complicated feelings and wish my mom could see me in my dress and all of that. My dad probably won't even know to take pictures of us, or if he does, they'll turn out all blurry like the ones he took of me and Luke at Christmas."

"My mom is like that, too, still," she says. "How hard is it to take a picture on an iPhone? *Not very hard.*"

I laugh and get my dress safely back into my closet

before flopping down on the bed. "Oh, so do you want to share a limo again, like last year?"

She gives me a look. "I think three in a limo is a pretty awkward number, don't you?"

"Everything is awkward in a limo! It's so long!"

James laughs again. It's nice it's like this and not like everything about me is annoying. "I'll pass. But thank you."

"Now I'm not even sure I'll get to be in a limo. Quinn thinks it would be more romantic to rent a cool car and drive me."

"You're the one who thinks limos are awkward," she says. Everything is so easy for James, just a decision and then moving on. Her brain is a machine. "You should let her."

"I guess I have to let her. It's, like, the only thing she asked for!"

"Well, you're making a really big deal out of prom," James says.

I just let it go because *of course* I'm making a really big deal about it. We're in the paper and changing history and also even if we weren't, I'm going to prom with the super dreamy girl I'm in love with.

"How was T&F?" I ask instead. "Did you run faster than everyone?"

She smiles a little. "It really isn't only about running fastest. I'm not sure how many times I can explain that to you."

I hear the front door, and I give James a look. "See how on-time he is now? Like he's not trying to live at his office anymore?"

"That's good," she says.

"Duh, I know." I regret my *duh,* but you can't put words back into your mouth. "I can still wish it was also, like, about me, and not just Diane. Can't I?"

Dad knocks on the door, and I call out that it's OK to open it.

"Hey, James, good to see you," Dad greets her. "You staying for dinner? We can order from the weird Asian place you guys like."

"Dad, it's not weird, they just have Thai *and* sushi," I say.

"I should actually get home," James says, *of course,* because of course this was too good to last very long. Like, longer than half an hour, apparently.

I wave good-bye to her and turn back to Dad. "Can we still get sushi and Thai?"

"Yeah, you wanna invite Quinn?"

"Dad, I can hang out with just you," I say, and he grins. It's funny how dads can be cute sometimes, like I can look at Dad and see what he was like when he was my age. I think about the guys I go to school with and wonder if someday they'll be having dorky conversations with their teen daughters.

We get our order placed and sit down in the living room to watch TV. Well, Dad turns on the news, but it feels like neither one of us is really paying attention.

"It's OK if I stay out all night for prom, right?" I ask.

"Yeah, yeah, sure, kid, that's fine. Just be careful. Don't drink and drive. No drugs." He shrugs. "So, uhhhh. Diane asked me to check with you if she could come over, take pictures, all that stuff. She thinks maybe I won't be the best at it."

"Oh, wow, it's almost like she knows you," I say, and he chuckles. "Of course she can come over. Diane's sort of the best."

"Yeah." He sighs. "Glad you're OK with her."

"Dad, I'm, like, way more than *OK* with her. I guess I didn't think you'd date someone so cool."

"I could say the same thing about you," he says, which makes me crack up. "I know it wasn't all easy on you—"

"It's totally fine," I say. "I just said it! Diane's the best."

I do wonder, watching him smile in his dorky awkward dad way, how much worse it would be if I said the other half, too. Does he also wonder if Mom would like Diane or if she occasionally has an eye on us and if she approves of how things are going? I still remember that Mom saw me wearing a choker made out of a ribbon only a couple weeks before she died and said, *Kat, leave the bad parts of the nineties back there.*

I wore it again the next day just to annoy her. I've never worn it since though.

Oh my god, I am thinking about a stupid ribbon choker instead of the millions of real ways I miss Mom. And then I wonder what the dumbest way Dad misses her is, like maybe how she always teased him that he legit thought that Target was pronounced *Tar-zhay* or that I'd hear him yelling about her hair clogging up the shower drain. But maybe Dad's lucky and he's not fighting all of it all the time, and the last thing I want is for him to *start*.

So I don't say anything at all, not then, and definitely not on prom night when I hear Diane arrive. You'd think I'd be too busy anyway, making sure my stylist-made-perfect hair doesn't fall apart and that my makeup is flawless and that my gel manicure hasn't chipped despite its strong promises. Somehow though I'm never too busy to miss Mom, worry about Dad, and consider how awesome I think Diane is and what that means for my family.

"Hey, kid." Dad knocks on my door. "Quinn's here."

I open my door, and he stares at me.

"Oh, no. Bad? What's wrong?"

He sighs. "You look really grown-up, Kat."

"Like, bad grown-up? Like when they say 'mature' but they mean old?"

"No, no." Dad shakes his head. "You look . . . beautiful. Go in there so Diane can take pictures."

I mean to walk in calmly like I'm sophisticated and as

apparently grown-up as Dad thinks, but I'm pretty sure that I race. Quinn's standing talking with Diane, and I had no idea you could literally swoon, but I think I'm literally swooning because Quinn's in a tux and she's never looked so gorgeous to me. She's never looked so gorgeous, period.

Holy shit, she mouths at me, which makes me giggle so hard I snort. It's super weird we're staring at each other *in front of my dad and his girlfriend.* Like, I want to kiss her so hard, but this definitely does not feel like the moment.

"You look amazing," I say.

"So do you," she says. "More than amazing. I need a better vocabulary."

"Your vocabulary is great," I say, and then, "Crap! Hang on. I was trying to be more prepared than this."

Diane super coolly hands me the box holding the boutonniere I picked out, which is the exact same shade as my dress. Matty thought it was environmentally irresponsible to buy flowers, so I didn't do this last year for him. And I'm glad, because sometimes something small like pinning a pink rose to someone's lapel can feel big.

"You're really good at that," Quinn says with a grin.

"I watched, like, six videos on YouTube. I was so afraid I'd stab your boob."

"I appreciate your diligence." She has a corsage of white roses for my wrist, and then Diane takes approximately a thousand photos of us. I catch a glimpse of Dad's face, and it sort of doesn't make sense how proud he seems.

I mean, it can't all be because he hated Matty and because of Quinn's lasagna.

"Be careful," Dad says as we're finally leaving. "Quinn, don't drink and drive."

"I would never, sir," she says, and the *sir* makes me giggle, and then we're out the door and finally alone.

"Quinn, you look so freaking hot I can hardly take it."

She kisses me in a sudden heated flash like lightning. Since I'm in heels we're the same height, and I curve into her as we keep kissing, kissing, kissing. I don't really care what happens tonight; prom isn't about winning. We've already won.

"You look incredible," she tells me, with her arms still around me. "And now I have bad news."

"Noooo!" I say.

"You don't even know what the news is. It's actually two pieces of bad news. My mom wants to take photos, too—"

"That's fine," I say, even though I know it isn't the same. I've seriously barely spent any time with Quinn's family, because unlike Dad, her parents took it as a pretty big deal that she isn't straight. It's weird to me that it could be a big deal to anyone, but especially if Quinn was your daughter, because she's so smart and thoughtful and kind. Like she must be a one-thousand-percent-better daughter than I am, if things like that were measured. Not that I wish they were. I'm lucky they're not.

"Also, you have to be twenty-five to rent a car," she says. "So instead of renting a classic convertible or having time to get a limo . . . I have my dad's car."

I can't help it. As I search the block for the bright yellow sports car that Mr. Morgan drives, a giggle bursts out of me.

"It's embarrassing," Quinn says. "You know this isn't me. Only assholes and my dad drive cars like that."

"Just assholes, your dad, and now you," I say.

"Whoa." Quinn opens the door for me. "I've never heard you curse before."

"It doesn't count when I'm quoting someone else," I say.

She pauses and just watches me.

"What?"

Quinn *blushes* and shakes her head.

"Hey." I take her face in my hands and make her look right at me. "I don't care about your douchebag car. I just want to be with you."

She kisses me again. "I just want to be with you, too. But I really wanted to drive up in a Mustang."

We stop by Quinn's house, and her mom raves over my dress, and I guess her parents are dealing OK with their daughter being in a tux and taking a girl to prom instead of the other way around because Ainsley is going with a junior and wearing a super cute green gown so it's out of their system or something. If I ever have a daughter I really won't care what she wears to prom as long as it's fancy enough, and I definitely won't care who she takes as long as they're nice.

It feels like a movie when we walk into the Beverly Hilton—and not just because we're at the Beverly Hilton, which feels like a super ridiculously nice place to be and probably has been in a bunch of actual movies. Our classmates turn to look at us, and I feel so proud to be standing here with Quinn. And it's not even the article or that we've been nominated for prom couple. I guess it *is* all of that, but it's more, too.

It feels like everyone wants to talk to us, even people we barely know, and it's hard not to get caught up in the spirit. But since I feel like I have to be super polite and well-behaved tonight—aren't Quinn and I kind of setting an example for the school?—I wish James would be less civilized and shove her way through to find me.

"You guys look amazing," Mariana tells us, and gestures over to her date, Bryan Owens. "His tux looks like garbage compared to yours, Quinn."

She grins. "I sprang for a good one."

"*Clearly*. Have you guys seen James yet?"

"I was going to ask you that," I say, as Sofia joins us. The three of us and James spent the morning together, getting our nails done and then waiting forever in line so we could get green tea pancakes at Bea Bea's. It felt just like last year but somehow more exciting, because last year we weren't seniors and last year I therefore had no chance at being prom queen. "Have you seen James?"

"I haven't. But I was going to tell you guys that the line for the photo booth is already *really* long and we should get in it now. James can butt in to join us by the time we get there."

But when we get to the front of the epically slow-moving line, James isn't there, so Quinn and I take photos first—and when we're done, James *still* doesn't show up to re-create last year's photo. Mariana tells Quinn to join us instead, and I feel my heart swell that she's so included by everyone. Still, no matter how much space Quinn takes up in my figuratively huge heart, there's a big James gap right now.

I take a second while Quinn's talking to Raina and Gretchen to text James. I see dots right away, which is a relief. If she was lying near dead in a ditch she probably wouldn't text right back.

I'm not coming.

Wait, what????! Why not? Are you joking or something?? (If so I totally do NOT got it.)

It's not a joke. I just don't feel like it.

J!!! It's our senior prom! You have a perfect dress! Your nails look amazing!

I don't have a date so . . .

SO? Like, EVERYONE is here. And also even if they weren't . . . I AM HERE! Your best freaking friend. We have to be at prom together! There's a photo booth again!

I just don't want to come. Period. And I tried to explain that to you, but you wouldn't take no for an answer.

"Are you OK?" Raina asks me, and I nod quickly.

"Totally," I say in my breeziest voice ever, even though my heart pounds louder in my ears than practically anything else. If I keep talking, nothing bad can happen. "It's prom! What's not to be OK about?"

Raina grins and nods in Quinn's direction. "I know she seems calm, but she was a wreck about *everything*."

I feel my heart settle. "Especially the car?"

"Oh my god, the car, your corsage, making her bow

tie look perfect—she practiced a *ton*—on and on. Pretty adorable."

"Super adorable," I say. "You guys look great, too."

"Oh, no, we're—Gretchen's my best friend."

"Uh huh," I say, though I laugh. "Not that people can't be friends, just that you guys don't really seem like friends. Like, James is my best friend and you guys don't seem like me and James at all."

Raina cocks her head. "James is your best friend?"

". . . yeah?"

"I just didn't realize. You guys don't seem that . . ." She shrugs. "Tight. But I'm pretty sure you're wrong about Gretchen and me."

I shriek without meaning to. "'Pretty sure'?"

"Oh, stop it," she says, but now she's laughing, too. The four of us end up on the dance floor together and it's easy to feel that everything's going perfectly until I remember that James isn't here, and Raina's words echo in my brain. *You guys don't seem that tight.*

I hope so, so hard that it's not because we aren't tight anymore. But do words echo when they don't mean something at least partially true?

Hey, seriously low pressure follow-up here! THIS IS ME BEING CHILL!

I hit send before I realize that ALL CAPS probably aren't very chill.

What?

Just come! I know people build up prom to be like SOME HUGE DEAL but it's seriously just everyone dancing and having fun. Everyone looks amazing. But you will look THE BEST OF ALL because your dress is 🔥🔥🔥 and your 💅 🔥🔥🔥🔥🔥🔥🔥🔥🔥🔥

GET IT? TEN FINGERS???

I get it.

I got you that 🔥 dress 'cause I wanted you to look amazing at prom! With all of us!

I'll pay you back next week.

J!! That's not what I meant!!

> Look, I'm in my pajamas and my hair's already in a shitty bun. There's no saving me now, even if I wanted to go. Which I don't. Also you're pretty much the last person who could convince me that prom isn't "SOME HUGE DEAL."

I stare at my phone and then I stare at Raina because now she seems like some kind of freaking fortune-teller. Quinn catches my eyes, and I feel like the hugest jerk because my sweet, hot, thoughtful girlfriend is the best prom date I could ever hope for but instead I'm frowning at my phone and wondering whether if I'd picked better emoji and used fewer caps, I would have been more persuasive.

"Everything OK?" Quinn asks me.

"Of course. Sorry. Everything's perfect."

I hate that I'm lying to her, but it's not her fault. And so I try with as much effort as I have to put James and her perfect dress and her apparent good mood earlier out of my head. I think about how we all laughed over giant plates of pancakes, and James never even hinted she wasn't coming tonight. Should I have insisted we pick her up even though it would be supposedly awkward with three people on the way to prom?

HEY is it that you don't have a way to get here? If I send you a Lyft now, you'll totally be here in time for the coronation.

?? I have my own car. I just don't want to go.

"K?"

"I'm sorry, I'm sorry." I carefully secure my phone back in my clutch and turn my full attention toward Quinn. "I'm a bad date."

"Oh, yeah, the worst," she says with a smile. "Everything OK? Really?"

"Really, everything is fine." I wind my arms around her, even though the DJ isn't playing a slow song. "I'm so glad it's you I'm here with."

She pulls me closer, and I accidentally whack my head against hers because we're not at all used to being the same height. We laugh and figure out, again, for the millionth time tonight, how we fit together.

"I really don't care how this goes," she whispers in my ear when Principal Ochoa takes the stage to announce prom couple. "I'm here with my dream date."

"I don't care how it goes, either," I say, but then I hear the principal call out *KAT RYDELL AND QUINN*

MORGAN and I know I've been lying because I'm flooded with so much relief, triumph, gratefulness.

Principal Ochoa grins at us as he places crowns on our heads, and the whole room seems to be cheering. I know that, on the one hand, it's silly; we're just kids at a prom in Beverly Hills like we're pretending to be rich and sophisticated grown-ups. But it's Quinn and me, and we have crowns, and just last year this wouldn't have even been possible. And thanks to us, now it is.

The DJ kicks off a slow song, and suddenly Quinn is *all moves*. She takes my hand and leads me to the center of the dance floor, as if every single night we dance for a ballroom full of people.

"This is nuts," Quinn says, while I'm wrapped in her arms and we're swaying to the music. "It's *nuts*."

"I mean, I totally wouldn't say this out loud, but . . . everyone was making a pretty big deal out of it. We were in *the paper*."

"The *Burbank Leader*," Quinn says, which makes me giggle.

"Still! I kind of thought this might happen." I lean my head on her shoulder. We've totally figured out our height nondifference. Everyone might be watching us, but the moment feels like it was made only for the two of us.

"You get that . . ." Quinn laughs softly. "You're, like, *super* popular. Everyone loves you. No one besides my friends really knew who I was until we started going out."

"That's not true," I say.

"It *is* true. And it's fine. This is just . . . it's a lot. I am not someone who thought this was how her prom night would end."

"Oh, please," I say. "If it wasn't me, it would be another girl. You're amazing."

"I seriously can't even imagine there being another girl," she says.

"Well, duh, me neither! If there was another girl, I'd fight her for you."

"Really." Quinn grins. "I'll just say that sounds unlikely."

"I can be tough if I need to be," I say. "I'm the one who taught my brother to punch."

"That *also* sounds unlikely."

I kiss her and hear a collective *awwww* around us. Quinn isn't wrong that people see us, especially right now in this moment. It hits me that it could have been me and Matty, slow dancing and kissing while wearing glittering plastic crowns, and, oh my god, I'm so glad that it's not.

The only thing I'd change about tonight is to have James be here. Of freaking course. And after prom's over, after we've Lyfted to the hotel, after we've left three separate parties in three separate rooms (Mariana and her date Drew Williams', Raina and Gretchen's—and I am now more than *pretty sure* Raina and Gretchen are hooking up or at least *about to*—and Miguel Carter's), James is still most of what's taking up space in my brain.

"I just don't understand why she wasn't there," I say, and it feels like it's for the millionth time, though I am very aware it's only the second time I've said it aloud to Quinn.

Quinn sits down on the edge of the bed. "Did you check that she's OK?" We're alone in our hotel room and my superhot girlfriend is on a giant bed, and yet all I can think about is James.

"Yeah, she just said she didn't want to come." I sigh. "I mean, I get that she's maybe still upset about Logan or something? And didn't have another date? But, like . . . it's prom. I thought we were all going to be there to have fun together. I freaking picked out her dress with her. James's was this really beautiful deep blue color and she looked amazing."

"Breakups are hard," Quinn says, taking off her shiny black dress shoes. Her socks have bright pink stripes that match my dress. "And prom is not *that* big of a deal, to people besides us at least."

"It's not just prom. It's . . ." Suddenly all I can hear is Raina again. *You guys don't seem that tight.* "James has been weird, like, a lot of this year. Things between us aren't . . . I don't know. I keep thinking how she's still my best friend, but it's not even like it feels like that? I don't know. Maybe I'm just being sensitive right now because . . ."

I turn to look at myself in the mirror, the sparkly plastic crown balanced sturdily in my curls. I still feel like a princess. Princesses in Disney movies, after all, always seem to have dead moms.

"Because?" Quinn asks.

"Because this was such a big deal. We changed freaking school history. Our classmates voted for us and . . . it just feels really special to me. And I really, really wanted it, even if that's gross and you're not supposed to want stuff like this. I know people just thought I was having a post-Matty freak-out or something when I started going out with you, but . . . it feels like everyone cares about us now. And I know it's just prom and it won't matter in ten years or whatever, but I feel like what we did actually *does* matter. And my best friend didn't even see it. I don't even know if she cares."

"I'm sure she cares." Quinn shrugs. "Maybe it's me."

"What do you mean, it's you?"

"K, I think it's now pretty well established that James doesn't like me."

"That's totally not true," I say as quickly as I can and blink my eyes a bunch to keep from crying.

"Hey." Quinn jumps up and hugs me. "K, are you OK?"

"Ugh, no," I say. "I'm not dumping all my stupid drama on you."

"You can dump all the stupid drama you want."

"It's just been . . ." I rest my head in the curve between

her neck and shoulder. "I like that you don't think of me as this super emotional depressing girl."

"I don't," she says, "because you aren't."

"You would, though," I say. "It's not like it's just James. Like if I talked about my mom or the day I found her or . . . or how my dad has a girlfriend and I actually *like her* and sometimes I feel like if Mom saw me getting along with Diane so well—"

I am in full beast mode. I'm crying and snotty and I don't believe Sephora's unspoken promises that my fake lashes will hold on through this storm.

Quinn just holds me really tightly. I feel it break through, this wave of emotion I've tried to dam off from her, and I cry like it's never been so safe to do so. Maybe it really never has been so safe before.

"What was your mom like?" is how she ends the silence, when my tears are finally over.

"Oh my god, Quinn, she was amazing. She was so sophisticated and funny, and she could make my dad laugh even when he was being grumpy and gruff with us. Her job was so weird—it was selling the ads on this website called HerMaturity, which was like a sex blog for middle-aged women? She was totally their best salesperson and she'd fly all around the country doing her whole business pitch for executives and stuff. And the articles would be like 'How to Choose the Right Lube for You' but she'd never get embarrassed, even though, like, can you imagine? And she'd always bring me back a fancy box of chocolates from wherever she went and would tell me not to settle for cheap chocolate, like, ever."

"That's a good life rule."

"Right? She was just, like . . . the kind of grown-up I hope I am someday. And I hope I can still figure that out now."

Quinn kisses me, and I taste her chai lip balm mixed in with my tears. Our crowns smash together and now there's glitter in the mix, too.

"I . . . I knew about your mom," she says. "Not that you found her, or what happened, but . . . you know how the school is. I'd heard that your mom had died."

"It was a cardiac arrhythmia," I say. "She didn't know she had it. She was always so healthy, you know? And then one day I got home and . . ."

Quinn holds me tighter.

"It still doesn't feel real sometimes."

"Seriously, I can't imagine," she says. "You're so strong."

"Oh, sure! I seem super strong right now, huh?"

"Yes," she says, looking right into my eyes. "You do."

"I didn't want you to think I was like this," I say. "Like this total emotional freak."

She leans in so closely that her lips are almost touching my ear. "I already knew."

I giggle and shove her away, but just a little. "Quinn!"

"K, you're one of the strongest people I know," she says. "If it wasn't for you, the school never would have changed this rule. Not now, at least. You, like, get out there and make people see what you're fighting for. It's a big deal."

I wave my hand. "I just wanted this super fancy plastic crown."

"You don't have to downplay it," Quinn says. "Not to me. You *inspire me.*"

"If you knew what a mess I really was," I say, "you wouldn't think that."

"You know you don't have to pretend you are or aren't anything, right?" she asks. "You're well aware I fall apart sometimes."

"I just liked being . . ." I sigh. "I like being this version of me, with you. The one who cried less and didn't talk about her dead mom all the time. Who didn't say, like, all her neurotic stuff aloud."

"You can cry and talk about your dead mom as much as you want. And I'm up for hearing as many of your worries as you want to tell me." Quinn grins and lies back on the huge hotel bed. "Is this how you pictured our prom night?"

I wipe my eyes for possibly the billionth time. "Oh, totally! Crying is super romantic and sexy, if you hadn't heard."

She traces her fingers down my arm. "I love you so much, Kat."

Oh my god, I burst into tears *again*. But they're different, and I hope she can feel that. They're full of joy, and relief, and somehow my future. Maybe it will be *our* future.

I've managed to stop sniffling—mostly—and I lie back next to her to kiss her. "I love you, too."

"I get that you think everything has to be perfect. But . . ." Quinn laughs. "It doesn't? That's all I've got."

"I don't—" I stop myself because I can feel how right she is. Even if this is one of the rare times I wish that she wasn't. "I've felt like a mess ever since Mom died. And then after Matty . . . you just made me feel like none of that had to define me anymore."

"None of it does," she says. "But you don't have to pretend none of it happened, or that you're fine one hundred percent of the time. Or that it wasn't a big deal to come out and start dating me. Or that whatever's going on with you and James isn't hard on you."

"It, like, weirds me out how well you know me." My skin tingles with the recognition. "And you still like me!"

"Also, you *really* can stop pretending that I'm perfect. We both know I'm not."

"You are to me," I say, sitting up. It feels more authoritative. "You have no idea, and if I have to keep telling you how I can't believe how funny you are and how hot you are and how when you kiss me sometimes I swoon so hard I can't even *think*. So, like, it's hard for me to imagine anyone not seeing all of that, too."

"I didn't kiss any admissions officers at Oberlin," she says.

"Well, duh. That would have been super unfair to every other applicant."

She blushes again.

"I get that you don't think I see you clearly," I say, "and probably I don't. It's all hazy like a perfect sunset. But also maybe you can't always see yourself clearly, you know? Like, none of your friends were shocked you got into college or were the other half of prom couple, were they?"

Quinn looks thoughtful for a moment. "You have a point."

I smile at her because I love her but also because I love being right. It hits me how much I work, all the time, to be perfect so that no one needs to worry about things that will hopefully be fine later. I could brush that off as easy, but feeling how much weight has been lifted off me tonight, I guess that it wasn't entirely. And maybe that's what I've been pushing on Quinn this whole time, this perfect mold to fill instead of letting her take her own shape.

"Seriously, though?" I touch her face, and she grins. "If I ever made you feel, like, not heard about being stressed out or whatever, I'm sorry."

"Thank you, K."

"Also, oh my god, Quinn. *Everyone knows you have to be twenty-five to rent a car!*"

Quinn just grins, and now it's too much; I have to kiss her, and kiss her, and keep kissing her. She carefully unthreads my crown from my curls but dodges me when I try to lift hers off her head.

"What? I'm leaving mine on," she says with a smirk.

"Oh my god, you're such a nerd." But I'm careful as I slide off her tuxedo jacket, untie her bowtie, and unbutton her shirt, not to jostle her crown. There are probably a thousand more things we could discuss tonight, but I'm done with talking, and from the swift way Quinn unzips my dress, I think she is, too.

CHAPTER ELEVEN

October of Senior Year

James

> Roommate's road-tripping this weekend! Ignore your Friday curfew, McCall.

I smile at my phone's screen. Last year, when I thought about Logan away at college, it sounded very adult and sexy. But it had actually been easier finding time to be alone when we—both only children with two working parents each—were still within walking distance of each other's homes. Apparently, roommates can be harder to shake than parents.

"You look happy," Kat says, walking up to my locker. "Like, boy-happy."

"You know me well." I start to hold out my phone to her but realize Quinn Morgan is right behind her. As usual, these days. And I have nothing against Quinn, but I don't know her well enough to let her in on my sex life.

"What are you doing on Friday?" Kat asks. Since she's glancing back at Quinn, I'm not sure who the question is for. I continue moving my books from my bag to my locker. "James?"

"Oh." I turn back to her. "I think I'm hanging out with Logan. Why?"

She makes a little frustrated noise. "Quinn's friend Raina is organizing a bunch of people to go skating at Moonlight Rollerway. You *love* skating."

Is it weird to ask my college boyfriend to drive out to the suburbs to go skating with a bunch of high school girls? Because Kat's right; now that even the idea of skating is in my head, I can feel the motion in my legs, picture the way the world curves around me as I fly around the rink.

She bounces up and down. "See, I can tell you want to!"

I'm used to Kat being practically a literal cartoon character, but I can see from how Quinn's eyes follow Kat that it's all new to her.

"I should check with Logan," I say.

"Of course!" Kat gestures down the hall. "I have to get

to class, but we can discuss more later at lunch? Quinn says there's tons of room at her table if we want to totally firm up plans with everyone."

"Oh, I . . ." I want to say that I don't think we need to switch tables just to finalize plans for roller-skating, but Kat's so eager and I can't figure out a way to say it that doesn't sound bitchy. So I end up nodding. And what Kat said ends up not even being true; Quinn's table is packed. Quinn, a red-haired girl named Raina, and Gretchen Bates, who runs track with me, all have to grab chairs from neighboring tables. We manage to mostly fit the additional chairs in, and I see how Quinn makes sure that Kat gets one of the non-shoved-in chairs.

"This is better," Kat says with a little glance over to our regular table. Matty is, of course, holding court, and maybe I'm an asshole for not realizing how rough it's been on Kat to sit near him after everything. Though I still hope this is for today only, because these girls aren't my friends, and I'd rather be catching up with Sofia and Mariana like always. Sitting here is already such a production. Over at the other section, if there aren't enough chairs, people just sit nearby without rearranging everything.

"Sure," I say, balancing my salad on top of my lap, while Kat's onion rings and tiny cup of Thousand Island dressing are in front of her on the table. Mom frequently starts sentences with *you know that I love your friend Kat—* but then there's always a *but*. And the fact that my best friend eats like a tiny junk-food-obsessed bird is often what follows the *but*.

"Oh my god," Kat says. "Quinn! Show James your list."

Quinn stares at Kat like she's just been asked to walk around naked.

"James'll think it's so cool," Kat says in the tiny sweet voice she uses when she wants to get her way. It's transparent but usually effective. This time is no exception, because even though Quinn lets out a heavy sigh, she flips through a small leather-bound book she's pulled out of her stack of school stuff.

"Amazing, right?" Kat grabs it from Quinn and shoves it nearly in my face. *Oberlin, Wellesley, Amherst, Vassar, NYU*. The list goes on in neat block handwriting, but I get the picture.

"It's the same as your list," I say.

"Yep! We're like college soul mates or something." She giggles, but I see a look of terror pass over Quinn's face, like the fear that everyone sees exactly what you're thinking. Her glances and the care she takes carving out space for Kat tell a lot already. To be fair, it feels like everyone's in love with Kat. She has that effect on people, and there's no reason Quinn would be immune.

• • •

Kat comes over after school ostensibly to do homework, even though I know she'll just want to talk and raid our refrigerator. I still get out my statistics homework while I hear her rummaging around in the kitchen.

"Can I eat this pink stuff?" she calls.

"It's *frosting,*" I tell her, but moments later she appears with a bag of pretzels and the tub of homemade frosting leftover from a cake Dad made this past weekend.

"Did Logan text you back yet?" she asks. "About skating?"

"Not yet," I say.

"He's probably, like, super super busy," Kat says, before I even have a moment to wonder.

"I'm not worried," I tell her. "You don't have to do that."

"Ugh, you're so freaking mature." She dips a pretzel into the strawberry frosting. "No wonder Logan loves you. Loving you is like loving the land."

What? "What?"

"Like it only slowly changes over time, it's all safe and good if you take care of it. Probably no one will ever love me again; I'm like loving a feral cat."

"These are both extremely inaccurate analogies," I tell her. "The earth is constantly changing, actually, and when you add climate change to that—"

"James, don't bring actual science into my science analogies." She giggles and checks something on her phone before looking back to me. It's at least a chance to get started on my statistics homework.

"So, do you have a whole plan? Like a Logan plan?" she asks. "Not your big life plan, like, your long-distance relationship plan?"

Is it possible there's a plan I've missed?

"Like, how often you guys are going to see each other in person, and if you're going to have actual phone calls or FaceTimes or whatever in addition to texting," she continues. "Relationship expectations, you know?"

"We didn't make a plan for it," I say. "But I trust him, and so I guess that covers everything? I don't expect him to be hitting on girls or avoiding me. If he's busy, he's busy. Logan's so honest . . ."

I suddenly hate my words, because Kat was literally gone for only about five days when Matty cheated on her, and even though she's the kind of girl everyone wants to be around, he left her feeling like a feral cat.

"OMG, James." She makes direct eye contact with me. "Like, obviously. Whatever bad thing you're thinking, it's OK. Logan has totally proved himself to be all honest and upstanding."

"Yes," I say. "I'm still sorry about what happened. You know that it has nothing to do with you, don't you? Matty's just . . ."

Kat shrugs. "I hope it doesn't. What if I'm just this depressing loser with a dead mom who's unlovable?"

"I'm sure that's not true," I say, and she throws her arms around me before returning to her snacks and her physics homework. "*Should* I make a long-distance relationship plan, though?"

"Ooh, a pro/con list about whether or not *to* make a long-distance relationship plan!"

I almost start to write that down before I realize she's teasing me.

Mom's home at her usual time, and I'm glad that Kat and I have managed to stay focused on homework and therefore seem as responsible as possible. My parents are younger than most people's I've known—they were both only twenty-four when I was born—and so I think Mom feels she's less removed from her own time of goofing off or whatever she's convinced we're doing. I've analyzed her box of high school memorabilia, and I definitely have better grades and a more solid extracurricular, so I have no idea why she's so judgmental.

"Hi, girls," Mom says, while flipping through the mail. She's wearing a simple black and purple dress instead of her usual jeans and a T-shirt or sweater (weather-dependent) and lipstick instead of Chapstick. Kat's commented recently that my mom's gone through a glow-up, which I don't think Mom appreciated. "James, since your dad's going to be at the shop awhile longer, I thought we should get dinner ordered."

It was just last year that Dad opened Vino Mag, and even though, like everything else around here, they close fairly early, he's often there later. On most days he's the only employee, so every duty—from counting down the cash register to taking inventory and restocking each shelf—is his to complete. I'd love to help out, but apparently it's frowned upon to have your seventeen-year-old daughter pulling shifts in a wine shop.

"Ooh, can we get those fancy hot dogs?" Kat asks. "If you use Postmates, they'll just bring them over."

It's almost impossible to believe that only a month ago she was, for all intents and purposes, a vegan who, on a regular basis, liked to join in Matty's lunchtime chats about factory farms.

"I'm sure your father's looking forward to seeing you for dinner," Mom says.

"Oh, OK." Kat takes one more pretzel before throwing her stuff into her bag and taking off.

"All right, let's get this over with," Mom says with a heavy sigh.

Dad's the one who loves food. At least half of the time, Mom and I would be happy in whatever dystopian future let us subsist on magical meal pills. So while in pre–Vino Mag days, we might be dining on homemade pasta or chicken grilled on the professional-grade barbeque in our own backyard, right now Mom is making me look over her shoulder as she scrolls through GrubHub's options. We're just lucky that we can pick out food online and have it delivered to our door. It's nearly as good as the food pills of our hypothetical dystopian future.

"Just pick whatever you want," I say. "You're going to do that anyway."

"You're very funny," she says. "Thai?"

I shrug. "That's fine. But, see?"

Mom laughs. "Yeah, yeah."

Logan's name flashes on my phone. "Can I take this?"

Mom waves me off, and I scramble to get myself locked inside my bedroom before answering it. I'm not used to my phone ringing. Texting's generally a much better option, but it turns out that I miss hearing Logan's voice.

"Hey!"

"Roller-skating?" Logan laughs. "This is our big night to ourselves?"

"I couldn't say no to Kat. I mean—I never can. You know this."

"McCall, you can't say no to skates. That is what I know."

I grin. "We'll do whatever you want after."

"Hopefully whatever I want is the same whatever you want," he says, and my face is hot. I'm sure life would be easier right now if I didn't turn into a prude over the phone, but it's just the way I'm programmed. If Logan asked something like what I'm wearing, I'd end up answering completely honestly about my workout clothes.

"Probably so," I say while scanning my brain for any possible topic to steer the conversation toward. "Do you miss being home? Or is that a stupid question?"

"You couldn't be stupid if you tried," he says. "Well, actually, you could. You're really determined when you put your mind to it. And, I dunno, maybe? Maybe not. I miss you being around every day. And potato balls at Porto's. And my mom's daal and rice."

"In that order, I hope."

"Definitely in that order, McCall."

I hear his smile in his voice. "I know it's cheesy, but maybe we could try to talk on the phone more. Or even FaceTime? Is that too much? We don't need a strict schedule, unless that's easier for you."

"I'll FaceTime whenever you want," Logan says. "You're probably wearing cute-as-hell pajamas right now."

"Logan, I don't even *own* cute pajamas."

"Oh, so completely naked. That's good, too."

"*Logan.*" I laugh. "I knew this would happen."

"I'm irresistible," he says. "That's what you know."

"Your self-esteem should be studied," I say. "Extensively."

● ● ●

When we get to the skating rink on Friday night, it hits me just how long it's been since I did anything social with anyone other than one of my usual groups. There's nothing inherently bad about that, but when you only hang out with people who are used to you, you forget that you may have qualities you don't even think about but are weird to others. Like owning your own professional-grade roller skates.

"They're *so* nice," Raina tells me.

Quinn crouches down to look more closely at them. The skates are polished black leather with a thick blue stripe running up the sides. "Really nice. You just *have* these?"

"James takes skating, like, super seriously," Kat says. "She can skate really fast. And backward. And fast backward."

"*Fastward,*" she and Quinn say at the same time, and then burst into giggles.

"She kicks everyone's ass on the track," Raina says. "So I'm *really* not surprised."

Practically out of thin air, arms encircle my waist and pull me backward. I know that Logan thinks this'll be a great prank, but I know what his arms feel like around me. And he's got a specific scent, this combination of his deodorant and hair product and something organic that's earthier and inherently *him*.

"Surprise!" Logan says.

"I invited you." But I laugh and turn around to kiss him. It's hard to believe it's been, literally, weeks since I've seen him. "Thanks for coming."

"Anything for you, McCall." His tone is sarcastic, but I know from his smile that he means it.

"Logan!" Kat runs over, as she's yet to lace on her skates. "I haven't seen you in, like, a billion years!"

"It's true, one billion years since I entered the collegiate halls of UCLA," he says with a grin. "How've you been, Rydell?"

"Super good," she says. "How's college?"

"Also super good," he says.

"Don't mock me," she says, but she's laughing. I don't have a word for the feeling that the two most important people that I chose to be in my life like each other this much, but I'm feeling it hard right now.

"Logan, you have to skate with me during one of the Couples' Skates since I don't have anyone."

He glances at me but agrees, and I decide to let it go. Even though I haven't seen my own boyfriend in record time, it's easy to forget that Kat was very recently heartbroken. How could I mind?

Raina and Quinn shout something to Kat, so she runs back over to join them, and I sit down next to Logan as he changes from his Adidas to rental roller skates.

"How long do we have to stay?" he asks.

"Sounds like at least through two Couples' Skates," I say. "Also you *love it*."

He gets up. "Introduce me to your friends."

I wave my hand. "They're Kat's friends. I just got roped into it."

"There's no roping necessary when skating's involved." He takes my hand and pulls me out onto the rink. "People were giving me shit for having a high school girlfriend, but

I proved them wrong about your maturity level by telling them all about our roller-skating date."

I feel a twinge of something in my stomach. Doubt? Anxiety? I keep skating though. "People give you shit about me?"

Logan squeezes my hand as we round a curve. I feel how my skates find the contour on their own. There's a feeling of magic out here, much like when I run. My brain seems to take a backseat and it's all my feet, my legs, my instinct.

"Like I care who makes fun of me?" Logan laughs his little boy laugh. "C'mon."

"Sure," I say, and I try to sound it. "I know."

Logan sneaks me a sincere look. It's not that he isn't sincere one hundred percent of the time; I'm not sure I've ever met someone who's so *himself*. But usually his honesty is piled high with charm. In this moment, it's like he swept all that off. "Really."

I smile. "*Really*. I know."

We pass up Kat, Quinn, and their whole group. No one—even Raina, whose track stats are impressive—is even close to as fast as Logan and I are. "God, they're going so slow."

"They're having fun," Logan says. "And the sign outside says there's no fast or reckless skating allowed. Not everyone's here to kick ass, McCall."

I glance at him and let go of his hand.

"Oh, you are *on*," he says, and then we're weaving in and out of the rest of the skaters on the rink. My long hair flies out around and behind me as I pick up speed. Running isn't something I do; it's something I love. But skating's the only thing that truly makes me feel like I'm airborne.

I lock eyes with Kat as I round a curve. *"Finish him!"* she mouths to me, and I give her a thumbs-up and keep flying until I loop around Logan. He's mostly perfect, but I know he has just enough dumb guy ego to be a little wounded by this. I smile plenty to rub it in as much as possible.

After two hours and exactly two Couples' Skates—both of which, somehow, involved Kat skating with my boyfriend—Logan and I take off back to his dorm. Being on foot again feels heavy and weighted-down compared to our hours on the rink, at least until we're alone in his room. I guess this feels a little like flying, too.

Plus it's *his room*. This isn't his parents' house. It's grown-up and separate and, right now, just for us.

"It's lucky for me that you still want me after you kick my ass," Logan murmurs as he pulls my sleeveless shirt off over my head.

"Yeah, thank god. Otherwise we'd never do it."

We both laugh so hard we ruin the moment, except that I love this. This *is* the moment. Standing so close, I can feel it in his muscles, how his whole body shakes with laughter. I had no idea how far away an hour could be, or that I could miss someone I heard from every day. I know how ready Kat is for next year, but even if I have Logan closer, my best friend will be what might as well be a million miles away.

"You still with me?" Logan's closed all distance between us, and even though we're alone in his room his words are flowing right into my ear. We could be the only two people left in the world for all I know.

"I'm always with you," I whisper, though he might not hear me as he's moved on to kissing my shoulders, my clavicle, the back of my neck. Before long, his lips have touched so much of my bare skin I've lost the ability to make a list.

Logan is the only person I've had sex with, but I'd definitely gotten close before. With those guys, there was always a clear goal to be reached—even if we never actually quite got there. Then there was Logan, and we'd lose time just leaning against each other, kissing. My mouth would ache and my head would buzz and somewhere in my core it was like I was being slowly consumed by fire. The destination doesn't matter when it's burning down anyway.

Right now, though, I'm already afire. So I pin Logan back on the tiny dorm bed so we don't waste a single moment.

"I'm not ready for next year," I say afterward, when we're lying next to each other, "but I am definitely ready for this."

We've only actually spent one full night together

before, after prom in May, when our curfews were both miraculously lifted completely. It's not like we haven't had plenty of opportunities to have sex, of course, and it's definitely not as if we haven't taken full advantage of those opportunities. Sleeping next to someone in bed, though, might be just as intimate. Especially in a bed this size.

"It won't always be like this." Logan hands me one of his T-shirts to sleep in, and I slip the familiar blue and gold of Magnolia Park High over my head. I have the same T-shirt, but mine doesn't feel so soft against my skin and doesn't smell like Logan. "Roommates exist."

"I know, but . . ." I glance around the room. Logan's half is decorated with concert posters, plus his giant calendar I've teased him could be seen from space. *You have to see your goals to achieve your goals,* he likes to say. Current goals seem to be *English comp paper due, Chem lab report due,* and *Math 31B study group.* Last year I knew all of Logan's classes, the teachers he had, and what his general course load looked like. I worry that part of Logan is a stranger to me now, but then I immediately feel silly. I'm naked except for his T-shirt and I'm curled up in his sheets, after all.

"Where do your parents think you are, anyway?" Logan asks me. "Kat's?"

"I tried to be vaguer than that." I watch him put on pajama pants that look like they're made for an old man. "Mom's always so happy if it seems like I'm living some slumber party lifestyle where my hair is being braided while I'm wearing a sheet mask."

"I find it weirdly hot that you're actually a grumpy curmudgeon," Logan says, and a burst of laughter flies out of me.

"I probably shouldn't be flattered, but I am." I wait until he turns out his bedside light to ask what I've been wondering the whole night, maybe longer. "Do you think we're naive to think we know what we want?"

I'm saying *we* but of course I mean *I*.

"Look, you're the one with the five-year plan," he says gently.

"It's actually a fifteen-year plan," I say, which cracks him up. "What? After pre-med, there'll be medical school, and then residency, and—"

"All I'm saying is, I'm trying not to get ahead of myself on any of it," he says. "I'm keeping my eyes right in front of me. But I like you right here next to me."

I hook my chin over his shoulder.

"Not *literally* next to me," he says. "Though that's good, too. I think we make a good team. And as far as I'm looking ahead of me, I can't see that changing."

I can't, either.

• • •

We get up early the next morning and change into our running clothes for an easy jog through the campus and then out to Westwood beyond it. I pretend for just a moment that it's already one year later.

"What?" Logan asks me with a grin, once we've cooled down into an easy walk.

"Can't I just be happy without an explanation?"

He cracks up. "You? Never. Your happiness practically has a bibliography, McCall."

"Don't worry," I say. "You're definitely one of the cited works."

"Hell *yeah* I am. Sidana, Logan. Ibid., ibid., ibid."

"You know, when Kat and I were little and talking about our dream future boyfriends, I never described an unbelievably arrogant guy."

"More like justifiably arrogant." He tugs on my ponytail. "You know I love the hell out of you."

"Oh, I know you do." I slip my hand inside his. "You know I do, too."

Once we're back on campus, I pack my stuff back into my bag and plan to head out. Mom and Dad didn't seem especially suspicious, but it's probably safest if I'm back in Burbank so I don't have to explain why it would take me an hour to get back if they called. That said, Logan and I end up having sex again, because, well, *of course* we do. By the time I'm in my car, Kat's texted that she's at Coral Café, so I drive there even though I'm far less into greasy diner food than she is.

I expect that she'll be alone with a book or her homework like usual, but she's sharing a booth with Quinn. They're so caught up in conversation that they don't notice I'm here, and now that I'm standing in a gross diner in sweaty running clothes, I wish that I wasn't.

"Hi," I say, finally.

"James!" Kat waves and gestures to the empty spot next to her. "How was your super romantic night?"

I shrug, because I'm not going to have this conversation in front of Quinn. Even if it seems like Quinn is suddenly my best friend's new best friend. Am I immature for how much dread that possibility fills me with? I know that a best friend isn't the sort of relationship where you make explicit promises and set expectations, the way you do with a boyfriend. It's like life sets up boyfriends to be the most important thing in a girl's life, when I probably couldn't even have navigated myself into a relationship in the first place without Kat's advice. There are a lot of things I can't imagine handling without her. But of course I've been so used to how things have been; just because Quinn's around a lot doesn't mean anything fundamental has shifted.

"If you guys are busy I can just—"

"We're only busy in the sense that we've had a lively debate about hash browns," Quinn says. This, somehow, causes Kat to burst into giggles.

"Sit down, James!" Kat pats the booth's seat more emphatically. "It's not fair how you still look super cute and all together after you've been running."

I shrug and push away the giant plate of hash browns Quinn offers to me. "No, thanks. And I don't look cute."

"Lies!" Kat laughs so hard she snorts. "Like this plate of hash browns!"

"How dare you!" Quinn says, and Kat sort of sinks under the table, as I believe she attempts to kick at Quinn with her short legs. I think about all the places I could be right now, instead of watching two people guffaw over some private potato humor.

A waitress stops by our table, and I don't think it's my imagination that we share a look over the giggling going on next to me. "Anything for you, hon?"

"Just a cup of coffee," I say. "To go, actually. I should probably get home."

"Already?" Kat asks.

"I don't want Mom and Dad to be suspicious," I say, which seems to placate her. It's also possible that she doesn't mind too much because she's got Quinn here. I wish I didn't care. Jealousy feels rotten in my gut. But with Logan off across town, the one positive thing that I could see coming from Kat and Matty's breakup was that Kat and I would have so much more time for just each other. I have nothing against Quinn, but she's eating into a lot of that time that I thought would be for me.

"What are you doing tonight?" Kat asks me. "Do you want to go to the AMC 16? Brett Bolton's having a party, but it might be more fun to see a stupid movie."

I do want to see a stupid movie, and obviously I want time with Kat that's just us, so I agree before saying good-bye to her and to Quinn. Mom's actually out when I get home, and of course Dad is at Vino Mag. I mean to catch up on the reading for AP Lit and Comp, but I get distracted looking at Instagram and texting Logan and Kat. I should probably feel guilty, but it's just so much more interesting than *Bleak House*.

"Hey there." Mom leans into my room. "Your dad and I need to talk to you, but he's still on his way home. Why don't you head to the living room now, though?"

I follow her in and search for some sign of what this very serious talk will be about. For a Saturday, she looks nice: dark jeans and a T-shirt that hangs in an expensive way. That in and of itself doesn't seem like a sign of anything, though.

"I thought it might be a good time to fill in your college application list," she says.

"Oh," I say. "I thought this was something serious, the way you sounded. It's really filled in already."

Mom raises an eyebrow. "Just UCLA?"

"UCLA, yes, and USC as a backup. I'm sure I can get into one local school."

"You realize that UCLA is actually more difficult to get into than USC, right, James?" she asks.

"Yes, I understand, but I still prioritize UCLA."

"I've been doing some research, and ideally you should be applying to at least six. Of course you can go with UCLA and USC as your target schools, but then two or three dream schools, and two or three safety schools."

"I'm sure that I'll be fine," I say. "My SAT scores are above what both schools are looking for, my track stats are strong, and Kat says she'll help me with my essay so I don't sound like a robot."

Mom sighs. "Honey. You have your whole life ahead of you. Are you really ready to commit everything to staying in your hometown, just for your boyfriend and your best friend?"

"It's not for 'my boyfriend.'" I use air quotes. "We both agree that UCLA's pre-med options are best, and I can run track there. I made this plan on my own; it wasn't that he decided and I'm following him. As for Kat, she's going more than halfway across the country, at the least, because she wants to be somewhere 'artsy and interesting.'"

"You're only seventeen." Mom's phone buzzes, and she glances at it with a little smile. But she quickly turns it over and her expression is serious again. "You're making decisions about your entire life."

"Uh, isn't that the whole point of college? How is deciding to move across the country and be away from my boyfriend any more of a decision than staying here?"

Mom sighs more. "James, I'm just worried that your world so far is so limited, and you're designing your future in the same manner."

"How is my world limited?"

"Well, you already seem to have committed for life to your boyfriend, you don't seem interested in living anywhere besides your hometown, you only have one close friend—"

"I know that you don't like Kat," I say, for the first time, though I've worried about this fact more often than I could keep track of.

"I like Kat just fine," Mom says. I decide not to call her out on it. "I just don't think that it's healthy not to have more of a social life at your age. And Kat's . . . a little self-centered. I worry there's no room for you in your friendship sometimes."

There's immediately a feeling that's double in all ways. It's fiery and freezing at once. It's wrong but it strikes dangerously close to something true.

"We just went skating last night, remember? Logan, Kat, a bunch of girls from school, and me."

"That's right." I hate how happy Mom looks at this reminder. "Did you have a good time skating?"

"It was fine," I say, and then, "I kicked Logan's ass, so."

"Good girl." Mom smiles again, and it hits me that I haven't seen her smile like this at me in a while. Is she that worried about my future? I've seen photos of Mom at my age—at all ages, really. My parents went to school together, starting in kindergarten, though they didn't start dating until high school. As they tell it, Dad was too shy and intimidated by everything about Mom. After all, she might clearly dislike my best friend, but pictures paint Mom as the Kat of her high school class. Everyone looked at her.

"I go out with groups of people all of the time," I say, which seems almost true.

"I know that you do, but you don't seem to be that close to anyone beyond Kat or Logan."

"You and Dad went to school together," I say. "Your life is perfect. Why can't I want the same thing?"

Mom laughs, but as if nothing is funny. "My life isn't perfect, James. I just . . . I challenge you to do something with your year that doesn't involve your boyfriend or Kat, OK? And add at least a couple more schools to your list. I did some research and I think UC Berkeley or the University of Michigan would fit you just as well."

"Fine," I say, as Dad walks in. "If you're as upset about my college list as Mom is, I'm fine adding Berkeley and Michigan to my list."

"That's not what we're here to talk about," Dad says in a snappish tone I've rarely heard from him before. When we were little, Kat and I had this elaborate conspiracy theory that Dad was a stoner because he was just that chill all the time.

"I'm sorry if you think my plans for—"

"This part isn't about you," Mom says, though not harshly. "James . . . god, I didn't think this would be so . . ."

"Your mother and I are separating," Dad says in the same horrible tone.

"What?" I look to Mom, and then back to Dad. There must be a moment coming where they tell me they're kidding. I'm ready for this conversation to turn back to my dismal future. I'll willingly go back to my room and read *Bleak House* all night if that's what it takes.

But there's no coming moment where the joke's explained. Mom and Dad just sit there with unchanged expressions.

"James . . ." Mom moves to sit closer to me and takes my hand in hers. We aren't that touchy-feely, and I jerk my hand away from hers without even thinking about it. "This is . . . it's incredibly hard to tell you. But I've met someone and—"

I pull back from her even more. "Wait, what? You've *met someone*? Like you're having an affair?"

"I don't like that phrase," Mom says.

Dad folds his arms across his chest. "Neither do I."

I feel like I'm watching a stranger who looks like my father. Nothing about his voice or the way he's holding himself is Dad.

"I wouldn't risk . . ." Mom closes her eyes and shakes her head. "I wouldn't make such a big decision that affects both of you if I wasn't so sure that this is what's right for me."

"For *you*," I say. "Clearly, not for me or for Dad, right?"

"For the three of us," Mom says. "Our lives are better if we're all truly happy, aren't they?"

Dad and I don't answer.

"Anyway, James." Mom keeps trying to make eye contact with me that looks like something straight out of a serious TV drama, but I don't want to be part of this episode. "I'm moving out, and Todd and I—"

"His name is Todd?" I ask. "It's like what you'd name a dog."

Dad coughs like he's trying not to laugh. I want to join in except that nothing's funny. How could anything ever be funny again, when Mom is leaving us for someone named Todd?

"Todd and I have found a house in Toluca Lake," Mom says. Toluca Lake is only one town over, but it's not retro or quirky like Burbank is. It could be almost any other personality-free town in the Valley. "It's less than a ten-minute drive from here—only five without traffic. You'll have a huge bedroom, and—"

"I'm not moving," I say. "This is my home. Not somewhere in Toluca Lake with someone named Todd."

"We're not asking you to move," Mom says. "Half your time here, half there."

"Half?" I don't want to live in Toluca Lake, even half of the time. I don't want to meet anyone named Todd. I don't want Mom to think that Dad isn't the best man she knows.

"I know this is a lot to process," Mom says.

I don't decide to, but I just stand up and walk away, down the hallway, to my bedroom. Nothing feels real, but it's not like a dream where deep down somewhere you know you could end it all by willing yourself to wake up. Everything might feel numb, but it's all actually happening.

"James, honey." Mom walks into my room and wraps her arms around me. "I know this must seem ridiculous."

"It doesn't *seem* ridiculous," I say. "It *is* ridiculous."

"I was fifteen when I started dating your father," she says. "I had no idea what I wanted then. And in a flash, I'm in my forties married to my first actual boyfriend. It's like I don't even know how I got here."

"Great," I say. "That makes me feel fucking great."

"No, James—that isn't what I meant." She hugs me even more tightly, but considering how numb everything feels, it doesn't matter at all. "I really thought that I was happy enough. And then . . . it turned out that I wasn't."

I stare straight ahead at my wall, at the framed square of pictures Kat had printed from Instagram. Five photos of her and me, four photos of Logan and me. Logan and me at prom. Logan and me after a track victory. Logan and me on his eighteenth birthday when he bought a pack of cigarettes he never smoked, just because he could. Logan and me holding hands walking down the sidewalk in a photo I had no idea Kat was taking.

The first photo of us together isn't up there—and I've always been grateful for that fact because it took me until fairly late sophomore year to make decent hair and fashion decisions—but if it was, I'd be fifteen in it. Just like Mom and Dad.

I didn't know that everything could break at the same moment.

"Can I please be alone?" I ask.

"Of course." Mom shuts the door behind her.

I've always been someone who didn't necessarily know the right thing to say, but right now I don't even know the right thing *to think*. Facts and research and plans have always made so much sense to me, and my life has *worked*. But this constant comfort I've had, since the fifteen-year plan gelled into place, was because I felt that my hypothesis had already been proven. This wasn't new, bold research. I had sources to cite, proven theorems, historical documents.

Maybe she's selfish, and maybe she's a bad person. But if Mom wasn't happy, my hypothesis is completely flawed. And, therefore, my fifteen-year plan is riddled with errors.

Dad's face flashes into my head, the way his eyes lost their light as Mom made her pronouncements. Then it's not Dad's eyes I'm seeing. It's Logan's dark brown eyes, and I'm the one breaking his heart.

When the best guy in the world has chosen you, you don't think it could be within you to ruin it. But now I feel it: my destructive possibilities, the new unproven formulas, the research yet to be written.

I don't want to be Mom. I can't imagine being a person whose own happiness is the only thing driving her. But it's better to know how things could end, isn't it? It's better to cut something off before it has a chance to bloom into malignancy.

I grab my phone with shaking hands. Kat's texted that Brett Bolton's party might actually be worth going to, but I leave those messages unread and maneuver to my ongoing conversation with Logan. What if the fifteen-year plan worked out and then suddenly it was twenty, twenty-five years, and then my unhappiness choked me until I had to leave him, leave our hypothetical kids?

Is your roommate still out?

Hell YEAH he is! Get your sweet ass over here, McCall.

I don't tell Mom and Dad where I'm going. I'm not sure if Mom's even still here. Why would Mom still be here? She's made her decisions about her priorities.

I let Waze tell me the quickest—and most stressful—path to Logan's dorm. My fist is banging on his door before I even know it.

"It's about time." He swings open the door and grins. "Just can't stay away, can you."

I wish that I could change my mind. If I were a

different person. If proofs meant nothing to me. If evidence never felt binding.

"Logan," I say, and the word feels heavy, hard to push out. "We need to talk."

He runs his hand through his black hair. He suspects nothing. I imagine Mom telling Dad, and Dad starting the conversation with that easy smile he has, for everyone, but especially for her.

"What's up?" Logan asks.

I step inside and dodge him as he tries to kiss me. "We have to break up."

"Great prank, nerd," he says. "Seriously, what's going on?"

"I'm serious," I say, and something shifts in his eyes. This is what it's like to carry this possibility, to be able to ruin someone. If time, if a life together, can only make it worse, this is the kindest I can be.

"I felt like I owed it to you to do this in person, not by text," I continue. "So I'm here."

"McCall." He wraps his hands around my wrists. "Slow down. What the hell is going on?"

"It doesn't matter," I say, and my voice catches on *matter* but I recover quickly. "This isn't going to work and . . . and it's stupid of us to pretend we have some big fifteen-year plan when—"

"What happened?" he asked, and his eyes are so big,

and so serious, especially as I pull out of his grasp. "Can we just talk about it?"

"Nothing *happened,*" I say, still moving back from him. "I've just been so stupid."

His eyes are still huge and earnest. I have to turn away.

"I have my whole life ahead of me," I say.

"OK," he says. "If you need a break or—"

"I don't *need a break.*" If only a break was some kind of magic potion. I'd take as much as it called for. "I need you to take me seriously right now."

"McCall," he says in a small voice, "I always take you seriously."

"Then, seriously," I say. "This is over."

"Please talk to me," he says, and now it's his voice that's catching. I have to get out of here, and so I leave without another word or look back at him.

Brett Bolton lives in the same little section of Magnolia Park as Kat and I do, and so even though I don't really know him, it's easy to make my way back to the neighborhood and find his house. Kat's hanging out with a small circle of people, including Quinn (of course), in the front yard, but she shrieks and flies over to me as soon as I walk up.

"James is here!" she yells with her beer-scented voice. "Yay!"

"Hi," I say, and a tiny sob escapes me before I can

help it. Kat's mouth falls open and she throws her arms around me.

"Come on." She drags me away from the crowd, down the sidewalk, around the corner. "What happened?"

"Logan and I broke up." It becomes real as I say it, and I try to imagine homecoming, Christmas, my birthday, Valentine's Day, prom without him. Mom in Toluca Lake, Logan gone forever. My world cut in two—no, three—pieces.

"James." Kat starts to cry, too, and hugs me tightly. "How is it even possible? You guys were like my OTP."

"You spend too much time on Tumblr," I manage to say, which sends her into snotty-sounding giggles. It's so tempting to lay it all out right now for Kat, but for all the horrible things I can't stop feeling, no matter how much I don't want to, the worst part is how stupid I must be, deep down. I might comfort myself with books, research, and carefully laid-out plans, but maybe these things mean nothing. Maybe I'm just a child who doesn't understand how life actually works.

Plus, my sweet *still recently heartbroken* friend believes the story, too, the fifteen-year plan, the fairy tale of Jamie and Valerie McCall who fell in love at fifteen and then lived happily ever after right here in Burbank, California. This amazing girl who's been my best friend every goddamn step of the way believes she might be no more lovable than a wild, snarling cat, because a boy made her feel small.

How can I do this to her, too? Someone still deserves the fairy tale.

"I don't want to talk about it," I say. "I just needed you to know."

"OK," she says. "We can talk or not talk about anything. Do you want to leave?"

"No," I say. "I want to have one of those ill-advised rebound hookups, actually."

I have no idea this is what I want until those words have left my lips, and judging by Kat's face, I think I might have scandalized her.

"Does that make me terrible?" I ask even though I'm not sure that I care. But I'd like Kat to think I care.

"No, no," she says. "Go get some! Who's cute? Who do you want to make out with?"

My brain literally can't conjure up even one guy, so I just head back to the party, arm in arm with Kat. I don't remember the last time that neither of us had a boyfriend, and suddenly our options seem incredibly open. Kat strikes up a conversation with Gabriel Quiroga, who's in our humanities class, and I feel myself a little giddy with excitement for her until she's disappeared, and I realize she's sent him my way.

"She's funny when she's drunk," Gabriel says. "I guess she's funny in class, too. Hopefully she's not drunk there."

"Hopefully." It's genuinely my best attempt at small talk. I really can't believe I've had multiple boyfriends.

It genuinely would have been a miracle even if there had been only one.

"Can I get you a beer?" he asks me, and I shake my head.

But, actually— "Sure."

He dashes off and returns moments later with a red Solo cup full of foamy beer-smelling beer. I get only halfway into my first sip before realizing that I hate it, but I take a few more sips because he fetched it and because who even knows what I should hate anymore?

"How's Sidana?" he asks.

"Oh, he's—we broke up." I want to feel freed by the words, and since I don't, I take a few more sips of beer. "What do you think of Mr. Wellerstein? Humanities isn't exactly what I expected."

He sort of laughs, and it makes me feel like I can read his mind. He doesn't care about humanities or Mr. Wellerstein right now. My head feels foamy like the beer and I think the beer is to thank or to blame. I don't want to remember the last time I was sorting out whether someone wanted to kiss me, because it's only bound to make me think about Logan and the way his stubble scratched my face the later in the day it became.

So I lean in and kiss Gabriel. He's about my height, which I'm not used to, so my nose bumps his on my approach. All of it's fuzzy, like a dream, like earlier when Mom was changing everything. I go with it because I'm already here, and Gabriel's a nice guy. I'd rather kiss someone than no one. Now it's proven: Logan is officially behind me.

"James."

I realize that my eyes are closed and that it's very bright and I'm on the floor of Kat's bedroom. There are hazy fragments of memories from the night before, but it would be a lot of work to piece them back together right now.

Kat lightly smacks me in the face with a pillow from her spot in her bed. "Your phone's buzzing like a whole freaking beehive."

I reach into my bag to scoop it out. My screen has never been lit up with so many messages and missed calls. Logan, Mom, Dad, Mom, Dad, Dad, Mom, Logan, Logan, Logan, Mom, Dad. "Shit. Shit, shit, shit."

Someone knocks on the door. "Kat, is James in there? Got her parents on the phone."

"*Shit.*" I pull myself to my feet—why the hell did I sleep on the floor when Kat has a perfectly comfortable queen-size bed we normally share?—and open the door. Kat's dad holds out his phone to me. "Hi, I'm sorry. I fell asleep at Kat's."

"It's fine, kiddo," Dad says. "I'm just glad you're OK. Can you please come home?"

I agree and, after giving Mr. Rydell his phone back, step back into Kat's room to get my bag. I notice another head poking out from under Kat's flowered comforter and realize why I was relegated to the floor. It's the same answer as it is to almost every annoying question lately: Quinn Morgan. I'm in too much of a hurry to care. Much.

"I'm sorry again," I call out as I let myself into my house.

Dad walks into the front room. "I'm not saying I want it to happen again, but it's OK. I know it was a rough day. I'm just relieved you're alive, and I know your mom and Logan were when they heard, too."

"When they heard? Is Mom not here?" I ask, and instantly feel stupid. Of *course* Mom isn't here. She's in Toluca Lake with Todd. While I was gone and my life fell apart more, Mom was leaving us all the way. "Did Logan call you?"

"Your mom texted him to see if you were with him, but he hadn't seen you in a while. I know he was concerned about you, too, so in case you didn't have a chance to let him know you were fine, I texted him."

"You don't have to text him anymore," I say. "Don't worry. We broke up."

"James, I'm so sorry," Dad says. "Do you need me to punch him or something?"

"Dad." I find myself laughing. Dad comes home sore from wine-tastings because he uses a corkscrew so much. There's no punching in his future. "No. I can take care of myself. And he doesn't need any punching, not that I think you're the best one for the job."

"Well, I could call a guy," he says. "How about breakfast? I'm the right one for that job at least."

I stare at the coat hooks near the front door. Six in all, two for each of us, for a light jacket and a heavier coat. The middle two are empty. "We're all alone."

"Yeah," Dad says with a sigh. "It really sucks, huh?"

I blink back tears. "It really does."

CHAPTER TWELVE

July after Senior Year

KAT

When we were only fourteen, James and I buried a time capsule in her backyard. We sort of took it seriously, but we also knew we weren't *really* saving something important for future historians. After all, we were fourteen, not idiots.

Mixed in with all the dorky stuff that seemed like a big deal at the time—on the one hand, I cannot believe just how hard I crushed on Justin Bieber, but, on the other, I did end up with someone who basically has his most iconic haircut—we decided to write each other letters about our friendship. I crammed in every single thing I could think of, even though I legit couldn't imagine what on earth James would say.

And so even though I know it was the wrong thing to do—and I for sure knew at the time—I couldn't bear the thought of waiting. James kept her feelings so close to her heart, and I had to know what she'd write down. As we closed up the time capsule, I sneaked the letter out and into my pocket. I even ended our hangout prematurely—super rare for us back in those days—to escape home to read it.

For a while I read it every night. It seemed like it answered every question, including ones I didn't know I had. Even when I was little, I was totally aware of how hard I felt my feelings, how close they were to the surface, how they rarely were just for me but for everyone else, too. James's feelings were somewhere else entirely, and I felt like a secret keeper now that I had this letter.

I never would have believed then that even a full day could slip by without speaking to her. But it's been nearly a month since graduation, and we haven't talked at all.

When I was seven or eight, I tried on one of Mom's fancy dresses and somehow got Play-Doh stuck all over it. She'd never yelled at me like that before (and maybe even after), but of course I was little and didn't get how royally I'd screwed up. I just thought my mom was the meanest in the world, and I somehow made it a full forty-eight hours without talking to her.

Obviously, I would give just about anything in the whole universe to get those forty-eight hours back now.

Losing Mom was the worst thing that's ever happened to me, and I pray all the time that it remains the worst thing that ever happens. And so it's hard to accept that I'm not talking to someone as important to me as James is when there's a choice in the matter.

But the truth is that I'm not talking to her, and I have no idea what to do about it.

• • •

Even though we're shopping for the same campus with the same list, Quinn and I decided not to shop together. We both agree it's important that even though we're going together we're not going *together*. We have different majors—well, she has one, and I'm figuring things out—and different goals, and of *course* we're not roommates or anything.

I'm considering two different sheet sets at Target—definitely an easier purchase when you're not with your girlfriend who you at least *assume* might sleep on them too at some point and has, like, strangely strong opinions on thread count—when someone turns into the same aisle.

"Hey, Kat," Hannah Padilla greets me. Her reddish-brown hair is up in a ponytail, and her face seems extra freckled. Even in Southern California, it's always interesting to see people's summer selves.

"Hi!" I hold up my printed-out list. "Dorm stuff?"

She holds up her own. "Dorm stuff. Where are you heading?"

"Oberlin," I say, and then, "Ohio," because it feels like most people need the full set of info.

"Oh, right. I'm going to Berkeley, but I'm sure you already heard that from James."

"Oh, I . . ." The list is suddenly wrinkled in my fist. "Sure. Yeah."

"Not to gossip, but . . . she seems like she's doing better, doesn't she?" Hannah asks. "I can't imagine going through your parents' divorce your senior year, but now that she's working so much with Habitat and getting therapy, it's like this . . . well, not a *brand-new James,* but she's *happy.* Though hooking up occasionally with Logan Sidana would do wonders for most of us, huh?"

A flush spreads from my face down the back of my neck, like that moment you're positive your allergies are actually the flu.

"Um, huh, sure," I say, and also just like the flu I calculate how quickly I can get away because honestly I could just totally barf right here and now.

"And I'm sure—no, I'm *positive* she feels shitty about everything she said at Jon's party way back whenever. Whichever version you heard. I think people were just at prom overload at that point, you know?"

"Oh, sure," I say, and stretch a big smile across my face. "I should probably go. Good luck at Berkeley."

I take off without waiting for her reply. I'm in my car stuck in traffic on Victory before I even know it. My brain's way too busy turning over all this information, pulling it apart, trying to figure out if there's an angle to look at it where James doesn't look like a huge liar. In another flash I'm parked, and then I'm outside the door at Quinn's aunt's.

"Hey," Quinn says, stepping out of the house with Buckley springing ahead and pulling his leash taut. "Did you get everything you needed?"

"I got, like, nothing." I lean over to pet Buckley, but he's way more interested in sniffing grass and peeing everywhere than my affections. "I ran into Hannah Padilla and had like the world's most awkward conversation ever, so I just ran away."

"Really?" she asks, as we start down the sidewalk. "Hannah's always been really nice to me."

"She's nice, but . . . I don't know. Just trust me."

"I always trust you," she says before leaning in and kissing me. "Are you OK?"

"I will be, I guess." It hits me how nice it is not pretending to be fine when I'm not. I'm so lucky this is how Quinn is, and this is how we work together. I start to say more aloud, but it's funny sometimes how words don't match their own gravity.

Buckley snarls at somebody throwing a soda can into a nearby trash can.

"He's *terrible*," Quinn says.

"You can't say that! He made us fall in love."

She laughs. "He did *not*! His escapades got us to interact. That's *it*. Maybe we would have fallen in love in humanities."

"I don't like risking that we wouldn't have. Humanities is *not* romantic, Quinn."

"Neither is chasing a Chihuahua on the lam!"

"More so, though! Maybe he's mad that guy didn't recycle!"

"You know as well as I do that we have comingled trash and recycling here, K."

Quinn grins at me, and I feel it course through me, that sunshiny rush of mutual love. It sounds *ridiculous*, but I didn't know how much more I could feel than the already amazing joy of falling for someone. Falling for someone, and staying fallen, and feeling *almost literally* the love in their heart, is something I barely even have words for. The secret about falling in love is how you can do it a million times over with the same person, when the person is the right one.

I have fallen in love with Quinn Morgan at least one million times already.

"I guess I just really need to talk to James," I say. "Like a super good and honest talk. It doesn't make sense everything should feel like this when we have, like, this total history, you know?"

Quinn is quiet, and I am pretty sure it's because to her

it doesn't even make sense that James is—*was?*—my best friend. And right now, I don't have anything that could convince her without a magic window into my heart.

"Senior year was just, like, a lot," I say. "Maybe now that it's over, everything will . . ."

I'm glad Quinn doesn't call me out on not finishing the sentence, because I've never wanted everything to stay the same, and even if I did, the end of senior year is the worst time in the world to expect it.

• • •

I text her the next day and try to sound as normal as possible.

> Hey it's been like super forever and I would love to see you!! Do you want to hang out? I'm totally open today but also whenever, just let me know!!!

If I ever have to be chill to save my life, I am seriously as good as dead.

She responds, though, without even much delay.

> Sure. Want to come over?

I do, so I change out of my gross sitting-around clothes because I'm pretty sure no one has mended a weird and potentially broken friendship while wearing grungy terry cloth shorts and a ragged tank top.

"Hey." She lets me into her house, and for a split second I can let myself believe everything's exactly the same. After all, she's done this probably thousands of times for me.

"So, um . . ." I glance around, but it looks just like it always has. I want to blame myself for not realizing something huge had happened, but you'd seriously never know that James's mom doesn't live here anymore. "I super hate how things have been, James."

She sighs. "Me too."

I sit down on the living room sofa, like I have a million times. Like it's all going to be fine soon, because, like, why wouldn't it be? Things can be really hard sometimes, but things can also find their way back into place. It wasn't really that long ago when it felt as if there was some hovering force between Quinn and me, but now when it's just us, it's just us.

"So, um, I ran into Hannah Padilla at Target," I say.

James shrugs. She's still standing, and considering our height difference, I'm practically craning my neck to look at her.

"It feels like she knows *everything* going on with you," I

say. "Which, like, obviously we both have other friends, whatever. But . . . it's weird I still feel like I know, like, *none* of it."

"You didn't ask," she says, like it's just that easy. Imagine being James! Everything is just simple and straightforward and only idiots complicate things.

"I assumed if something was going on, you would have told me," I say. "I tell you *everything*."

"God, don't I know it," she says. "When would there have been room for my problems? For me at all?"

Whoa. "James . . . it's not like that. I tell you everything because you're my best friend."

"But it's *not* like that," she says. "It's like I've been your therapist. You dump all over me and then you don't even stick around to reciprocate. At least therapists get paid. I'm just doing all of it for free."

"I *ask* how you are," I say. "I ask about Logan, and college, and . . ." I don't know what else I ask about, honestly. I didn't ask about her parents, because as far as I knew, Mr. and Mrs. McCall were still living out their amazing, true, and beautiful love story. And maybe I didn't ask a ton about college, but James seemed so tight-lipped when I did that I took it as a hint. I tried as hard as I knew how to, but it's like, looking back now, it was never enough. No matter how I tried, James needed some other thing entirely.

"It's like you don't think I can see how you are," she says.

"How I *am*?"

She seems to be gathering her words, and so I try to gather mine. How *am* I? I really just want to be good for everyone, for my family and for Quinn and for future me so she'll look back and be proud and of course for my mom just in case she can still somehow keep an eye on me. But I feel like my thoughts are coming faster than I can fully comprehend them, because maybe not everything James is saying is super untrue. Maybe not the things about me, at least. I just don't know another way to be. Especially around James, who I thought had loved me with super unconditional friend love for more than a decade now.

"In front of everyone else, you're perfect," she says, and I feel it, like how I think getting punched would feel. Because Luke's said it and Quinn's said it and now it's James saying it.

"I know," I say.

"Oh, god. Of *course* you know. Because Kat Rydell doesn't do anything wrong or by accident."

"I didn't say that!" I stand up even though it only evens out the height difference a little. "I just mean that I know it's a thing with me, and I'm working on it."

"OK, fine," James says, and walks out of the room and into the kitchen. I'm not sure what to do, so I follow.

"I sorta feel like you hate me," I say, not because I believe it but because I need her to tell me it isn't true. "Like, to leave me out of so much. And assume the worst of me."

James watches me but doesn't respond. She just gets a glass of water. And so maybe she does hate me.

"I mean, you've *never* taken my relationship seriously." Now it's like I've punched myself in the gut. Somehow I couldn't even fully see this until the words were out of my mouth.

"Not at first," James says. "That's fair. It was all so fast, and suddenly everything in your whole life was Quinn and being prom queen, just whatever you could do to get attention."

I wish we were fighting like dumb boys do, because I'd rather James's strong fist in my face than hear those words from my very best friend's lips.

"I can't believe you'd say that to me," I say. "Like I couldn't figure out other ways to get attention, Jesus."

"Are you serious?" She enacts an extremely dramatic eye roll. "When you were with Matty, you were a vegan and told *everyone who'd listen* what went on in factory farms. When you went out with what's-his-face—"

"Ryan," I add for some stupid reason.

"—you went to all those black-and-white movies. You joined the swim team for, like, half a minute. You were going to try out for the school musical freshman year and you made me watch all those PBS videos of *Great Performances*. You knit three-fourths of a scarf and then tried to give it away to someone short like they wouldn't notice."

"I like trying new things," I say. "Not that Quinn is a new thing to try. Not like *girls* are."

"I promise you," she says, and she sounds extra serious, "I didn't mean that at all."

"Right now, it sorta feels like it." I'm actually not sure that it does *right now* but it sure has for plenty of the rest of the year. I guess I need to say it.

"I'm sorry," she says. "Obviously being a vegan is a choice and being bisexual isn't. They're absolutely different things, and that isn't what I meant. It's that you throw yourself so hard into whoever you're dating. It can feel like the rest of us disappear."

"I totally get it can seem like that. None of that before was love, though," I say. "I *love* Quinn. I love her more than I knew I could love a person."

"You're barely out of high school," James says in a way that suggests she's decades older with miles and piles of experience and wisdom. "None of this means anything now. Don't you get it?"

"Just because your parents got divorced doesn't mean none of it matters," I say.

"You don't know anything," James says.

"And you don't know everything!" It's honestly shocking that it's taken me this long to burst into tears. I know there's no point in trying to stop them. "I know how I feel, James. I know what's in my heart. And, no, I don't know if I'm actually going to stay with Quinn and marry her someday or who knows. But right now, it's one of the realest things I have."

"Once Quinn showed up, it was like I was nothing to you," she says.

"Oh my god, I can't believe how freaking unfair you're being. Quinn tried so hard to be your friend. I tried really hard to include both of you all the time."

"I didn't *want* to be Quinn's friend," she says. "You never forced me to be Matty's friend. I have enough friends! I didn't want to switch lunch tables and stop hanging out so much with Sofia and Mariana or anyone else."

"Then why did you?" I ask. "You totally could have been like, hey, Kat, I know you want to sit with Quinn but I still want to hang out with everyone else."

She's silent.

"Stuff was clearly bothering you! You didn't say anything about that, either. If you thought I was being a crappy friend, you should have said something."

"And you should have *known*. I just wanted you in my life, like before, like when it felt like it was me and you against everything."

"But we *weren't* against anything. You were my best friend, and then suddenly you weren't. Suddenly you didn't tell me anything and I had to find out stuff from Logan, and from Hannah Padilla. Like, are you freaking hooking up with Logan again?"

She looks guilty for just a split second.

"Great, I'll take that as a yes. And what did you say at Jon Kessler's party? I hear you didn't really mean it but everyone was just sick of prom or something? So I'll assume"—I realize for some stupid reason I hadn't let myself accept this already—"you were saying something horrible about me or Quinn or both."

She stares at me. "Look, I was sick of hearing about this great civil rights struggle, when you know as well as I do that it had nothing to do with equal rights. I'm thrilled our school finally caught up with the times, but for you to act like it had something to do with anything but still getting to be prom queen . . ."

"Is that . . ." I take a few deep breaths and try to get my crying under control. "Is that seriously what you think of me?"

She doesn't say anything.

"You know what? You can *like* being prom queen and still want equal rights," I say. "Even if Quinn and I had lost—"

"But you didn't lose," James says. "You *never* lose. And so you had no room for someone like me, who could only lose."

"I *had* room for you! You locked me out."

"You were impossible to talk to," she says. "You wouldn't have understood."

"I wouldn't have understood having your family suddenly split up in a way you could never have imagined? I couldn't have understood what it was like having your parent fall in love with someone new? That's, like, my whole freaking life, James."

"Your mom *died,*" she says. "Mine left. It's not even close."

"Oh, yeah, I'm so lucky. I get to know my mom was perfect, while thinking about the fact that I will never see her again, never be hugged by her, never get to tell her about prom, or college, or whatever else happens to me. I'm sorry your mom maybe did something selfish, but you're freaking right it's not even close."

James stares at me. "I'm sorry. I'm so sorry that I—"

"Don't. That you could even think it . . ." I turn from her and start crying again. Continue crying? Does it even freaking matter? "I really, really feel like you hate me."

"I don't," she says. "I could never. It's just . . ."

I turn around, and we stare at each other for a few moments.

"James . . . if I wasn't a good friend to you, I'm sorry."

She kind of laughs and shakes her head. "Really? *If?* I think I laid out the reasons that you haven't—"

"Oh my god, seriously? I'm trying to talk to you, and you're so super ready to jump down my throat about—"

"*Jump down your throat?*" She sighs. "So much fucking drama. I'm over it."

"You know what I hate? How people say things all super calmly so they can say someone else is being dramatic. I can't help how my voice sounds."

"You can help what you say, though. You can think about how you choose your words. And I don't know why I thought you could manage not to be selfish for even five minutes. Somehow you've turned into the most selfish person I've ever known."

"Keeping yourself all locked away from people who care about you seems really selfish, too."

We watch each other some more.

"I don't think you're my best friend anymore," I say, a little because I believe it, and a lot because I'm hoping she'll fight to contradict this, to do *something* that makes me see how horribly wrong I am right now.

"Yeah." She folds her arms across her chest. "I don't think you are, either."

I hate every single thing about what's happening. I hate that once things are out of your mouth, it's already too late to put them back in. Worse, I hate that it's the same when it's someone else's words.

Or is it worst of all when it's your own?

"OK, then," I say, and then it's like before, when my brain couldn't keep up with its own thoughts. My mouth seems to be talking without my full input. "Have a good life, James. Have fun in Berkeley or wherever you're going."

"Yeah," she says. "You too."

I know that I basically came over here to yell at James. I feel justified, and it seems fair. And no matter if that's true or not, I don't expect to leave her house in tears, no longer her friend, no longer *anyone's* best friend.

My phone buzzes as I walk home, and I desperately grab it from the pocket of my shorts. It's just Quinn, so I ignore it for now while sending a silent plea up into the blue skies that James will text anyway.

But James doesn't text. James doesn't text all afternoon, evening, and night. There are only more messages from Quinn when I wake up—if you can even call it sleep if all you do is toss and turn—the next morning.

I'm still not even sure if I can fully wrap my head around just how angry James made me. In some ways, I'm used to being hurt. Isn't everyone? Life hurts you, and you do your best to heal. But anger is something different. I hadn't prepared for it. I'm not sure it was ever my default for anything. Even when Matty slept with Elise, and I *should* have been angry, what I remember most is how sad I was, how betrayed, how suddenly alone a person's absence could make you feel. Matty was no one compared to James, though, not even a blip on the radar where James was the brightest light.

I was going to talk at her wedding, and I had these dumb thoughts that we'd have babies who would grow up to be best friends, and whoever she ended up with would also love the Dodgers and we could make him take Quinn to games while James and I did something way more fun instead. Whenever I thought about being old, I thought about *The Golden Girls* and how, even if really sad things happened, James and I would be there for each other until the very end.

I was not going to walk out of her house one summer day when I was only eighteen with that part of my life behind me, with all those future possibilities immediately deleted.

Except that it's what happened.

The thing is that I know I could text her, and I know that people can fight and end up OK later. Finality is one of those things you can feel, though, and even though I hadn't been prepared for it, I can't deny that it's what's hitting me now.

"Hey, kid." Dad knocks on my bedroom door. "Quinn's here."

I check my phone again and the day has gotten much later than I realized, and, also, I have about a thousand messages from Quinn. Not even one from James, though.

I rush into the kitchen. "Hey, sorry."

"K, are you OK?" She throws her arms around me and holds me, and it's way too much niceness and so of course I start crying again. "What happened?"

Dad eyes the scene warily and then walks down the

hallway to his room. Quinn and I laugh at exactly the same time.

"I had a huge fight with James," I say.

"I'm sorry."

"We're . . . we're not friends anymore."

"That sucks." She's still holding me tightly. "I can't imagine how bad it would be if Raina and I . . ."

"You and Raina never would," I say. "She believes the best in you. And James . . ."

"I'm seriously so sorry, and I feel like an asshole that I kept texting you about the game when you had something major going on."

"Agh, oh, man, Quinn! That's why you're wearing your special Dodgers shirt!"

She glances down at it. "It's called a jersey."

"Whatever! We are still going to the game. It slipped my mind but—"

"You don't have to."

"Nope! I promised my girlfriend an evening of baseball, so we are baseballing."

"Oh, boy."

"Do I have time to get ready? I bought a special shirt, just for the occasion."

"Do you mean *a jersey*?"

"No! It's, like, a super cute T-shirt. You'll like it."

"Yes, go get ready," she says. "But, really, we could just stay here and do nothing. Or I could see if someone else—"

"I think it's good if I don't stay home," I say. "If I keep crying, I might never stop."

She squeezes my hand before letting me go. And even though my face is wet and my eyes are puffy and red, I change into jeans and the cutest Dodgers T-shirt I could find at Target. Quinn drives us over to the stadium, and I stand in line to buy Dodger Dogs so she can watch batting practice. I still don't care about baseball, but I care a lot about the tense faces Quinn makes during the game when players go up to bat, and I find myself as happy as she is when we win the game. Almost as happy, at least. No one's smiling like Quinn is.

"This was actually super fun," I say as we walk out of the stadium. "We should see a game when we're home for break."

"Kat . . ." She gives me a very worried look. "You understand there are seasons, right? They don't just play all year 'round."

"Oh, right. Because of snow in other places."

"Since I think you're just being cute now, I'm going to ignore that." She slides her arm around my waist. "How are you feeling?"

The win seems to slip off of me as we reach her car. "Not great. Can we go eat like one million cheese fries at that weird diner?"

"You'll have to be a little more specific than that, but, sure."

I buckle myself in and lean over to kiss her. “How are you?”

It feels awkward to ask, for some reason, but she just smiles. I feel weird that while things might be forever lost with James, her words are maybe helping me be a better person. Ultimately, though, being a better person is the most important thing. No matter where it comes from.

“My team won, I’m on my way to cheese fries with my girl, and my sister’s about to leave for camp for two whole weeks. I’d say I’m pretty great.”

“Coding camp?” I ask. “Isn’t that, like, where you go to kiss cute girls?”

“It’s cheer camp,” she says.

“You could definitely go to cheer camp to kiss cute girls!”

She grins. “Trust me, that’s definitely not what Ainsley’s going to get up to.”

We’re silent for a few minutes as we sit in traffic bottlenecking out of the parking lot. I start a playlist of pop music that I know Quinn likes in spite of herself.

“Hey,” I say, and I try to use my nicest voice because sometimes it’s scary knowing in advance how things will come out. Especially when you’ve decided not to be perfect anymore, as much as you can help it.

“Hey,” she says.

“I have to figure out how to still be super in love with

you and also, like, someone who has time for everyone else. Everyone else who deserves it, at least."

"OK," Quinn says, as traffic clears long enough that we pull out of the parking lot and are actually on our way. "Direct me to cheese fries."

"That wasn't a weird thing to say?" I ask.

She gives me a very cute *what-the-heck* look. "No?"

The funny thing is that when I lost my boyfriend, it was fine because of my best friend. But no matter how amazing Quinn is, nothing could make losing James OK.

We still eat a giant plate of cheese fries, and make out in her car, and talk about the classes we hope we take next year. My life has a new sad chapter, though, and it's hard to imagine I'll ever see events again as anything but before and after losing my very best friend.

• • •

I don't hear from James, and I don't hear from James, and then, somehow, every day, it gets a little more normal that I don't hear from James. I don't want to burden Dad with my girl drama, but I think Luke fills him in, because Dad surprises me with a pair of Dodgers tickets—better seats than the ones I'd bought earlier in the summer—and a scrawled note to *have some fun with Quinn*. I think he's mainly just relieved that one of his kids sort of cares about sports in any capacity. Two baseball games in one summer is way more baseball than I ever expected in my life, but it just goes to show how love can change everything. Even sports.

It's not like other summers, and not just because James isn't part of my life anymore. There were always so many parties, trips to the beach, hunts for the best and cheapest ways to access pools. But now I think we're all looking forward—to leaving, to knowing our new friends and classmates will be from other places. I'm pretty sure I'm now messaging my future roommate, Rochelle, as often as I message anyone who isn't Quinn. Quinn's future roommate loves baseball but is apparently a fan of the Giants, so hopefully a baseball rivalry won't tear their room apart. I'm sort of excited to find out, though.

I guess for a long time now, since we lost Mom, I've been sad. I know how to be sad and still have a life. And it's what I'm going to keep doing now.

• • •

Dad calls me out from my room on a late Saturday afternoon because Diane's here. I can hear Luke already being all chill and charming, and I aim to do the same, until I realize Diane's not alone.

Stacey smiles as I walk into the room. "Look at you. Mini-Jennifer."

"No," I say, embarrassed and flattered and relieved that this is how my mom's best friend looks at me. I was so convinced she had no use for me at all. "Hi. Dad didn't say you were coming over."

"Diane and I were getting drinks and when she said she was headed to Charlie's later, I decided to figuratively crash the figurative party." Her gaze goes to my neck and I see the realization in her eyes. "God, I made fun of her when she got that."

I touch my necklaces. "Really?"

"I know it's hard to believe, but we were pretty cool back then," she says. "I knew where all the great clubs were, and your mom could talk any guy at the door into letting us in. And then she started wearing this preppy little necklace, and I thought, who even *are* you? You know how it is when you're—well, your age. Friendships are so big and dramatic, and everything seems symbolic of something."

I blink to keep from crying, but Stacey sees it.

"I miss her, too," she says. "Every day."

"It's not just her," I find myself saying. "My best friend—well, she's not my best friend anymore. We had a fight and it's over and . . ."

"Take it from me," Stacey says, once I've trailed off. "One day you're angry at someone about a necklace, and then before you know it, none of it matters."

"I hope that's true," I say, even though already James seems so far away. I can't imagine something that would delete that distance, pull her right back to me.

"It's one hundred percent true." She smiles. I don't believe her, but I smile, too.

"So, Oberlin, Charlie says. That's great."

"Oh, it's, like, nothing, really," I say as quickly as I can. "I don't have a major yet and I know I'm doing it all wrong and—"

"I didn't declare a major until the last possible minute," Stacey says with a smile. "Which is somehow sooner than Jennifer did."

"OMG, really?" I look over at Luke, who's home for only a couple of weeks in between important intern things. "Did you hear that?"

He shrugs in his insufferably chill way. Is my brother turning into a freaking hipster? He *is* wearing new and cooler glasses and growing a weird beard. "You're the one who was making such a big deal about it."

Stacey snickers, and I realize it's because I'm rolling my eyes.

"Brothers are the worst, I know," she says.

"The super serious worst," I say, though I smile at Luke.

"When you're home on break, call me—we'll get dinner or something, OK?" Stacey asks me.

I nod and try not to look too enthusiastic. Luke calls me over to settle some faux-argument with Dad, and I love how crowded our little house suddenly feels. I love that Luke and I are just back to bickering like we did as kids, before we lost Mom and suddenly it didn't feel OK to be kids like that anymore.

Diane sneaks me wine, and she and Stacey promise they'll take me to the guy who cut Mom's hair so I can maybe finally get my own curls under control. We all give Luke girl advice, though of course he won't take it and will whine later anyway.

The feeling comes over me like when it's cold out but suddenly the furnace kicks in. For almost three years I didn't feel like a family, and right now, I can totally feel how we are one after all.

Later, after Diane and Stacey have left, and Luke is out probably just drinking beers in Keith's garage, I find Dad alone in the kitchen. And I know it's time to ask.

"Dad?" I take a super deep breath. "Where's Mom's stuff?"

"What stuff?" he asks, and I realize there's no stiffness in his shoulders, no weird itchy look. He looks OK.

"The stuff that used to be in your room. Her *stuff*."

"Oh." He nods. "I put it away. Do you—"

"Of course I do! I wish you would have offered."

"Kat, in case you had some idea that I know what I'm doing . . ." Dad sighs and rakes his hand through his hair, just the way Luke does. It's wild how gestures and looks can be passed down. I wonder if there's anything of me that's just like Mom.

He walks down the hall to his room and comes back

with a small box. When I open the lid, I smell her perfume. For just a second, it's like she's here again. From the look on Dad's face, I'm pretty sure he's thinking the same thing.

"She'd be so proud of you," he says.

"No," I say, for some stupid reason. I laugh and cry at the same time. I think of James's words, how I never lose and I don't have room for other people. What if she's right? How could anyone be proud of me then? "Why? I'm not a big deal."

"You're a big deal, kid." He puts his hand on my shoulder, and he still doesn't look itchy or jumpy. "*I'm* really proud of you."

I hug him so tightly. I don't remember the last time we hugged like this.

"Everything OK with you?" he asks.

"Not really," I say. "But I'm surviving."

"That's all we can do, huh."

"What about you?" I ask. "How are you?"

Dad glances at me like he's surprised, and I feel it in my heart. I have to be the girl who asks, even when it's hard and weird and maybe even itchy. Everyone in my life deserves that, and even though she isn't my friend anymore, James deserved it, too. And I can't undo that or give her any of the attention she deserved when she deserved it, but I can be this girl moving forward. I can be better every day, if I keep trying.

"I'm doing pretty good, kid," he says. "You want a beer?"

"What?"

He shrugs and gets up. "You're going to college soon. It's fine."

Dad returns a moment later with two bottles. I clink mine against his and hope that it's OK that I don't actually have a toast ready. He nods at me and looks back to the TV, so I think everything at this exact moment is OK as it is.

Later that night, I get a new follower notification from Stacey, and later still she directly messages me an old photo of her and Mom I've never seen before. Stacey's delicate diamond nose stud was a shiny silver hoop back then, and Mom was wearing a ripped-up T-shirt that said BABES IN TOYLAND. I can see how the necklace was an affront to their friendship, and I can also see that I look more like her than I realized. We stand just the same way.

I message Stacey.

How long were you and Mom mad at each other?

Her response is fast.

Which time?

I have no idea if James and I are Stacey and Mom. But Mom stood just like me and Stacey's tight with words like James. I know that soon I'll be in Ohio, for the majority of the next four years, and of course I think I'll meet new people and make new friends to confide in. But they won't be James, with our shared histories or her quiet knowing smile. They won't have known my mom, not at all, much less the way I remember Mom teasing James, and how James could always dish it right back. Not even Quinn knows that part of my history.

And so maybe I can let all of this mean something besides my future having a big James-shaped hole right in the center of it.

I'm about to get into bed later that night when I unfortunately think about the time capsule, about James's letter, about how it's still tucked away in my desk drawer. I know younger James wrote it, not current James, but I miss her words so much that even old ones sound better than none at all.

The thin, crisp envelope is under the stack of birthday cards from my parents and then just Dad, and I touch those birthday envelopes written in Mom's handwriting (always *Katherine*, never *Kat*) before grabbing for James's letter. I hug it against my heart for just a moment before sliding out the piece of heavy, pale blue stationary.

Dear Kat,

I know that you think that I'm writing this only because you're making me, and I suppose on some very technical level, that's true. Also true that I don't talk about *my feelings* all the time (or ever?) but I will make an exception for you.

I'm so glad we were paired up in kindergarten, though I don't think it was fate like you (probably?) do. We were just lucky. I think I already wanted to be your friend, though. Everyone wants to be your friend, and I get to feel smug that I already am. Your best friend, at that. It's like being best friends with Beyoncé. (It's actually probably better, because Beyoncé would always be leaving to go on tour, and you're always around.)

It's true that I don't always know what to say, or that I do and am not always sure how to go about saying it. I'm glad this hasn't ever mattered to you, as if you always miraculously know anyway. And so you probably know better than I do what to say to my future self in your letter. I don't think the passage of time will really matter, though, because once you've forged your friendship in kindergarten mortarboards you're linked for life. (That's a saying, right? ☺)

Love, James

CHAPTER THIRTEEN

August before Senior Year

JAMES

Something about Los Angeles that seems to surprise people from anywhere else is how big it is. I know that it doesn't sound like a big deal to live in Burbank and have your boyfriend move into the dorms at UCLA, but, well, it's not nothing. Even today, a Saturday, it took me nearly an hour to drive over. Finding parking that wouldn't get me a ticket—or worse, towed—took fifteen minutes more.

But it's fine, because now I'm sitting on the green grass of the UCLA campus, with my college freshman of a boyfriend. I can't believe in one year I'll be the freshman here—as long as I get in. And as long as Logan doesn't skyrocket past me in maturity and not need me anymore.

"Oh my god!" Logan's overcome with his dorky little laugh. I hope he never knows how stupid weak it makes me. "That guy was skating past those girls and trying to look cool, and he completely wiped out."

I follow his line of vision. "Well, Logan, not everyone can be as cool with the ladies as you are."

"You jest, but I'm the coolest guy you know."

I laugh and lean back on the lawn. "Only because I don't know *that* many guys."

"I'll take what I can get."

"Logan . . ." I don't know why this is coming out of my mouth now, but I don't feel like I can stop it. Normally my feelings seem so within my control, so maybe it's the campus. "I know what we said, but if you—"

"Nope, McCall, nope." He collapses back next to me. "We're in this. As long as you still wanna be."

"You know that I still want to be."

"That's what I like to hear." He pushes up my sunglasses and kisses me. "Seriously. I love you and wanna make this work. Us. College. Semi-long-distance. The whole shebang."

"God, you're a nerd." I laugh but end up kissing him more. My brain had conjured up a new Logan, who'd be instantly more mature, more serious, more quick to judge. The new Logan wouldn't need a high school girlfriend, much less one like me who wasn't like him in ways I worried would someday matter.

But it's just a campus, and while the drive wasn't exactly fun, it's not *actually* that far. He's the Logan who asked me out by waiting outside the girls' locker room after track practice and who once took my best friend to Throwback Thursday at Moonlight Rollerway because I'd suddenly come down with the flu and Kat couldn't drive yet.

We lie silently next to each other for a while, and I imagine this moment, exactly one year from now, when I won't have to drive home afterward. This is all assuming I get accepted at UCLA, but my plan feels so right that I can't imagine it not working out.

My phone buzzes in my pocket, so I risk ruining the moment and take it out to read the screen.

OMG I am home!!!! California air!!!! J you have to see the size of my hair. I look like a mushroom cloud.

I glance over at Logan, who is now on his phone as well. "Would you kill me if I left?"

"McCall, murder is never on the menu." He shoves his phone back in his pocket. "What's up?"

"Kat's home from Indiana."

"Go," he says, instead of reminding me that she's been gone for a shorter time than he has. "Tell Rydell I said hi."

"It's only because I love her more than you," I say, and kiss him. "It's still weird you aren't a few blocks away anymore."

"We'll get used to it," he says. "I'll escort you to your car, my lady."

"No," I say with a laugh. "I'm good. I'll call you later. But if people want to go out or you get invited to a party, *go*."

"Aye aye, Captain McCall."

We kiss once more and then I'm back to my car and fighting weekend traffic on my drive northeast back to Burbank. By the time I park, I've got what looks like two dozen texts from Kat.

🎉🎉🎉🎉🎉🎉🎉🎉🎉🎉🎉🎉🎉🎉
🎉🎉🎉🎉🎉🎉🎉🎉🎉🎉🎉🎉🎉🎉

Are you still coming over?

Is everything OK??

J what is up!

Is this because you're scared of seeing what Midwestern humidity has done to my hair??

> I went to get coffee which will seem heartless if it turns out YOU'RE DEAD!! but hopefully you've just forgotten I exist, wait, no, that would be MUCH WORSE!!!!

I turn around and rush over to Simply Coffee. Kat is sitting outside and leaps to her feet when she sees me.

"You're alive!" she calls out as she tackles me into a hug, which is impressive, given that she's nine inches shorter than me.

"Sorry, I was actually in Westwood with Logan," I say.

"Oh my god, thank you for journeying so far to see me." She gestures to her hair, which does resemble a mushroom in shape. "This is what I'm going to look like in college, so it's good I've already locked down your friendship, James. I cannot imagine I'm going to pick up a bunch of new friends starting next year."

"Only if you get in," I tell her, which makes her giggle.

"Thanks! That's totally the silver lining I needed."

We walk inside together so I can get a coffee and Kat can get a(nother) chai. We risk losing the table outside, but it feels ridiculous to stop talking.

"So Luke is settled in?" I ask once we've ordered our drinks.

"Totally. Him and his new roommate had already been

emailing about, you know, all their engineering stuff, so he seems completely at home. And I know I texted you about it, but it was so cool Dad drove me all the way to Oberlin."

"So you're sure you want to go there?" It's not that I want to deprive Kat of her dream college experience. It's only that going to Ohio seems so *random,* and, for god's sake, I'm struggling to adjust to Logan only forty-five minutes (plus parking) away from me.

"I'm not one hundred percent sure. But I felt super at home on campus, and it would be kind of cool to not be too far away from Luke. It just feels so smart and creative there. They have this first-year student seminar program that sounds so good for me. And I know your James brain wants all these logistical reasons that add up to some perfect formula, but . . . ?" She laughs and takes our drinks from the barista, and we walk back outside into the sunshine. Our table's still open for us. "It just feels right, you know? Can't something just *feel right,* James?"

"Well, sure." Of course, I like facts and reasoning, stats on how fast I ran this year compared to last, SAT scores to aim for, percentage of local students accepted at UCLA. Life isn't all so tidy, and even though it might surprise Kat, I'm glad that it isn't. Is there sense to make of our decade-plus-long friendship? Is there logic and sound reasoning to falling in love with Logan? All of that *feels right,* but I know if I said that aloud it wouldn't sound passionate and interesting the way it does from Kat.

“I need to see more of the world,” Kat continues. “I know that you’re about to say that *Ohio isn’t exactly more of the world, Kat,* and I know that you’re right, but it’s not LA, and that’s all I know. I barely know that! I know freaking *Burbank.*”

“Hopefully Ohio has everything you’re looking for.” I try not to smile as I say it, but Kat cracks up and then I’m laughing, too.

“I have no idea what I’m looking for,” she says with a little shrug. She doesn’t look terrified, even though that feeling would chill me to my core. “It seems like a good place to find out, though, maybe. Who knows! Senior year could hold anything, though.”

I don’t realize I’m smirking, but then Kat elbows me.

“Oh, stop. I know, I know, the next years of your life are completely figured out while I flail about. Whatever.”

I sip my cold brew. “Have you seen Matty yet?”

“James! I literally just got back and now I’m here with you. Matty can wait.” Kat fidgets with her necklace. “So, like, not that you should have been, but were you nervous to go see Logan? Did you worry he’d be all . . . collegiate?”

“*Yes.*” Last Thanksgiving, my aunt asked me if Kat and I were still friends, and why we got along so well. When you’ve been friends with someone as long as Kat and I have been, it can be hard breaking it all down. And I didn’t know what to say, because Kat and I just *work*. Kat knows the things that scare me without me having to name them.

"But Logan loves you," she says very firmly. "So I'm sure he wasn't collegiate and everything was normal, right? Like perfectly normal. Normally perfect? Whatever. You guys are my proof love exists."

"Not your own boyfriend?"

She giggles. "My own relationship can't be my own inspiration, dork. It's all you guys."

I can't make fun of her considering it's probably much dorkier for your relationship inspiration to be your own parents.

"Urgghh," she says, and then sips a bunch of her iced chai. "Don't you wish it was already next fall? You're all cute with Logan on the UCLA campus, and I have mush-room hair in Ohio?"

"I think I'll like being a senior," I say. "And not having you more than two thousand miles away."

"We'll FaceTime," she says. "Lots! Think of all we'll have to talk about. We already have a million things to talk about and that's with us doing almost all the same stuff all the time."

I'm not sure that I'm ready for any huge changes, but—besides Logan—all of that's a full year away. What I am ready for is senior year, right here, with Kat. And I love that I don't have to say it. With Kat, I never have to say it. I just smile at her, and she knows.

Acknowledgments

Thank you to my editor Maggie Lehrman for fighting for this book. Working on it with you was a dream come true. Thank you to Hana Nakamura and Christine Almeda for the beautiful cover that brings James and Kat to life. Thanks to the entire of the Abrams team for your hard work!

Thank you to my agent Kate Testerman, who continues to be more tireless and optimistic than I could ever manage. This book found its home because of you, and I'll be forever grateful.

Thanks to early readers and cheerleaders and note-givers: Christie Baugher, Meghan Deans, Jessica Hutchins, Gretchen McNeil, Sarah Skilton, and Jessie Weinberg. Thank you to Tess Sharpe for your genius nonlinear thoughts. Thanks to Zachary Wilcha for your incredible help regarding Habitat for Humanity, and Darien Wollman for the helpful information about Tree People. Thanks to Jasmine Guillory for always knowing what characters should be cooking. Thanks to Britta Lundin for knowing the worst car for prom. Thanks to Laura Birek for brainstorming how one could be romantic via coding. Thanks to Scott Singer for all of the information about running track.

Thanks to my amazing writing community. I will be sure to inadvertently leave people out, but encouragement and support from, but not limited to, these people has kept me going: Robin Benway, Kayla Cagan, Heather Cocks, Audrey Coulthurst, Elizabeth Eulberg, Maurene Goo, Adrienne Kisner, Aditi Korana, Kathy Kottaras, CB Lee, Nicole Maggi, Jessica Morgan, Julie Murphy, Becca Podos, Isabel Quintero, Marisa Reichardt, Zan Romanoff, Rainbow Rowell, Lance Rubin, Aminah Mae Safi, Tiffany Schmidt, Robyn Schneider, Stephanie Strohm, Robin Talley, Julia Whelan, Kiersten White, Sara Zarr, and all the pals I forgot. Writing is stressful and isolating and weird sometimes, and yet because of the people in my life, it's a little less so.

And, finally, thanks to my mom, Pat Spalding, for all of your encouragement.